donald dewey

aLL THE ALieNS in the Neighbor hood

short stories

MILFORD
HOUSE
an imprint of Sunbury Press, Inc.
Mechanicsburg, PA USA

MILFORD
HOUSE

an imprint of Sunbury Press, Inc.
Mechanicsburg, PA USA

For information about special discounts for bulk purchases, please contact Sunbury Press Orders Dept. at (855) 338-8359 or orders@sunburypress.com.

To request one of our authors for speaking engagements or book signings, please contact Sunbury Press Publicity Dept. at publicity@sunburypress.com.

ISBN: 978-1-62006-818-2 (Trade paperback)

Library of Congress Control Number: 2018947641

FIRST MILFORD HOUSE PRESS EDITION: June 2018

Product of the United States of America
0 1 1 2 3 5 8 13 21 34 55

Set in Bookman Old Style
Designed by Crystal Devine
Cover by Riaan Wilmans
Edited by Lawrence Knorr

Continue the Enlightenment!

For Sardi

STORIES

The Trolley Barn

DURKIN felt antsy. The mutterings in his ear were irritating, and telling Gregory Ribant to raise them to a prattling level didn't seem like much of an alternative. The topper was the numbness in his right foot. Had he developed a circulation problem? The last thing he needed was to open another medical front. He was already swallowing enough pills to keep the drug industry in the black.

Somebody out in the church dropped something that sounded like a can of soda. It clattered and rolled across a pew before being snatched up. Durkin wondered if Gregory Ribant realized he was also aggravating the Cola gods. Or was it Durkin himself who was doing that? His restlessness almost certainly had to do with his 25th anniversary on Tuesday. For a week or more, he had sensed the plot in the air. Perez and Mayfield had made coy allusions to the day as if pretending to recall an old forest fire in Idaho. Geis had called from the bishop's office with far too much nonchalance about whether he might be free for a drink Tuesday. Most telling of all, Vera Trimble, who had not let a birthday or anniversary pass without making his favorite roast lamb, hadn't said a word about the Tuesday menu. What else could he conclude than that they were all in on some surprise dinner?

And so what? Why should that make him so anxious? Durkin had enough experience faking things to affect a look of dismay when he was ushered somewhere so people could jump out at him. If there was one thing he should have been confident of by now, it was his ability to dissemble under pressure. Without that skill, at least two people would have committed suicide and a couple of others wouldn't have surrendered weapons to the police. Instead, though, he felt itchy about having neglected something. Was he overreaching, taking too much for granted? The only thing that threatened more of a jolt than a surprise dinner, as he had been reminding himself, was anticipating a surprise dinner that hadn't been organized in the first place.

Gregory Ribant had fallen quiet, and Durkin rushed to fill up the awkward silence with the stern but reassuring. He knew what had inspired this particular confession: Ribant wanting to screw his wife. About once a month, the saloon keeper was all but elated to unburden himself in confession. This dollar gouged here, that one palmed off the bar there—all the petty misdemeanors had to be declared. Durkin didn't know what perverse neurons went into a thief who had to clear his conscience before tackling Cynthia Ribant in the bedroom, but he had heard enough from both over the years to know that was the game afoot. Instead of a cassock, he should have been wearing the striped cherry suit of a pimp.

As soon as he had dispensed with Ribant, Durkin stretched his toes and shook his right foot. The numbness folded back vengefully, every capillary around his ankle running up his leg to jangle out that it was back in business. He chided himself for his jitters. They were preventing him from appreciating the odd entertainment Saturday afternoons could provide. Compared to others he had been listening to for 25 years, for instance, Gregory Ribant represented a Barnum and Bailey spectacular. At least the man's banal greed had been thievery in action. He preferred hearing about the filching at the Green Giant Bar & Grill to the usual Saturday afternoon catch—bedtime visions of chained up women, naked children, or supermarket managers bleeding to death in the meat aisle for overcharging on the sirloin. Catechists or no catechists, he had never been comfortable granting absolution for thoughts and fantasies; it seemed the smallest of presumptuous steps away from rendering moral judgments on breathing. Anything short of actual deed—trivial or horrendous, whatever it was—wasted everybody's time.

That went for surprise dinners, too, because he had to admit he *would* be disappointed if Perez, Mayfield, and Geis weren't ganging up to pull something on Tuesday. His 50th birthday had been one thing: Anybody who survived to 51 had a 50th birthday. A few beers with Geis at the Green Giant had said that as well as it could have been said three years ago. But the silver jubilee of his ordination seemed worth a little more ceremony, if only as a celebration of choice. He hadn't become another stock analyst, house painter, or serial killer, he had chosen to become a priest.

It had been an earthly, deliberate decision made by a human being with a free will and the powers of reason—qualities that didn't enter into having a birthday. And who better to plan the surprise than men who had made similar choices?

Durkin didn't recognize the scraping feet coming in, and gave himself a demerit. Especially after his sneaky sweep of the front pews while walking from the altar to the confessional, he had expected to know everyone who parted the curtain. But even more tantalizing than the sluggish walk was the froggy voice; *that* he should have recognized immediately if it belonged to anyone in the parish. Was he dealing with a parachutist from St. Anthony's who had feared being identified by a confessor in his own parish? "And how can I help you, my son?" he asked.

"I'm older than you," the eerily hoarse voice snapped. "Only place I'd be your son is on Mars."

Durkin sat up. He was in the mood for a smart mouth; it was usually a shield for something serious. "All right, we're not related. How's that?"

"I'm gonna tell you the worst thing you ever heard."

"That a boast?"

"Just a fact."

Durkin couldn't think of a hollower claim, not since Kate Harper had drowned her two-year-old daughter 12 years ago. He would never have a problem recreating the sour churning in his stomach at hearing about how the gaunt blonde woman with the doe eyes had kept Melanie Harper's face under water in the tub until the little girl had stopped squirming; worse, he would always feel even that nausea being gutted out of him at Kate Harper's casual footnote that she had planned the killing for a Saturday afternoon so she would be able to run straight to him to tell him what she had done. "Why don't you just say what you want to say?"

"You have visions, Father?"

Durkin told himself to control his temper, that he was back to the usual Saturday afternoon haul. "You mean daydreams?"

"I guess. A priest like you, you probably think a lot about Paradise and all those things, right?"

"We've got a lot of people waiting outside. Could we get to it?"

"All those puffy clouds. People kind of sailin' along in their white togas. 'Hello there, angel! How are you today?'"

"That the way you'd like it to be?"

"I like the one about the Garden of Eden better. You're with all the fruit and the flowers and you're naked as a jaybird with the beautiful babe next to you. Even the snake looks happy."

Durkin ran down the list of suspects. Marty Weyhauser was out because he was in the hospital for a hernia operation. That he knew, nobody from the seminary had blown into town. No school pal from his old block would have pulled such a gag. And besides, the voice belonged to someone 20 years older than he was. "Who put you up to this?"

"What're you talking about? Can I make a confession or not?"

Durkin was bewildered; the man's annoyance was too genuine. "Well, go ahead. What's this vision that bothers you?"

The frog took a moment to make sure Durkin understood he was clearing indignation from his throat. "It's a trolley barn. The one that used to be down in Coney Island on West Fifth. Remember it?"

Durkin tried to imagine something as grotesque as Kate Harper drowning her daughter that involved a trolley barn; he couldn't. "Trolleys were before my time."

"Yeah? You look old enough."

"Sorry to disappoint you."

The man fell silent for a moment. "That's too bad," he finally said. "When I saw you, I thought you'd be the one to understand."

"Maybe if you told me what I have to understand, I'll surprise you."

The man clicked his tongue, then sighed. Durkin played back the click as "Unlikely" and the sigh as "Well, I've come this far . . ." He made up his mind that whatever the old bastard told him, he would be reciting rosaries in penance for the rest of the weekend.

"All right, try this. When I was a kid, I had this favorite place down in Coney Island. Not the Cyclone or the Wonder Wheel or any of the rides. I mean the trolley barn at the last stop. The roof of the place was these sooted over glass panels. A couple of them weren't so dirty so sunlight still got through them. And the pigeons! Pigeons all over the place up in the roof. Whenever they'd fly from one spot to another, their wings sounded like drums. Because they were inside, know what I mean?"

Durkin said he did. Anything to hurry the man along from his trip down memory lane to whatever it was he was confessing.

"All over the place you had these single tracks runnin' every which way. They crossed and they recrossed, then they went curvin' off on their own, but always stayin' inside the barn walls, you know? Like they could go anywhere they wanted, but only *some* anywheres. That make sense, Father?"

"Sure."

The old man didn't hear his impatience; on the contrary, he sounded relieved. "The trolleys, they came into the depot from every part of Brooklyn, the conductor bars always spittin' sparks on the top as soon as they hit the shed," he said. "And the smells, Father! When the conductor bars spit, it was like somebody was solderin' the whole place. Like one big burnin'. And you had the ocean thick in the air, too. Don't forget, the Atlantic Ocean was right outside, for Christ sake!"

"For His sake, too? Good to know."

"All right, all right. Don't get on your high horse. The thing is, you had so many choices in front of you, know what I'm sayin'? Every line had a little island for the passengers where you got off or stood to get back on. Islands all over the place. And the trolleys, they had these outsides that looked like plastic and curved right down to the tracks. Like some big hatchback on the sides. Somethin' almost . . . well, almost like a woman about it. You look at a bus, and it's all like some dumb block. But the trolleys had humps."

The old man paused, started picking at something on the screen in front of his face. Durkin suspected he was getting closer.

"I can't tell you how much I loved that depot, Father," he said after a moment, a new mellowness in his voice. "When we'd get off the McDonald Avenue trolley, my old man would take my hand and ask me where I wanted to go first—the roller coaster, the whip, what. I never had the guts to tell him I wanted to stay right where we were, that there was no ride down there that could be better than the trolley barn. Everythin' was screwy, but there was a kind of order to it all, is what I'm sayin'. Each of the trolleys knew what it was doin', knew where to go. Nobody had to be tellin' it what track to follow. They'd all just keep passin' one another all day goin' this way and that way."

Durkin waited. Only when somebody slammed the church door as if escaping a tornado did he say, "I'm sorry, but I still don't know what you're getting at. What's wrong with remembering this trolley barn?"

He went back to sounding miffed. "To me, it was like this mornin', that's what I'm sayin'. There probably hasn't been a week my whole life I haven't thought about it."

"Okay. I can hear that. But . . ."

"What I'm sayin' to you, Father, is that I'm 72 years old and don't figure to add too many more weeks to that. But in all that time the only thing I've ever really given a damn about is that trolley barn!"

Durkin heard depression and heard despair; he was annoyed he hadn't picked up on them sooner. "You're ill?"

"Who the hell cares? That's not what I'm gettin' at! If I lived to be 172 in perfect health, I'd be sayin' the same thing to you!"

"Okay, but there's something about it you regret. What?"

"You don't listen too good, do you?"

"You're telling me your idea of happiness, I think."

"I'm tellin' you my idea of *everythin'*! Listen, for a change!"

It wasn't a gag-gag, Durkin thought; it was Perez sending somebody to show him the consequences of not listening. "And why's that a weight on your conscience?"

The old man's cackle was sarcastic, but also too resigned to be merely mean. "What's the opposite of everythin', Father? Nothin', right? Well, that's where you and the rest of the world are—in nothin'. Anybody I ever knew—a couple of wives, two sons and a daughter, my sister, the whole goddamn world—you're all in it! Gee, all those people killed in that earthquake over in Turkey or wherever last week? The ones slaughterin' each other in Africa, cuttin' off one another's arms and legs? The old lady upstairs dyin' of cancer? The welfare kids? The crooks in Washington? I don't give a goddamn about any of that crap, Father Dur-kin. I don't give a crap about you, either. The only thing I've ever given a shit about is that trolley barn! Get it now?"

✳ ✳ ✳

Durkin thought he did. Over the next couple of days, he told himself he had been talking to a man so consumed by fear of approaching death that his last defense against despair had been trying to make it sound like defiance. He had heard that desperation countless times, and had been prepared for it with encouragements, admonishments, and more of both. Couldn't they have talked further in the rectory after the confession hours were over? What about if he suggested a psychologist friend they could call that very evening? At bottom, didn't the man's coming to confession mean he wanted to get beyond his truculent pose and deal with his problem as honestly as he could? No, no, and no, the man had growled, jumping up from his kneeler and sounding a lot more limber leaving the confessional than he had entering it.

Durkin wondered if he should have chased after him, to hell with the reaction of the people waiting outside. No doubt the man would have been even snippier in public with other eyes on him, but should that have been a consideration? Of course not. And yet what would have been accomplished by pursuing him to the door? The only answer that came back to Durkin was a demonstration of his own solicitude—a vanity act that wouldn't have nudged the man an inch closer to coming to grips with his terror or with the despair he was obviously battling to reject as his sin.

The old man's fixation on the Coney Island trolley barn gave Durkin something to think about besides his 25th anniversary. In the middle of his sermon on Sunday, he went further than think about it when a reference he made to a subway train suddenly caused him to stall at the pulpit with a mental picture of the single trolley tracks the man in the confessional had described—a pause that apparently lasted so long his altar boy had to cough pointedly to get him back on his own track. Later that same day in the rectory lounge, his attention drifting away from a *Times* book review of some history of West Virginia, he envisioned the roof the man had talked about—brown grime over most of the panels, the sun shining brilliantly through the odd remaining clean pieces of glass, the pigeons fluttering from one section of the eave to another. He saw the pigeons so clearly that one of them began to resemble Pepper, the black bird he had fed as a child in his backyard for more than a year. He was on the verge of making his old tweeting call to Pepper when Mayfield came barreling into the lounge looking for the Arts and Leisure section.

The images were more elaborate on Monday. During a marriage prep session with Jill Anton and Tom O'Dowd, he pictured the passenger islands in the depot, how people lined up smartly but separately throughout the building for their individual trolleys. If Tom O'Dowd hadn't intruded with some question about the meaning of marital rights, he was sure he would have made out the calliope sound of a carousel coming from somewhere out in the street near the barn. Even odder, he would have sworn he was picking up a whiff of cotton candy. But how could that be since the froggy man had mentioned neither the calliope music of a carousel nor the sickly-sweet smell of cotton candy? It felt ridiculous to have to remind himself that he had never been to any trolley barn.

At lunch an hour after the marriage prep talk, he had more reason for feeling ridiculous. Watching Vera Trimble walk her plates from the kitchen to the dining room without making the slightest attempt at deceiving him about Tuesday's dinner, he suddenly *did* smell the cotton candy. It was like a middle layer between the salt from the ocean and the burning from the trolley conductor bars—three tiers of strong odors with each one somehow also maintaining its own identity. And as the old man had said, what ride along Surf Avenue could possibly have been more exciting than the ramshackle building containing all the smells? Without moving beyond the barn, the visitor to Coney Island did indeed have absolutely everything. Not just the entertainment to be had from the parachute or the Wonder Wheel, but the practicality to be had from a trolley going to a specific destination. Not just the seductive order of the Ski Ball holes, but the meticulous planning behind the tracks crossing, running parallel, then curving out on their own. A ticket to the bumper cars bought a five-minute distraction, but the fare for the trolley was an investment in real life! It would have been stupidity *not* to want to stay in the barn.

"Something wrong, Father?"

Durkin looked up into Vera Trimble's censorious eyes; seldom did she see anything that didn't merit wariness, if not total distrust. But for once, her attitude was an inspiration. "You went to Coney Island as a kid, didn't you, Vera? You remember the old trolley depot they had down there?"

The housekeeper glanced at his plate to be sure her food wasn't the reason he had turned into an idiot, then nodded reluctantly. "It was a smelly place. Mice and rats all over the place. Why do you ask, Father?"

"Somebody just mentioned it. They didn't mention any rats, though."

"People see what they want to see, Father," she said, shuffling out to the kitchen with his dirty tomato juice glass. "And they don't like you openin' their eyes, neither."

It was while waiting to fall asleep that night that Durkin decided to take a trip the next day to see what had happened to the trolley barn. Because it was his anniversary, Perez and Mayfield had volunteered to take over all his usual duties for the day except for the seven o'clock Mass. They were also adamant he stay away from the rectory, visit friends, go to a museum, or disappear into some multiplex to watch one movie after another—anything to keep him away from a house phone bringing an emergency. Durkin didn't object; on the contrary, it seemed an omen that his curiosity about the depot dovetailed with their desire to have him out from under foot for whatever it was they were planning.

The next morning, he took the subway to Coney Island—a trip he hadn't made in 20 years. He regarded it as an achievement of sorts that he didn't start feeling like an idiot until he was a few stops along. This he promised to make good on by confessing his sin to the only appropriate person—Vera Trimble. Because it was a weekday, there were only a few preschool children and their mothers going to the end of the line with him. Whatever fancy he could indulge for himself, he couldn't believe the fat blond boy already scooping at imaginary sand with his plastic yellow shovel would have had more fun in a trolley terminal than at the beach. He wouldn't have blamed the mother for worrying if the boy had made such a claim. So what did that say about the froggy man, what kind of a kid must *he* have been? There was only one plausible answer: What Durkin and his schoolmates would have called a weirdo.

When he stepped out onto the elevated platform of the last stop, Durkin was immediately invigorated by the sea air. He inhaled deeply, returning the smile of the blond boy's mother as she took the child's hand to guide him down the staircase. The exchange made him feel furtive, tempted him with the thought that, instead of searching for the goddamn trolley barn, he could still pass himself off as just another visitor hungry for a Nathan's hot dog or eager to see the dolphins in the aquarium. He didn't know where such an impulse had come from, but it was unsettling in its tiny, pointless hypocrisy. Who was he supposed to be deceiving, and why would either he or they care one way or the other?

It took him less than five minutes to discover that the trolley barn on West Fifth had been razed for a high-rise housing project. Its successor was a three-story subway and bus terminal on Stillwell Avenue. The new terminal resembled the froggy man's depot as much as a car resembled a horse. Just the gleaming blue and white solar panels in the vaulted canopy of a roof seemed like overkill to the man's memories. The strongest odors were of McDonald's coffee and burgers on the building's main floor—an aroma he could have had three blocks away from the rectory.

Durkin got a coffee and sat down at a bright orange table near a street window. It was barely eleven o'clock and he had traveled little more than a half-hour on the train, but his arms and legs were loggy, as though he had been hard at work since midnight. He practiced a little abstinence by refusing to dwell on whatever new exotic disease was taking hold of his body, focusing instead on the desultory groups coming off the trains. Two men went across the street to the Mets minor league ballpark where a sign advertised season tickets on sale, while most of the other clusters of couples and family groups set off down Surf Avenue toward Astroland. He tried recalling if the housing project had been on the site of the barn when he had last been to Coney Island. He was pretty sure it must have been, that back then he just hadn't given a second thought to it, the people living in it, or whatever it had replaced. He still didn't know why he should.

He got back on his feet before a full grouch descended. For the next hour or so, as he wandered through the Cracker Jack, corn on the cob, and cigar smells of Surf Avenue, seeing the kids shrieking over water gun races and adults fuming for not knocking over enough milk bottles, he felt a growing sadness for his frog man. The old timer had missed so much by wanting his *every-thing.* How could he possibly have enjoyed himself in something like the House of Horrors if he had still been thinking of being back in the trolley barn? There couldn't have been an amusement anywhere on the street that hadn't reminded him of how little he had settled for, of how much he was being cheated. Why hadn't it at least ended in childhood? Why hadn't somebody somewhere along the line—a parent, a lover, a professional man—persuaded him of the difference between his *everything* and debilitating ob-session? Whose sin was it that he was still battling the same illusions at the age of 72?

Durkin had to stop in front of an arcade. He was seized by a melancholy he hadn't experienced in years, and it seemed to weaken his legs. To shake it off, he sat at a poker ball table for almost a half-hour, feeding quarter after quarter into the slots in quest of something besides a lousy pair. When he finally scored a flush, even the change man alerted by the bell looked happy for him, presenting him with a couple of extra tokens so he could claim a hand-sized white bear with a red ribbon around its neck. Revived by his rest, Durkin walked with the bear for a couple of blocks, determined to choose well. A boy wailing at an older brother for another ride on the bumper speedboats was just a pain in the ass and didn't deserve a reward. He would have given the animal to a cute girl in a stroller who smiled up at him, but the sister walking alongside the carriage wasn't that much older and he had no intention of instigating a family quarrel. Finally, he gave his prize to a redheaded girl chewing on her thumb who seemed mesmerized by his collar. It was only walking away from the girl and her mother (who acted as though they had been handed the lottery prize) that he wondered why he had worn his collar instead of civvies.

His clothing seemed like some last reason for Durkin not to like himself on the day. Would he have gotten the same smile from the mother on the subway platform, the same extra tokens from the change man at the poker ball table, in a sweatshirt? Durkin knew he wouldn't have. When he found himself back at the subway station, he had no reason not to take the train, to get away from so many exercises in self-aggrandizement.

✳ ✳ ✳

Durkin followed orders for the rest of the afternoon, burying himself in the neighborhood multiplex for some boxing world nonsense and then some louder intergalactic nonsense. It was a little after six when he returned to the rectory. He was putting his key in the lock when Perez yanked open the front door. "I just left you a note. Vera's feeling under the weather, so we're having dinner around at Vesuvio. Why have her on her feet when we could all use a break from Celtic calories anyway, right?"

Durkin had to control the imp in him that wanted to go inside to see if Perez had left a note or had just drawn the assignment of watching for his return and accompanying him around to the restaurant. "Italian sounds good," he said. "Busy day?"

Perez jumped over to the curbside of the sidewalk as they started their two-block walk to Vesuvio. "Nothing out of the ordinary. What about you? What'd you do?"

Durkin backed into it, talking first about the movies he had seen and about why he would probably forget their titles within a week. Perez nodded far too enthusiastically, savoring every word as another footstep closer to the restaurant. Only when the slight man threatened to make up the rest of the distance by talking about something he had seen recently did Durkin mention his morning in Coney Island. Perez looked quizzical, even lost a couple of steps when he heard about the discovery of the new terminal on Stillwell Avenue. He all but stopped completely out of curiosity when he learned the trolley barn wasn't there anymore. "That's nice to know," he recovered with a broad smile. "Of course, I didn't know it was there in the first place, so pardon me if I don't have a crying fit over it."

"You're excused."

"Why?"

"Why what?"

"Why this sudden interest in Coney Island terminals?"

Durkin couldn't tell him, of course; the frog man was still protected by the seal of the confessional. He couldn't even mention it in personal detail to Perez in his own confession. So he just shrugged and shifted the conversation to the bear he had won at poker ball.

Perez was watching him with another knowing smile as they waited at the corner for the light to change. "We haven't been very subtle about it, have we? You've figured it out."

Durkin looked across the street to Vesuvio. Marty Weyhauser was obviously out of the hospital; or at least his Buick with the WEY plates was. And if he wasn't mistaken, the man taking off his coat inside the entrance was Bishop Glaudini. "Don't worry about it. I can pretend."

"That would be good," Perez said as the light changed. "It would make a lot of people feel better."

MRS. ROANOKE

MILLER started his day with Mrs. Roanoke. That wasn't her name, and Miller had never been to Virginia, but he was sure that if the city of Roanoke ever resembled a person, it would resemble the old lady who peddled her bike past his window morning after morning between 7:30 and 8:00. And old Mrs. Roanoke was. He hadn't realized how old until the day a gust of wind blew her canvas hat off her thinning gray hair in front of the house and she had braked her bike, dismounted shakily, and gone casting after the hat through a couple of sadistic breezes. As she stooped over and then stooped over again, Miller saw she had to be closer to 80 than 70, her oval face set in the squint of a wrinkled squaw who had seen too much to remember tribal details. Her daily exercise up and down the hilly block had to sap her strength for hours afterward because she was certainly no once-upon-a-time athlete with stored up re-sources against aging. The shoulders under her blue print shirt were almost curved to a hump and the legs inside the loose tan slacks defined the spindly. If he hadn't met Mrs. Roanoke through his window, he would have most likely encountered her in one of those dusty mantle photographs where a great-grandmother sat surrounded by generations of family members and tried to look oblivious to the drunk next to her shoulder and the brat on the floor in front of her.

Miller being Miller, the fact that the woman was so scrupulous about her exercise worked its way up through an initial dismay to an incredulous anger. How could her regimen end except with the stroke or heart attack she appeared so dedicated to keeping at bay? At least if she had been punched out at home, she could have fallen on a chair, a bed, or at worst a carpet. But in the street? Suppose she had her attack as she was pedaling across in front of a bus? She not only would have been dead, she would have been mangled painfully beforehand. Every time she went churning by, he was tempted to run outside and remind her of all the fitness gurus who had collapsed in the middle of their exercises.

That he never actually did run out to her was Miller: Not only given to regular angers, but to abandoning his most urgent ideas at a temptation level. The angers he had learned to negotiate by avoiding contact with people; the habit of not carrying through on his impulses he had long entrusted to the tragedies recorded when others *had* done more than think about acting on some inspiration. He wanted no further part of that destructive motion, and hardly felt poorer for not volunteering for more of it. For himself he had his computer and his telephone, mostly venturing out his front door only when the city threatened him with citations for sidewalk snow that had turned to ice or for the latest assault on his garbage can by the neighborhood cats. About this too he had learned to take the long view since as long as he appeared every so often at the front of the house to shovel or re-bag, the kids on the block had no reason to play Scary Freddy games through his windows and their parents couldn't gripe he was a spooky neighbor. In a way, the city's periodic threats had come to make an essential contribution to what the TV chatterers called his life style.

Miller hadn't always been so reclusive. Well up to his 40th birthday, he was Mister Congeniality, always the first to suggest evenings out and equally first about fishing out a credit card for handling what charges the evenings had racked up. There had been women, there had been movies, there had been ball games, there had been trips to Europe, the Caribbean, and Latin America, and there had been more women. At many junctures on this odyssey he could have sincerely replied to the curious that yes, he was a happy man. No one lived in Eden, but how far from it could he have been if he occasionally got a whiff of its aromas? And if he was wrong about the source of that scent, the self-delusion alone seemed like enough to get on with.

There had been no specific cause for the marked change in Miller's behavior—no traumatic car crash, loss of a job, death of a friend. He had been well along in his seclusion before becoming aware of it. One month he had been knotting his tie in the morning to go off to his office, the next he had been scraping directly from his kitchen table breakfast of cereal and coffee to his studio desk. If he could satisfy his employer as much from home as from the middle of the city, why argue? The closest thing to a distinct fork in the road was the day his broker had informed him they had underestimated the potential windfall from a start-up in Nebraska and had made twenty times more than what even their optimism had foretold. With that profit safely ensconced in his bank account, Miller saw no reason for continuing his office employment even at electronic remove. There had been a couple of obligatory farewell evenings with colleagues, but these he mainly remembered for his impatience for the check to arrive so he could say goodnight and walk out into the future with an empty promise to keep in touch. He had been grateful his ex-colleagues had shown enough understanding of his attitude to wait on him to carry through and not to precipitate starker tones with their own calls.

Thanks to behavior developed years before his strict domestic routine, filling the day didn't pose much of a challenge. If people could be described by a single adjective, Miller's would have been *avid*. The piles of stock reading printouts that accounted for most of his paper garbage every day said he was an avid investor. The floor-to-ceiling shelves in his studio, living room, and bedroom said he was an avid reader. The hallway train of bookcases for his CDs and DVDs said he was an avid listener of music and watcher of movies. His refrigerator said he was an avid consumer of fruits, yogurts, and chicken, his closet that he was an avid wearer of black jeans and solid Caribbean shirt colors (mango, lime, rose). His credit card and phone bills said he was an avid customer for anything that could be delivered to his door. In this sense, his avid pursuit of isolation was not at all odd: It was just a different avidity.

He had also collected new relationships, and of the best kind—people who, like his broker, claimed from him only what he had been ready to cede anyway. It had taken weeks to find them. First, he'd had to maneuver through chat rooms that were screens for on-line sex numbers, phishers disguised as former classmates, and other Internet con artists. Truth be told, it had been an aggravating search, and just to have someone to communicate with he had been tempted for a few days to reply to the president of the Nigerian State Bank who had millions of dollars in an inheritance for him if he would only send along his bank account number. But being a mere temptation, this potential relationship with Lagos was quickly forgotten, and he returned to hunting for serious correspondents. Ultimately, he found several.

One was Marco in Lucerne, who really wanted to play chess. For all Miller knew, the man might have been Pierre in Geneva or Hans in Zurich lifting his personal anecdotes about Lucerne from some obscure novel only the Swiss knew about. That didn't matter to Miller. The person he knew as Marco in Lucerne was as eager—and as inept—about chess as he was. The two of them had plenty of e-mail laughs every game about how it was already a miracle that they knew how to move their knight pieces.

Another correspondent was Lena in Copenhagen. She had come on so flirtatiously that Miller had thought she was another phone sex worker, but then he realized she wasn't being flirtatious at all, simply typing more frankly than he was used to. When she had asked if he had a lover, she had wanted to know only if he had a lover, not if he had a citizenship she could borrow. After a few weeks she had admitted she wouldn't have liked it if she had been part of confidences he hadn't felt free to share with a lover. As Lena had put it: "You would be dishonest with two of us. You would be making us halves of some whole that exists only in your mind." Miller reassured her immediately. "The only reason I'm even in contact with you," he told her, "is so nothing genuine exists only in my mind. You are my sanity."

And so were others. Frank in Monterey knew everything there was to know about movies made in the 1940s and 1950s, and constantly tested Miller with the names of actors (those who had played the four killers in *High Noon*, who had played the jurors in *12 Angry Men*, etc.); it was thanks to Frank that Miller kept Netflix hopping after one forgotten title after another. Julia in Milwaukee knew every group Miles Davis had ever played with, Billy in Memphis every backup shortstop to play with the Brooklyn Dodgers, Raymond in Boston every politician who had been denied a likely vice-presidential nomination. Miranda in Miami Beach went on incessantly about Spanish language dialects, Sebastian in London about royal families. Everyone was an expert on something, but not so overbearingly that he or she couldn't be dismissed with the click of a single key.

Inevitably, there were pests. One was old man Christian next door who used any pretext at all to ring the bell. If it wasn't to borrow something, it was to come right out with a blatant invitation to his house for a coffee, iced tea, or some other concoction Miller had plenty of in his own kitchen. Miller was polite the first few times, claiming work deadlines or the need to remain home for a phone call. But then he made the mistake of saying he had a contagious disease; instead of responding to the outrageous lie for what it was or just simply backing down from the front door in fear, Christian had taken it as an excuse for a dirge about how his two daughters had left him alone by marrying husbands on the other side of the world. It had gotten so bad, Christian had confessed, he had begun drifting down to the local Catholic church for the weekly bingo games to have company. The exasperated Miller had finally cut off the whining by advising Christian to look for a card with a B6 on it at the next bingo evening and had slammed the door.

John Fazio, the UPS deliveryman, had also become irritating. First there had been the jokes about how he could have made a living just delivering to Miller. Then there had been the calculatingly idle remarks about the contents of the packages and the sulking when he hadn't had his curiosity satisfied. The third and latest stage had been the absence of any greeting, the shoving of the clipboard into Miller's chest for signing, and the leaving of the package on the ground in front of the door. Miller considered calling UPS to lodge a complaint, but he had the feeling he had already become John Fazio's favorite topic of conversation back at the warehouse loading platform and that any new deliveryman would feel compelled to be twice as snippy in an act of solidarity. He let it go.

There were others, as well. The cable man came practically every month to fix a tiled television picture caused by squirrels chewing the wires in the control box and acted as though Miller should have exercised more control over the neighborhood wildlife. Despite all the blockage lists he had signed up for, he was bothered regularly by telemarketers pitching life insurance, politicians, or phantom charities. And no, he didn't want to take just two minutes out of his busy schedule to answer some public opinion poll about global warming. Nor had he ever been sure where Jehovah fit into the mythological pantheon, so drop him from the potential Witnesses two eerily smiling women kept coming back to find on his street every other Sunday.

It was Mrs. Roanoke who weighed on Miller the most, though. She almost never missed her morning grind, the major exception being when a blizzard had left the streets impossible for walking, let alone bicycling. As the old woman had kept at it day after day, Miller had also observed how totally absorbed she was in her pedaling. Not only Christian but several people on their way to work had waved to her as she had passed, but they might as well have waved to the clouds for all the acknowledgment they received from her. Not counting the day she had been forced to go after her hat, in fact, she saw nothing around her except the next few yards in front of her wheels.

The woman's blinders gave Miller the shivers. Was she mocking him in some allusive way, taunting him that he wasn't the last word in concentrating on self-generated projects? There wasn't much reassurance in the thought that she couldn't have been doing that because she had never glanced at his window long enough to know he existed behind his curtain. However she knew he was there, he was certain, she knew, and the bottom line was mockery. As foolish as he felt raising the subject with her, he shared his misgivings with Lena. "Tell me I'm being stupid," he implored her.

Lena waited a whole day before getting back to him. "The woman sounds like she's in her own world," her message from Copenhagen said.

"I know that much. That's why I mentioned it."

"So what is the problem? You want to compete with her at some game? Why would you want to do that?"

"It's no game!"

"Good."

As e-mail brush-offs went, it was the sharpest one Miller had received since Julia in Milwaukee had teased him for mixing up the Adderley brothers. He regretted having given so much of himself to Lena, and made a mental note not to repeat the mistake.

His anxiety about Mrs. Roanoke continued to build. Just attending the morning ritual produced a hot fluttering in his chest. Day after day she chugged past—slowly enough that no one protested her using the sidewalk instead of the street, ruthlessly enough that she might have had a demonic gleam in her eye for being more predictable than some of Marco's chess moves. She seemed to be counting on him to watch her go by so he would be forced to remind himself he would be doing the same thing the following morning. None of the rest of Miller's activities were so preordained. If he wasn't in the mood to talk about old movies, he simply left messages from Frank unopened in his In Box. As obsessive as he was on the topic, Sebastian knew not to make the Windsors daily fare. But not Mrs. Roanoke: She came wheeling down the street morning after morning, totally indifferent to the capacity of others' tolerance.

Miller was tempted to respond to her arrogance. Maybe startle her by running out the door one morning, planting himself in the middle of the sidewalk, and bursting out with a cheerful Hello. Before she got over her shock, he might even relate an anecdote or two about his former life style, swamp her with meaningless-ness. Did he care about her reaction? No, he didn't. The only important thing was to interrupt her relentless flow.

Because he was only tempted to stage his little street scene, Miller let the idea ride for more mornings of watching from behind his curtain. His growing anger with Mrs. Roanoke he dealt with by ignoring everyone in his mailbox and turning on cooking shows, talk programs, and sitcoms that reconfirmed for him how little of the world was worth saving. When that didn't do, he reached for one *film noir* DVD after another, nodding through the cynical deliveries of the Garfields and the Mitchums until he felt naked in his lounger without a cigarette and a wide-brimmed fedora.

Then one morning Mrs. Roanoke didn't come. At his post behind his curtain he checked his watch three times, and three times his watch said he hadn't been late for her usual appearance. To be on the safe side, he submitted to the gougers at AT&T for a time check; for once, wasting money felt like a secondary consid-eration. He was furious. Had she succumbed at home the way he had often imagined? Or, short of that, maybe collapsed and been admitted to a hospital for too much exertion? He didn't feel like guessing, so he called every hospital and then every funeral home in the district, claiming the old woman as a grandmother he had lost touch with. All the polite, suspicious, and brusque replies came down to the fact that no one answering Mrs. Roanoke's de-scription had been admitted on their feet, on their backs, or any other way. She had simply changed her schedule!

"There is another possibility," Lena pointed out. "Maybe the riding was too much for her and she just decided to stop."

"Why?"

"I don't know why. You would have to ask her."

Miller laughed at the notion. Instead, he paid greater atten-tion to the death listings in the local paper. Old women appeared to drop dead every day, but none of them was Mrs. Roanoke. They were the wrong age, the wrong ethnic group, or in the wrong fam-ily situation. How did he know? He just did. When Mrs. Roanoke died, he didn't have the slightest doubt he would recognize her between the lines of the agate type.

The days turned into weeks without any trace of her in the obituaries. Putting the paper aside one morning, Miller realized he had become as used to not detecting her presence in the death listings as he had grown accustomed to not seeing her pedal past his window. He risked saying as much to Lena.

"You don't sound angry about it anymore," she replied.

"It'll be there one of these days," he reminded her.

"Then what? You'll be angry again?"

"I'll probably be tempted to be," he typed out to Denmark.

SECURITY CHECK

SHE was furious she had left the ticketing up to Abel. If she had done it on her own, she wouldn't have had to explain at the ticket counter, at the security checkpoint, and at the boarding desk that her name was Sheryl, not Cherry, and that her passport was right and her ticket reservation wrong or not wrong exactly but okay, maybe confusing because Abel preferred thinking of her as Cherry rather than Sheryl, had in fact never called her anything else after she had introduced herself to him that way two years ago in that Ninth Avenue Chinese restaurant Marlene claimed was the only place in the city that served the kind of food she had eaten in Shanghai. So whose fault was it he had made the reservation in the name that he still sometimes cried out while he was coming inside her? If he had cried out Sheryl, wouldn't she have been the first to suspect he was no longer excited by Cherry, that he had been storing up some exotic Sheryl in his fantasies who wasn't the woman who lived with him, the same woman or not?

She liked herself for conceding that doubt, for being objective enough to admit some of the mess might have been on her. But that still didn't excuse what Abel had put her through with all the morons who couldn't see beyond their noses. If you had two first names, you were a terrorist and had to take off more than your shoes. She was going to hold that against Abel—when she landed and called him to say she had arrived, when she got back home from her trip, all the way to the next life where he would precede her and be on hand to greet her. The least of it was that he had put her in a bad mood before she had planned to be in one. She needed neglected facial muscles to smile back at the stewardess or air support technician or whatever the hell the woman was now called who seemed to be congratulating her for knowing how to clasp her seat belt. From the second she had stepped out of the cab and walked into the terminal, she had been in the clutches of people for whom condescension was the height of virtue.

Getting into the air helped. She began blurring the faces of the two security women who had brought her into the bare room and demanded to see that she didn't have bombs attached to her underwear; one was white with a big nose and a musty smelling uniform, the other black with thick eyebrows and an odor of lilac toilet water, but that was all she could still recall clearly. She was safely away from them, no need to continue sounding apologetic to them in her anger. The boarding desk guy was history, too. She didn't have to put up with any more of his looks insinuating she had been very clever to have penetrated the terminal as far as him. All gone, back on earth. She could even feel a little giddy at being suspended in the clouds between the Cherry she had left behind with Abel, her friends, and the office and the Sheryl who would be awaiting with her mother and father when she landed. In the air she could be both and neither and one in place of the other and none of the above. Was there a specific border in the sky when she passed from Cherry's sphere into Sheryl's? She didn't think so so she could be anonymous for the whole trip. She was She Without a Name, and that seemed especially right for a flight where everything was pretty much without identity. Had Abel specified she be given the front row in Economy to have more leg room? The backs of people's heads might not have been the worst sight, after all. There was nothing whatsoever on the gray metal cabin wall in front of her, not even an ad for the airline or a rack for a puke bag or a card instructing her how to inflate her life preserver when they dropped into the ocean. Only the unused seat buckle sat next to her in the sunlight. The couple behind her could have been complaining about a grown son or a pet cat. And the long-legged cowboy across the aisle had all his character in his silly mustache and in the tight jeans and boots he had propped up against his cabin wall before nodding off to sleep.

The attendant-now-waitress smiled again with her clumsy beverage wagon to offer water. She Without a Name said yes, and was glad it came in a plastic glass. Cherrys and Sheryls might have paid for wine, brandy, vodka, scotch, and tequila in fancy flutes or shot glasses or whatever, but She Without a Name was just fine with K-Mart plastic glasses for free water. It even tasted like plastic.

She thought about looking at the work she had brought along in her shoulder bag, but decided not to. Work would have reminded her of ground things, of what she was supposed to be responsible for when she was Cherry to most people she knew and Sheryl to those who liked thinking they knew her more intimately than the people who assumed they knew her. She didn't want to be any closer to ground things than the greenish mountain or plateau way down below her window. If whatever kind of land it was could get along without her, budding and growing and dying in her absence, she could get along without it. She was perfectly fine with her plastic glass of water and the blank cabin wall in front of her.

She closed her eyes to see if that brought even more anonymity. It didn't. Just the opposite, the blankness immediately wanted to be filled—with the testiness of the couple behind her, with the squeak of the attendant's wagon wheels, with the whining of a little boy in the back for Seven-Up. She Without a Name opened her eyes again and felt better to be back in her private blankness. The cabin wall in front of her was hers, the dozing cowboy was hers. With her eyes open she felt reassured; more than reassured, entitled. She existed: Her lap and legs and shoes told her she did. She occupied space, and it didn't depend on what others called her. She had wasted too much time worrying about things like that. She had been born, that was what was important, not what her mother and father had called her. She had friends and Abel and a good-salaried job, that was what was important, not her rebellion against her birth certificate and compulsion to turn into somebody else once she had moved out of her parents' house.

She would have thought more about herself, about what she had done right and what wrong, about choices she wished she could make over and those she hadn't realized at the time were in fact choices, but that would have spoiled the blankness she was past craving and now felt comfortable within. Her particulars were neither here, there, nor any place in between. She compromised only to a smidgen of gratitude to the security women for helping make that kind of thing irrelevant. She Without a Name had paid her dues by being treated as a terrorist threat and by being forced to strip within hearing distance of hundreds of passengers—men, women, and other children who wanted Seven-Up—trooping past her. She had earned where she was. She was higher than the plane itself, flying over what it was flying over. She felt strong about that.

Her sense of vindication didn't last. She wouldn't have imagined having competition in her mood, but she did. She envied the glistening of the silver buckle on the seat belt next to her; not the sun or the buckle, but the glistening the two of them together produced. And it came completely from natural forces, not from her kind of manufacturing She Without a Name. It looked blissfully unaware that it would lapse back into dullness once the plane got out of the sun's way. Or once . . .

She Without a Name dismissed the idea. She certainly didn't see herself reaching over to the buckle and sweeping it down between the seats, out of the sun's glare before the sun itself had a chance to end the glistening. She could no more do that than listen to what the couple behind her continued to go on about. Inertia was all. It was a gift that had come to replace the snacks aboard.

She didn't know whether to be glad or not when a cloud darkened the window and the glistening stopped. She was glad for now, but also knew it wouldn't go on forever. The cloud would be left behind, the belt buckle would glisten again, and she still wouldn't have been as natural. She would have to remain private to herself for a long time yet, at least until the plane landed and her mother and father came up to her to kiss their Sheryl hello.

MORE THAN LESS

THE superfluous detail was a Kubel family trait. Kubel's brother Ray couldn't tell a story without taking biographical detours on everyone he mentioned. Older sister Regina was incapable of setting the table without procrastinating over which fork best suited her son, daughter, and husband. Younger sister Shelley couldn't admit her latest beating without identifying the liquor her boyfriend had been drinking or the book she had been reading when he had exploded against her. All were aware of the foible and could laugh at it in themselves when they weren't being criticized for it with impatient sighs and scowls. As a library researcher, Kubel liked thinking he was the most practical symptom of the family disease in at least converting it into a paycheck. He had lost count of the people who had thanked him for revealing the relevance of tiny footnotes or appendix additions for the project on which they were engaged. And when he was feeling especially philosophical, he could also fancy the notion that he, his brother, and his sisters were on some cosmic assignment to encompass as much reality as there was to gather, neither the directly pertinent nor the excruciatingly tangential escaping their vigilance, all of it to be forwarded to some intergalactic laboratory for sorting out in the study of the human species.

But then Shelley was strangled by her boyfriend, and Kubel didn't feel like being philosophical.

Within the wake of shock, mourning, insinuating questions from the police, cryptic questions from the district attorney's office, and crass questions from TV stations and newspapers, Kubel kept at his job, telling himself his hatred for Shelley's boyfriend had to be sublimated for his own sanity into his daily tasks at the library. He considered it fortuitous that his workload suddenly became heavy in the minutiae of such repugnant subjects as the Nazis, Stalin's labor camps, and the bloody consequences of Britain's divide-and-conquer tactics for one-time Empire possessions. Rarely did he have to labor to find a particular that satisfied his thirst for fury: It was usually right there in the first old journal or water-logged folio he ferreted out from the shelves of the dank library basement. The vengeance he wanted for Shelley had been a comprehensible option for entire peoples throughout history, and he subsided professionally within their tribulations. If only in passing for a conceit he had decided was inappropriate, he wondered if the intergalactic laboratory he, his brother, and sisters had been serving had provided these precedents for him so he could go home at the end of the day more weary than furious.

Instead of a fantasy about an intergalactic laboratory, his brother Ray and sister Regina had only their rage about what had happened to Shelley, and the more open they were about it, most often in guilty shrieks and tears that they hadn't intervened to help her when there had still been time, the more uncomfortable Kubel became. At the funeral and for weeks afterward, while they seethed with what they would do to the killer of their sister if given the chance, he found himself sitting silently or walking out of rooms when they erupted. He understood their readiness to go on shows to support campaigns for the death penalty, or even just to tell the public about a Shelley who had lived her 26 years unknown to it, but he couldn't share their zeal. At the end of his workday he was exhausted by brutalized Jews, Russians, and Malayans, and didn't see how his visible fatigue could contribute anything to Ray and Regina's radio and TV appearances. On weekends he preferred to stay at home with his cat Brandy than to continue with the semi-rituals of going to a bar with Ray on Saturday night or to Regina's for dinner on Sunday afternoon. In his most morose moments the apprehension crept over him that, more than just Shelley, he had also begun to lose a brother and another sister when a drunken psychopath had choked a girl friend to death for not explaining why it had taken her an hour to pick up orange juice, frozen yoghurt, and a box of Shredded Wheat at Key Food.

He didn't say as much, of course. There was still always that fraction of a second of joy at hearing their surviving voices when he phoned Ray and Regina or they phoned him. It took whole instants for everyone to remember they were supposed to be edgy with one another for not having reacted identically to what had happened to Shelley. Only past those instants did the new aloofness settle, Kubel hearing some of his own caution in his brother and sister for avoiding conversational land mines. He despised Shelley's boyfriend for introducing so much superficial tact into the family.

By the time the murder trial started, Kubel had to be urged by the assistant district attorney to show up at the courtroom in a demonstration of united family anguish. He knew the man was right for practical reasons, but he wouldn't have minded a little bit more persuasion that this was an accurate description of his feelings. Grief he certainly felt for Shelley's death and—work or no work in the library basement—the kind of loathing Ray and Regina had for Shelley's boyfriend. Did grief and loathing add up to anguish? He supposed it did, but he wished the assistant district attorney, more experienced in such matters, had spent a few more minutes winning him over to the idea. He was also taken aback by the alacrity of his boss to give him the morning off to attend the opening of the trial. He had barely gotten the request out of his mouth before the woman jumped up from her desk with a lot of *of course* this and *of course* that, making a bad job of diverting his attention from the tabloid on her desk with Shelley's college photo on the front page. He didn't like his growing impression that everybody in the city seemed to know how he should have been behaving before he did.

When he arrived at the court building, he found reporters already gathered on the front steps around Ray, Regina, and the assistant district attorney. With their backs to him, he thought he could slip into the courtroom without being seen, but he had barely started for the far side of the steps when one of the prosecutor's aides spotted him and steered him into the circle. When Regina clasped his hand, he didn't know if she was giving him sisterly solidarity or just warning not to blurt something stupid.

He got through the press conference without having to answer any questions, but was disconcerted to discover that the three seats reserved for him, Ray, and Regina in the courtroom were in the front row directly behind the prosecution table. He had seen countless TV dramas where the relatives of the victim had been seated in less conspicuous places and he was annoyed with himself that he hadn't gone over that point with the assistant district attorney before agreeing to show up. He couldn't have been the only one who had watched *Law and Order*, *Matlock*, *The Good Wife*, and all those other lawyer programs. Didn't their popularity over so many years suggest that people from the district attorney's office had to have watched a few episodes of them, too? What had they been thinking to put him, his brother, and sister on such display? Were they supposed to sob for the cameras on cue?

The boyfriend Shelley had still insisted on calling "Ronny" when she had been talking about her beatings, as if he had retained his rights as a familiar person despite acting like an animal, came through the side door with two lawyers who were half his height and twice his age. All three of them wore pinstripe suits, the one on "Ronny" blue, the other two gray. Kubel had first met "Ronny" at Regina's at a surprise birthday dinner for her husband and had tried to get him to talk about his brokerage house job. But "Ronny" had fenced off his curiosity, laughing that Kubel needed to take time off from researching facts that had no meaning for him and then turning to Regina's husband to talk about football. Shelley had sidled over to him to tell him not to get mad, that "Ronny" had just been joking. Now, though, as "Ronny" made a screeching noise pulling his chair out from the defense table and tried to look comical about it, Kubel was astonished to recall how much he had always detested the man, even before what he had done to Shelley. How could he have forgotten that? Had "Ronny" also put on a funny face hearing Shelley's last gurglings on their living room floor?

Kubel chided himself for being slow to get to his feet at the entrance of the judge. He was sure the newspaper people in the courtroom had noticed and he could see the next day's headline: KUBEL TOO DISTRAUGHT TO STAND UP FOR JUDGE. And then he made it worse by also being the last one to sit down again. He saw the second headline: DISTRAUGHT KUBEL ALSO TOO UPSET TO SIT BACK DOWN. It was as if the assistant district attorney had paid him to do the anguished thing.

The judge, a big man with a layer cake of a head of bushy salt-and-pepper hair, pushed his microphone away from his face, and that was a mistake because his voice wasn't as strong as he assumed it was. Not even the sight of Regina having to lean forward to pick up what he was mumbling got through to the man: He rambled on about what could just as well have been the morning news as the procedures he would be presiding over.

Kubel guessed that once upon a time the judge had either been criticized for barking too loudly into the mike or complimented for being naturally equal to courtroom electronics, and, offended or flattered, had never gotten over the observation. One way or the other, he didn't like so much vanity sitting in judgment of "Ronny." The empty seats in the jury box seemed twice as empty at the prospect.

He had been surprised when Ray had told him it would be a bench trial. Apparently, "Ronny" didn't trust jurors to understand how he could have been so "emotionally distressed," as the defense claimed, that he had been powerless not to throttle Shelley for good one last time. Maybe his lawyers were afraid of a juror who had suffered his own emotional distress listening to the investment advice of a brokerage house. But what did a bench trial imply about the judge? The plaque in front of him said he was Barton Pitt, almost like Brad Pitt, the actor who had lived with Angelina Jolie. Kubel had heard worse names for a kid growing up. What else could Barton Pitt's schoolmates have taunted except "Here comes the Pitts, here comes the Pitts!"? As schoolyard teasing went, it fell a little short of the traumatic. He decided Barton Pitt had been lucky: If he had suffered for anything at all as a kid, it had been for his double-tiered head. Kubel imagined a strawberry filling between his ears and the black-and-gray ringlets on top.

He pulled his attention back as Barton Pitt looked over at him, Regina, and Ray. Whatever he was going on about had driven Regina back into her chair and Ray into more of a glacial expression than usual. There was sadness in the man's eyes as he addressed them, and "Ronny" seemed doubly intent on studying his hands in his lap. Kubel figured the judge was extending his sympathy to the family of the deceased, and probably also throwing in a warning that this didn't give them license for any outburst. He didn't want to hear it, so he nodded quickly in agreement. But Barton Pitt continued to mutter at them behind full eye contact. Kubel wished Regina and Ray would also nod so they could all move on. The man's stare was embarrassing, made Kubel's throat itch. He coughed to get rid of the tickle, and one of the defense lawyers looked back at him as though coughing was outside trial protocol. That made him feel better about the itch.

As the judge finally began reading the indictment, Kubel was amazed to see how threadbare the right knee of his suit pants had become. Had one of the machines at the cleaner's gotten stuck

on that patch of material? He would have had to be a gardener
or nun to be down on his knees as regularly as the worn area insinuated. But then he remembered an article he had once looked
up on the haberdashery trade, something about how the knee
area wasn't threaded as densely as the rest of the leg to allow for
greater give. That had made sense when he had come across it in
the library basement, but now it made for the cost of a new pair of
pants. Fortunately, they were slacks and not part of a suit, or he
would have been even more out of pocket. One way or the other,
though, he was going to have a little talk with Mrs. Rosen at the
cleaner's.

At long last Barton Pitt shut up, and the assistant district
attorney got to his feet. Kubel didn't understand the necessity
of opening remarks when there was no jury. Surely, Barton Pitt
must have already heard about the fingerprints around Shelley's
throat that had been matched to "Ronny" and about the next-
door neighbors who had heard Shelley screaming her boyfriend's
name just before a last sound of a body being thumped on the
living room floor. And if he had heard all that, he must have also
anticipated what the two defense lawyers were going to say. So
why did Barton Pitt have to hear it all over again?

Kubel's grunt of disgust was so loud the assistant district attorney stumbled in his speech to look at him, accusation in his
eyes. Kubel stared ahead to the flags behind the bench until the
prosecutor went back to talking for the record. He knew what the
man was up to—wanting to remind Barton Pitt he wasn't sitting
in judgment over a corpse found on a living room floor, but over a
savaged woman named Shelley Kubel who had once inhaled and
exhaled as naturally as he did and who hadn't known she would
be dead seconds before she was. Kubel felt the itch coming back
to his throat, certain by now that it was an allergic condition he
had picked up in the library basement. What was the purpose
behind reanimating Shelley for a stranger like Barton Pitt, only
to remind everyone, as he had to, that Shelley really couldn't be
reanimated? There was a cruelty in that, a procedural conspiracy
to kill Shelley all over again.

The low sniffling to his left wasn't from Regina, but from Ray;
his brother's eyes were watery red even as the rest of his face
remained rigid. The assistant district attorney just kept talking, more gratuitously with every word. There had been so many
details from Shelley's life he was eager to cram in because Ray

and Regina had passed them along to him and his secretary and he didn't intend for that information to go to waste on a steno pad. Shelley had grown up with her older brothers and sister in a house that was really a bungalow with airs, had liked drinking milk from old jelly jars, had played in a community soccer league, had led a group of teenagers in a street protest to reopen a municipal pool during a heat wave, had obtained her B.A. in English Literature, had gone to work at a shelter for single mothers, had signed up for every marathon organized against disease. Kubel almost gave in to an urge to cackle out his suddenly overwhelming sense of futility. Where could he have started? When had he become the brother of Mother Teresa? The truth was that Shelley had never lacked for the smart crack or the arrogant push. She had even borrowed money as her due. Their own mother had said more than once that Shelley might have been the youngest but could take care of herself better than any of them.

So why was she the only one dead?

Kubel didn't know. Nobody around him did. The courtroom was a crowd scene of ignorance; with its venerated rituals, but of ignorance nevertheless. More frustrating was that the person closest to knowing why Shelley was alone in being dead was "Ronny," now trying to look like an interested but dispassionate observer as the balder of his two lawyers got to his feet to address Barton Pitt. Only "Ronny" knew what nobody, not even his mother, had figured out about Shelley.

Kubel tried to take in nothing but disconnected words as the bald lawyer went on and on. He counted the letters in the Latin motto on the shield behind Barton Pitt and divided them by four to see if they would fit evenly into his four front teeth; they didn't. He waited for the stenographer to come up for air, to notice anything at all around her, but she didn't and she didn't. He wanted to see the court guards throw a greedy look at "Ronny," give away how they thought of him as their meat, but they were on bland innocent-until-proven-guilty behavior. Finally, the bald lawyer stopped talking and the morning session ended.

Kubel managed to regain the street without being trapped by Regina for lunch and without saying anything to the TV news people waiting for him in the corridor. His boss looked astounded when he stopped by her office to say he was back for the afternoon, but he closed the door between them again before he had to hear the sound version of the protest forming on her face. Only when he reached his desk in the basement and saw his project files still waiting for him did his heartbeat slow down. At least his work hadn't been farmed out on the assumption he would be gone all day.

The top file was from a university professor asking about the novels written during Stalin's reign in the Soviet Union. The one under it was from a soap company vice-president needing information about bathroom sinks. Kubel didn't know why the professor's campus library didn't have the Soviet novel material and the soap executive didn't have enough subordinates to spend the day surfing the Internet for what he wanted. For some time, in fact, he had been surprised in arriving for work in the morning that institutions or corporations needed his help for anything. Aside from assisting individuals coming in off the street for documents that could be sent to them upstairs immediately for consultation, he couldn't see his position lasting too much longer. If his job wasn't on the endangered species list, as he had joked to Ray one night at their favorite saloon around the corner from Ray's house, it was only because the list hadn't yet been posted on the Internet.

The professor's request had no deadline delivery date on it, so Kubel assumed the information needed was for some book still being written, maybe only at a planning stage. He slipped that file to the bottom of the pile and looked more attentively at the request from the soap company executive. Did the library have any materials tracing the first use of soap dishes as an accessory for bathroom sinks? He was sure the library did, and probably within one of the numerous volumes in Section GH on the history of domesticity and household conveniences, but again he was stumped on why the soap man hadn't found that information on his own. At times, it seemed like the word had gone out to keep the poor researcher named Kubel busy, no matter how redundant he had become.

Kubel felt a frizzy warmth spread throughout his chest at the idea. Only now did he realize how cold—even bloodless—he had been back in the courtroom listening and not listening to what everyone was saying about Shelley. Simply put, he had been out of his element, defending himself against all the lawyer talk, trying to play the anguished role the assistant district attorney had assigned him. If Ray and Regina wanted to play along, fine. But he would produce his own anguish, thank you, and not just for public consumption. In the meantime, he still had work to do.

As he suspected, the history of soap dishes was hidden away in a book on bathroom accessories on the second shelf of Section GH. He wondered if Shelley remembered how, in her everything-is-disgusting teenage years, she had reamed him out for leaving a bar of Ivory soap caking in bubbles in the dispenser. It was as though he had been responsible for every fragment of soap even when he hadn't used it to wash his hands.

The Opals Man

MALEK sentenced himself to stay out of sight for a year. But that didn't mean locking himself up in his apartment or fleeing to some desert island. Instead, he rode the #2 train day and night, every day, with his only break the six hours between midnight and dawn that he needed for sleeping in his own bed, feeding the cat, and changing his clothes. He could afford his sentence: He had both enough money and enough pain to see him through 365 subway fares. He was also confident he wouldn't run into any friends on the train or going between his stop and his apartment.

While riding, Malek guarded against slipping into any expertise about the #2. He didn't want his time turned into some kind of fertile experience. It was enough to read his paperback thrillers, eat the hot dogs and hamburgers he bought at the station stands, and indulge his daydreams. Approaching specific stops, he immediately began musing about other stations on other lines so they would all be a jumble in his mind and he wouldn't be responsible to his memory for somebody who entered the train through the same door at the same hour every day. That he wasn't wholly successful, that almost every day he encountered a familiar commuter getting on, didn't bother him much: The tepidness of his industry seemed appropriate to the circumstances.

Naturally, he thought a great deal about Eileen. How could he have avoided it when she was the occasion for his sentence? At first, he thought of her exactly as she had predicted—what she referred to as the "CAWA of a broken relationship." Just as the terminal cancer patients she dealt with at her hospice job went through stages of Confusion, Anger, Withdrawal, and Acceptance in coping with their illness, she had told him, he would go through those phases in dealing with their breakup. And in fact, for the first couple of weeks on the train, Malek spent most of his ruminations on trying to pinpoint how far along he had progressed on the CAWA scale. It wasn't all that easy to figure out since the Confusion, Anger, Withdrawal, and Acceptance didn't always parade past him in rigid order. Some days he was so angry at her he could imagine beating her, some days he was confused their three years together had crumbled so quickly, on other days he could stir to some warm thump in his stomach to wish her happiness wherever she was. And of course, there were also the days when he merely had to take in his surroundings to agree that he had very much fallen into withdrawal.

But soon even Eileen's ferociously inclusive categories for his feelings palled, and he began thinking of her differently, in ways as odd to him as they were uncontrolled by her. For one span he thought of her as a mythological goddess—as Artemis who loved but who couldn't be touched, as the vengeful Hera who turned him into a bear condemned forever to serve as a light in the sky, as Aurora the Dawn who had left him with the most precious of all gifts in being able to start every day with renewed hopes. When the goddesses no longer captivated him, he thought of her as literary creatures—as Meg in *Little Women*, as the firebrand Carmen, as the melancholy Camille. Then came movie stars and singers and women artists and animals and flowers. Each realm of reference filled his mind for a day or two until he had explored all its possibilities and moved on to the next one. Eileen Cahill was all things that had ever been created, ever been imagined, simply ever been.

Including the bitch who had thrown him out of bed.

By the third month of his routine Malek began to feel Eileen's presence less obtrusively. She was still close, but presumptively, as though she had somehow gone from being a person outside him to an organic part of him. He had less and less reason for singling her out in his mind because she was already of a piece with it. She didn't need to hear his thoughts about what he was doing since she was doing it along with him. Together, for example, they realized that the basic appeal of the mystery stories he bought from a station newsstand every day was that they weren't in the least mysterious, that by the last page all doubts and confusions would be resolved. What could possibly be more entertaining for them than being able to identify all the killers and to clarify all the motives?

One consequence of not having Eileen breathing as a distinct person was that Malek felt progressively removed from all the things they had once done separately together. As the weeks went by, it became harder and harder for him to recreate his feelings when they had phoned one another to make dates, when they had sat in a favorite restaurant or bar, when they had undressed for one another in his bedroom or hers. He retained bits of conversation and some of his movements, but only to the point of making even these seem abstract. Had he said such-and-such to her or to somebody else? He couldn't remember, and with a finality that seemed to dissolve both of them physically. Parts of her remained vivid, but the whole was never quite there. There were days when he pictured her thin waist and tiny ass, other days when she was just a sardonic smile under her bangs, still others when he could make out only a yellow towel around her as she had sat on the rim of his bathtub and leaned over to pat dry the calves she doted on. It was parts, never the whole. Somewhere deep in his mind, he remained certain, she was still all there waiting to be reassembled, but now like every other experience he'd had in 41 years—coded for a subterranean archive that only the most unpredictable of remarks or fortuitous of meetings would have had the power to summon back up to his attention.

With his train Malek had fewer problems. Most other lines would have brought him into the neighborhoods of people he and Eileen had known together; the #2, not. The only troublesome patch was between 34th and 96th streets in Manhattan, where he risked running into acquaintances from the Upper West Side; but, as he recalled, even those people preferred the #1 local for Lincoln Center, 79th Street, and 86th Street. And it wasn't as though someone in that area would have had the time to ask a lot of questions before getting off again, anyway. He didn't look like a recluse. He wore good clothes, was always shaved, made sure he didn't break out his thermos or eat his fast food until he was uptown or in the Flatbush section of Brooklyn. To all appearances he was somebody going somewhere.

If he was surprised by anything over his first four months, it was by how complete his isolation was. The closest he came to having to talk to somebody was in his third week, when Martin Ambrose entered his car. Ten years before he had crossed paths with Ambrose in the faculty room of St. Barnabas High School— just long enough for Malek to understand that the balding algebra teacher with the pelican jaw didn't appreciate people who used the teaching profession as a temporary solution for money problems, just briefly enough that they could pretend not to recognize one another over the heads of an evening rush hour. For all that, Malek still felt a twinge of lost opportunity when Ambrose arrived at his Brooklyn station and hurried out the door.

He got over it. He didn't really regard his days as a fill-in Social Studies instructor as all that significant. No matter how much Eileen had said she was sure he must have been good at it, he really hadn't done it long enough to know one way or the other. About that Martin Ambrose had been right: He had worked at St. Barnabas only because he had been broke and on the verge of losing his apartment. For the same reason he had manned a hotel lobby desk, donated blood, checked off boxes for a market research house, flogged tickets for an afternoon TV quiz show, written promos for a radio station, waitered, assisted a cab dispatcher, sold cheap bracelets by telephone, and washed windows. He had never considered any of these way stations as the Essential Malek, either. Who the essential Malek was, the years had told him by now, was the comfortable opals dealer who warned all his customers from the start that they were investing in eminently finite stones and who then went along with their smiling indifference to pocket a 40 percent markup on his sales. Working from his apartment or from the office of some middleman, the Essential Malek was a dealer whose principal overhead was his honesty about the frangible nature of opals—something he insisted on (he was the first to acknowledge) to the point of obsession. The fact that he lost a sale here and there because of his obsession never worried him. As he had sometimes had to note to colleagues irritated at watching their brokering percentage walk out a door with an enlightened customer, overhead was overhead, simply had to be paid.

As he also had to pay for losing Eileen Cahill to the fatally ill hospice patient named Andrew Brewer.

By the fourth month Malek could go whole days without feeling aggrieved. In fact, there seemed to be many more things to pay for besides losing the only woman he had ever truly loved. There had been the time as a nine-year-old, for instance, that he had bullied Matthew Gold out of his bicycle; a week later Matthew Gold had gone to the hospital, eventually dying there of leukemia. There had been the time he had spent a weekend in the Catskills with

Alice Sterling—two weeks before her wedding. There had been the afternoon at St. Barnabas that he had overheard a student named Creighton boasting to friends about having deceived Mr. Malek with promises to study harder, with the result that he had flunked the slug on general principles. There had been dozens of times like that, when he had been something less than splendid in his behavior, and suddenly they began marching into his car like passengers who had been waiting years on their platforms. At times Eileen Cahill seemed like just the most recent, not the worst, of it.

Near the end of the fourth month Malek found himself starting to nod off for 10- and 15-minute stretches. In no mood for a cop to bang him awake with a nightstick, he forced himself to remain in bed an extra 15 minutes every morning so he would have no excuse for not feeling sufficiently rested on the subway. But this remedy also left him with less time in the morning for washing up, doing the laundry, and feeding his cat Boris, so he was forced to eliminate other parts of his routine, starting with shaving and making the bed. It was the first time he had grown a beard, and he wondered why it had taken half a lifetime to get around to doing it. Were there other things under his nose he had never done?

Midway through Malek's fifth month, an elderly black drunk staggered into his car at the Eastern Parkway station. The man had a rheumy, wild look in his eye and reeked of piss. Ranting about somebody named "Big Blake," he stumbled directly over to a student sitting alone with a lapful of books, pulled a long knife from his coat pocket, and began flailing away at the boy. Thanks to the scream of a Latin woman sitting adjacent to him, the student saw the knife coming and threw himself to the ground just as the first slice of the blade cut the air where he had been. The next few seconds were pandemonium as the boy scrambled away from the books he had fallen with, the crazed drunk tried to find him at his feet, the woman kept screaming in Spanish, and somebody at the other end of the car yanked the emergency cord.

Already halfway out of his seat, Malek was flung full force into the drunk as the train came to a screeching halt. Even as he was telling himself that he hadn't really intended tackling the man, that another second would have counseled less instinct and more reason, Malek rammed into his chest. For what passed like minutes he and the drunk looked at each other in a stupor. Then, just as he brought himself to remember the big knife behind the fold of the ratty coat, he saw the glint of understanding in the drunk's spottled face and shot out his forearm as hard as he could into the man's Adam's apple. For another eternity the drunk just stood and stared, seemingly too numb to feel the slam that had left Malek's arm tingling. Malek was already thinking of repeating the blow when a hand clasped him from around the back of the neck and pitched him over his own feet back to the door. Through the door glass he caught sight of the conductor taking the drunk's arm and jerking it up behind his back in one swift move. The last thing Malek saw before blacking out was the drunk twisting his neck back, trying to get a look at who had attacked him from the rear. The man appeared absolutely indignant.

When Malek opened his eyes again, he was half-stretched over the three-seat bank near the door. The Latin woman and a natty dresser with a tie clasp and collar pin told him he had been out for five minutes. He couldn't believe it. Neither the drunk nor the conductor had hit him on the head, and he hadn't banged it against the door. His first thought was that it was the fault of his eating regimen: He had been going on too long on hot dogs, hamburgers, and the other greasy crap from the midtown subway platforms. Only later did another possible explanation occur to him: He had *wanted* to black out.

Otherwise, the episode with the slasher dismayed him more for what didn't happen than for what did. As soon as the Latin woman and the smart dresser saw he wasn't hurt, they ignored him, turning their attention to where the conductor and a Transit cop had pinned down the drunk on a seat and handcuffed him behind his back. The train was moving again, but by inches, sounding like more of the coughing static coming from the cop's radio. For a moment Malek was seized by panic: He was going to be forced to get off at the next stop and go sign a statement about what he had seen. Even as he told himself it didn't matter, that he had never planned to make his routine *that* rigid, he entertained the fancy of making a run for a window, jumping down to the tracks, and hiding in the tunnel until everybody had forgotten him. But even his mental whim proved unnecessary. When the train finally pulled into Grand Army Plaza, only the cop, his handcuffed prisoner, and the student got off. None of them said a word to Malek, and only the muscular conductor who had grabbed him around the neck even looked over to inquire if he was all right. The Latin woman went back to her religious tract, the well-dressed man took a seat at the far end of the car. Malek might not have been there at all.

Over the next couple of days, he chewed on the incident until it had lost all its flavor. Who had picked him up in front of the door, then helped him over to his seat? Why hadn't the student at least nodded thanks to him? Was it just his imagination, or had the Latin woman and the suit been averting their noses even as they had asked him how he was? Had the shaggy hair on his face put them off? Did he stink? Granted he hadn't been using his deodorant as zealously as he might have, but he still managed to shower every other morning. Had the other passengers seen him and the drunk merely as different degrees of outcast? Had the cop ignored him because he didn't look like a reputable witness?

Malek came up with no satisfactory answers. Instead, he turned his attention to the crossword puzzle books he had become more in the mood for than his mystery stories. The mysteries had lost their excitement for him and Eileen. There were just so many formula plots, formula clues, and formula motivations for them to discover together. At least the crossword puzzles allowed them to admit the mechanics of their effort from the beginning, with no illusions they were dealing with people of any kind. In killing hour after hour with the white squares, they were being more honest with one another. Never, not even when they had hungered to do new things together, had they entertained the prospect of encountering a real African silkworm, a real Roman official, or a real medieval ascetic. Never had they wanted to travel to the capital of Guam, to an Arabian gulf, or to a town in Oklahoma. Doing crossword puzzles together was a totally accurate reflection of how they had come to feel about each other.

Near the end of the fifth month Boris died. Malek discovered the cat stretched rigid on the kitchen floor amid its food dishes; ants were already marching boldly around the carcass. As he knelt for a closer look, he thought he should cry, that Boris represented his last line to all that had been. But instead of crying he suddenly felt grateful to the animal for using its death to send the clear message that the past was over.

Without taking off his coat, Malek found a plastic bag in a cabinet and, using only the edges of his fingers, nudged Boris into it. Going out to the garbage cans on the street in front of the house, he realized he had a second reason for being grateful to the cat—that because it had been 16, he was in no way responsible for its demise. He felt good depositing the carcass in one of the cans, and even better when he clanged the lid down on the mess evenly and finally.

Because he had to spend extra time disposing of Boris's litter box, dishes, and yarn spools, Malek didn't get to bed until a half-hour past his usual retiring hour. He made up for it the next day by leaving the house as it was and skipping his every-other-day shower. Without the shower he didn't bother changing his socks and underwear, contenting himself with the last of his favorite clean shirts to mark the morning. Safely ensconced back on the #2, he was surprised to see that some squares from the previous day's puzzle book remained blank. Not only was that a first, but it prevented him from tossing the book in the trash next to the kiosk where he bought his new puzzles. When the train pulled in at 14th Street, the stop for his breakfast and work matter, he sentenced himself to not getting off. He simply hadn't earned his new day; if he was still chewing on yesterday's puzzles, he would also have to continue chewing on yesterday's food. It seemed like the only just solution.

Three hours into his ride, Malek still hadn't come up with a single letter remaining to be filled in from the old puzzle book. What seemed like the easiest of the clues— "Piano Concerto in A Minor"—bedeviled him after the initial letters *S C H U*. One moment he was sure the other four letters had to be *B E R T*, the next that they had to be *M A N N*. He simply couldn't make up his mind, and the vertical clues intersecting the solution were no help at all. The longer he stared at the empty boxes, the more they seemed to be mocking him. At home he had hundreds of CDs and cassettes, the overwhelming majority of them classical music. He belonged to two classical music clubs, had a subscription to Lincoln Center, and often taped televised concerts if he couldn't be home for them. The answer should have been obvious. And would have been—to the old Malek.

By one o'clock he felt drowsy. The combination of staying up late and skipping his breakfast and lunch made it easy to welcome the warm enfoldings that came over him when he closed his eyes. For the first time in months he imagined the shimmerings of his favorite opals. He imagined the clean black opal he had sold to Mrs. Campbell, teasing her that she could delight her friends by explaining why black opals weren't black. He imagined the green and red brilliance of the stone from Nevada he had sold

Weizmann. He imagined the smaller white opals, worth no more than $20 apiece, that he had given his niece Andrea one Christmas and that she had received as the rarest of emeralds. Each took a turn in dazzling him closer to sleep. He had been honest with everyone about the fragility of the stones, even with his niece (thereby earning him the same scowls from his sister as from people in the trade). With his stones and his customers there had always been truth.

When Malek awoke, the train was jammed with evening rush hour commuters. They had crept aboard to occupy every seat and standing area around him, and some eyed him as though he had stirred just in time to foil their attack on his seat, as well. He didn't blame them. As tired and edgy as they looked, most of them were still dressed neatly and smelling of an incredibly sweet variety of perfumes and colognes. He didn't belong in their society any more than in their seat. Nevertheless, the seat was his, and he had no intention of surrendering it. It seemed like submission enough that his puzzle book had fallen off his lap and was now torn and blackened under so many shoes. He went the rest of the evening without even the few open squares of the crosswords to occupy him.

Returning home that night, Malek admitted for the first time that his six-hour break in the apartment was the most dispensable part of his routine. Without Boris to worry about, there was no practical obstacle to writing a check for covering his rent for the rest of the year or to having the phone and electricity shut off. He went to bed that night without getting out of his shirt and pants. It wasn't going to be his last night in the house, but he wanted to work as smooth a transition as possible to that deadline.

Midway through the sixth month Malek recognized a second acquaintance. Like the algebra teacher Martin Ambrose, Kathy Hunter eyed him indecisively from the safety of the door over other heads. But Malek also grasped the difference: While Ambrose had debated the wisdom of saying hello, Kathy simply wasn't sure it was him. Three times she looked over at him and three times she immediately turned away to reposition her bag on her shoulder and argue her doubts. For his part, Malek was surprised how little Kathy had changed in the six or seven years since he had last seen her. She hadn't added a single ounce to her tall, slack frame, and her face was still a composed elegance. He wondered if she was still as tentative about her life as when she had worked as an office manager for Grossman. It was that profound passivity that had once attracted him to her, that had made them on-and-off lovers for several months, and that had finally parted them with little sense of loss. The last time he had seen her, he remembered, was at a party thrown by Grossman. He had gotten into an argument with her about never wanting anything, she had chugalugged her third or fourth scotch, then had wandered over to a sapphires hustler named Rick and brazenly flopped down on his lap. His last glimpse of her had been 10 minutes later at Grossman's door: As he had closed the door behind him, he had seen Rick taking off one of her shoes.

Seeing her standing now at the train door, Malek suddenly felt fragile in his self-pity. He had fantasized about all sorts of people coming up to him, looking at him in disapproval, and lecturing him about getting back on the straight and narrow. Somebody like crusty Cy Green, the Baron of 47th Street, for instance. Or his sister, back from her husband's embassy job in Singapore specifically to complain that he had been answering her letters even less than usual and to warn him that he was about to lose his status as her sibling. He had even played with the idea of Eileen unleashing her new lover Brewer from the hospice so he would be compelled to hear how losing a lover was nothing compared to losing a lung and then a life. But not once had he imagined Kathy Hunter upbraiding him. Kathy Hunter who had never dared criticize a living soul, who had been so insecure she had ambled through lovers and jobs with equal meekness, hoping only that "things" would work out, that somebody somewhere would give her what she wouldn't ask for. Any chastisement from her would have emptied him, mortified him beyond guilt.

He didn't give her the chance. Jumping up from his seat, he pushed his way through to the rear door. He didn't care how many feet he stepped on, how many passengers barked at him, how he stank more strongly even to himself in wading through so much perfume, cologne, and deodorant. He didn't care about the briefcase that (he realized too late) he had left at his seat; there was nothing of value in it anyway. His timing was perfect. No sooner had he gotten to the rear door than the train rolled into the glazed lights of the station. Another couple of seconds, and he was out and careering down the platform to the last car. Only when he had pushed back onto the train, not giving a damn how many people were trying to get off first, did it dawn on him how stupid he had been, that some cop might easily have come after him thinking he was an absconding pickpocket.

In the weeks that followed, what Malek most regretted about his encounter with Kathy Hunter was losing his briefcase. As unnecessary as it had become for carrying things, it had also evidently been his last line of defense against the sneers of the Transit cops and the condescension of the conductors who had by now picked him out as too much of a regular. Especially for a cop named Alexander and for a conductor named Martinez who identified himself belligerently one night as "somebody who don't need you stinkin' up my train," the bag's absence worked like a red flag. Alexander, a thick-necked rookie who resented his train duty, never seemed to be without a warning when he passed through Malek's car, even after Malek had shown him his money and credit cards. "Just fall asleep and see where it lands you" became the cop's daily greeting. Martinez, on the other hand, usually left it at glares. though one night he also made sure Malek was out on the platform of the Flatbush Avenue terminal before closing all the doors and signaling the motorman to get moving.

It was in the seventh month that Malek began thinking about Eileen again. As he had predicted to himself, the occasion was completely fortuitous—two women sitting across from him and talking about a mutual friend named Eileen. Yes, Malek thought of saying to them, he too had known an Eileen—way back when, in the days when he had been given to unpremeditated behavior. What a distance he had traveled from those days! But then, as the women turned their conversation to Eileen's mother and *her* problems, Malek felt himself surging toward some peak that he knew was going to offer an equally sheer drop on the far side. And he didn't want to stop his flight, anyway.

He pictured Eileen as she had been in their most precious hours together—swinging her big skirts in a mockery of embarrassment if she entered a public place after him and had to cross over to him under other eyes; raising her short arm up to his neck to kiss him hello and subsiding again with a breathless, perky laugh; frowning over her sharp nose as she spoke about her work, blocking out the deaths that occurred weekly to talk about the hopes and new hobbies she encouraged in her patients hourly; sitting down to London Broils or other pieces of meat that seemed too big for her; bouncing on the legs under her as she talked about something she was enthusiastic about. Once again, a couple of yards away from people who were making every effort to keep their eyes off him but who also knew an Eileen, Malek remembered with an overwhelming sadness how Eileen Cahill had represented life itself where he was concerned.

How else to say it? There was nothing she hadn't given him, nothing she hadn't inspired him to do or think for himself, nothing she hadn't made him want to give her. She had understood his obsession about being honest about the opals. She had understood his need to spend at least an hour a day in Central Park or in the rear of St. Patrick's Cathedral, where he could put together his thoughts and recharge himself for the sensation of then returning to the world. She had understood that their love making was going to be all things to them, that sometimes he needed everything and sometimes he needed practically nothing, but that, most important, they were going to have the time to go from everything to practically nothing and then back again. And had he not made her feel the same way? Had he not looked up and down into her shimmering green eyes over and over again and known that no fuller honesty was possible?

In the train that afternoon the tears rolled down Malek's cheeks helplessly. He felt the kind of choking giddiness he had once surrendered to at the movies—watching stern, implacable men look upon their sons with some culminating approbation; watching prodigals finally persuade the skeptics around them that they had been laboring for a great good all along; watching a dying hero bring together a woman and her true love and bless them as a couple for all the eternity he was about to embark on. The giddiness was silly, of no reason or credibility, but it was insistent and real. He had seen Eileen Cahill for the last time. He had nothing more to give her or get from her. He had loved her even more than his hurt at losing her had admitted.

Malek went home that night for the last time. He could no longer tolerate the possessiveness that had fueled him for so many months; even to himself he had become tedious. As he did every evening, he snatched the mail out of the box, made sure there was nothing with a Singapore stamp on it. then dumped it all into the trash basket at the foot of the building stairs; whatever it was, it was junk mail. In his apartment he made certain the gas was off and all the windows locked; however he wanted to lead his life, it couldn't be an excuse for abetting burglars or making the super's life more difficult. The water taps he secured only after he had taken the last shower he knew he would be taking for some time and had dried himself off. In the bottom drawer of the dresser he found the old flannel shirt he hadn't worn in years and had never really liked, but that was now his last article of clean clothing. He threw the shirt on a chair with the most passable pair of jeans and sweater left to him, then went into the kitchen to rinse out some underwear and socks. These chores done, he gathered up all the cans, boxes, and bottles in the refrigerator and closets and, except for the olive oil, dumped them into a duffel bag. The bag he placed at the front door so he wouldn't forget to dispose of it in the morning.

Lastly, Malek got out the five stones he had on consignment from a Brazilian dealer named Rao whom he hadn't seen in five years and who, for all he knew, had been dead that long. He gave the stones an olive oil bath in the kitchen sink, then wrapped each one in toilet paper and spread them around in the pockets of his jeans, flannel shirt, and coat. He had never really had a reason for holding on to the pieces, since two of them were doublets, another probably a triplet, and the other two possessed of only the most modest of rainbows, but now there seemed to be no reason for leaving them behind, either.

Falling asleep that night, Malek dwelled serenely on all the people he was no longer part of. One by one they marched through his thoughts—not festively like a parade of Fellini characters, but sedately, separately, like a procession of tradesmen showing him their wares, then moving on in either mild satisfaction or mild dejection. They would survive him, he would survive them; whatever.

Over the next couple of months little happened on the trains that Malek had not—or shouldn't have—foreseen. With little else to think about, he doted on the mural work of the downtown Manhattan stations, the computer institute ads in the cars, and the passengers who came and went. After a while he had gleaned enough Spanish from the ads to string together sentences of his own, sometimes testing himself when he saw a slogan written only in English. He became expert in the stations that had broken locks on the john doors and that had the best musicians. He learned how to slide his underwear down to his thighs when it began feeling too grotty, then how to slide it back up over his ass when his jeans required the relief.

As he had also counted as inevitable, the cop named Alexander tossed him off the train whenever he saw him, twice even escorting him through the turnstile and watching until he had made a show of starting up the staircase to the street. Malek didn't mind: It was victory enough that Alexander never carried out his threat to have him arrested as an Emotionally Disturbed Person. Another cop, a young woman with a heavy Bronx accent named Forte, announced herself one day as somebody who knew "all about" him, but thereafter did nothing more than make sure he didn't rest his feet on another seat. One evening she even placed herself a few yards away from him in an otherwise empty car and tried to get him to talk about his monotonous travels back and forth. Malek appreciated her curiosity, but soon diverted the conversation to the rigors of her job and her ambition to finish her courses at Pace and become a certified accountant.

Most of the surprises Malek could have done without. The most painful was that the additional midnight-to-dawn hours on the plastic seats aggravated a hemorrhoid problem, forcing him to stay on his feet whenever he was sure his seat was safe. Neither had he expected to be so defensive about the stones and money in his pockets. Rare was the rider sitting near him whom he didn't scrutinize as a potential thief. At first, he was alarmed so much paranoia festered within him; it was exactly the kind of emotional shabbiness he had always been fast to condemn in others. But then he stopped fighting it. After all, he had little in common with the old Malek.

And then there was Abdul.

For some weeks, and despite his vow not to interest himself in other #2 regulars, Malek had taken note of the blond in the dirty white caftan who sauntered through the train, not so much asking passengers to drop money into his peeling Dixie cup as simply assuming they would when he held it under their noses. Abdul, looking like a preppie gone to seed, said nothing, begged for nothing, promised nothing. If riders wanted to think of him as a white Muslim, as a mocker of the blacks who were plying the same route in similar garb, or as merely somebody wearing something he felt comfortable in, that was all right with Abdul. In his canter through the car he barely gave riders time to understand what he wanted, let alone lingered to hear what they thought of him. Nonchalantly flashing his Dixie cup, he could have collected a $100 bill as easily as a nickel and not noticed the difference until he was off the train counting his take.

But he did notice Malek.

Early one morning, after the #2 had disgorged the last of its stock market clerks and managers at Wall Street and had entered the tunnel for the crossing into Brooklyn, Abdul flopped down next to Malek and, behind a disgruntled glance into his cup, launched into a rambling monologue about how he had been "demoted" from the more affluent E and F lines going to Queens. Even as he tried to look deaf to what he was being told, Malek grasped that Abdul belonged to some group known as the Fourth World Beggars Association, that the group's members had to wear readily identifiable Third World clothing, that the group was very meticulous about analyzing what sort of clothing elicited the most money, and that members were absolutely forbidden to speak with riders during solicitations so as not to soil the purity of the findings on the comparative appeals of the various kinds of clothing. The money collected, Abdul told Malek, was divided evenly among members every Tuesday morning. It went without saying that members gave a full accounting of their collections, since honesty was at the core of the association's charter.

Malek listened to Abdul's ludicrous monologue with a growing infatuation. So many details were monumentally arbitrary! Why, for example, had Abdul chosen to wear a caftan instead of a loin cloth or Vietnamese pajamas? How could the group be so narrow-minded as not to realize that the people inside the clothes, not the clothes themselves, triggered a passenger's decision about donating a quarter or not? And why did they share out their proceeds on Tuesday mornings? What was wrong with Thursday afternoons or Sunday evenings? The whimsicality was colossal. For the first time since he had started riding the train, Malek felt a lift from something outside his own meditations.

The train rumbled into the Clark Street station just as Abdul was beginning to explain the association demotion system that had landed him on the #2. With no acknowledgment of Malek, he stood abruptly and ambled out the door. For the briefest instant, watching Abdul go over to the other side of the platform to await a train that would take him back to Manhattan, Malek considered getting up and going after him to hear more about the association's bizarre rules and regulations. But then he decided against it. It seemed enough to know that Abdul had accepted the demotion in the right spirit, and was still a working member of his group.

Malek was buoyed by his encounter with Abdul. Later that day he could still smile at the awkward attempts of two Fordham students to muffle their cracks about him while keeping their eyes on the ground. The red streaks running up the sides of their faces to their ears made him think of how he had tried to cover the dreadful burning in his chest the night Eileen had told him she didn't want to see him for a while, that both should get away by themselves and think things through. He hadn't known about Andrew Brewer that night, not explicitly, but he had sensed enough not to linger in her kitchen, to grab his coat and get down her linoleum-smelling stairs before she had put it into words. Over the next few days he had let this fear so preoccupy him that he didn't return her calls to his machine. Cy Green had scolded him: A hopeful man would have called her back at once, Cy Green had said. But Malek, as he was able to admit standing above the Fordham kids, had known better than to nurture any such hope. His dread had been luminous: The only reason for her calls was to provide him with details he didn't want, to give him a chance to be more honest with her and himself. He had never wanted so much honesty.

It was well into the tenth month that Malek saw her again. The train had just pulled out of 96th Street, and he looked up to see a tall, gaunt man in a red suede jacket jerking at the handle of the locked door at the end of the car. Malek was already lowering his eyes again when the man looked sheepishly over to the woman observing him from the bench near the door. She was amused by his attempts to open the door, and her amusement made the man smile, as well. With a theatrical wave of his arms the man sagged down on the seat next to her and rolled his head over on her shoulder in mock resignation. She took a small hand out of her coat pocket and comforted him ironically. She was all nose and teeth, her eyes covered by huge sunglasses. Even as she caressed the man's cheek, she seemed to be bouncing up and down on her seat.

Malek swallowed hard. A sheet of sweat covered his forehead. He stared down at his worn jeans, telling himself that if he kept looking at the white splotches, he would detect a pattern. He searched for islands and continents, for uncharted places between them where he could submerge and never be heard from again. But there was nothing to see but the splotches. He began to tremble. It seemed absurd he couldn't imagine an escape.

The train kicked into its blazing tear toward 72nd Street, the fastest stretch of the ride. The local stop at 86th Street flashed by. Malek wanted to be outside, on the tracks, running as fast as the train, pile-driving through every stanchion and post that threw itself across his path. After so many months Eileen Cahill was still real, still a separate person, still breathing, still bouncing up and down wherever she sat, still a woman who moved, walked, and talked on her own. She hadn't ceased to exist since he had last seen her. She still got up in the morning, peed, savored her bubble baths, stood before her dresser mirror to inspect a waistline that barely reached the bottom edge of the mirror. She still went to work and thought a hundred things of her own on the way. The only big difference was that, over the last several months, her thoughts had been less and less about him.

Malek felt a greater panic than he had the night he had fled her kitchen to avoid hearing Andrew Brewer's name. It was he who had deliberately driven himself out of her life. Instead of being on the train, he might as well have spent the last months shadowing her on her morning walks to her job to whisper in her ear that he was no longer worth thinking about, to brainwash her of his existence drop by drop. It hadn't been her at all, it had been him, only him, from the start.

But then the panic subsided, and he immediately recognized it as his last grasp to keep her chained to him. And such a transparent grasp, at that.

He peered over at her. Her glasses made it impossible to see the line of her eyes, but he was sure she wasn't looking in his direction. Andrew Brewer was talking about something as he lolled on her shoulder; she was nodding as she squeezed his hand between them. Brewer was thin, but he didn't look quite like the sick man she had described. What he mainly looked like was somebody who *had been* sick.

Malek understood. Andrew Brewer had come through for her. Brewer had needed her, surviving precisely because he had been honest enough to admit that to her. He, on the other hand, had never done any such thing. About that Eileen had been right from the beginning. Not once had he shown her how much he needed her. He had always acted beyond the reach of destruction or disintegration. How could he have pretended to be something he wasn't, even for her? He had never been in danger of crumbling overnight like one of her charges at the hospice. Just the opposite, he had been infrangible. Hadn't that been what had attracted them to one another? He had never thought of her as a nurse, but as a friend and lover. He had been incapable of believing in the corruption that had been so vital to her. He was Malek—whole, in one piece, honest to the edge of mania. Ask anybody . . .

The cry died in his throat, then stayed there, making it hard to breathe. He waited it out; he had no choice. It was much too late to show her. The simple, brutal fact was that even now he wasn't beyond repair. What had been done to him he had done. He hadn't come any closer to her; if anything, they were even further apart. For good.

He smiled to see her strong calves as she stood with Brewer to await the slide of the train into 72nd Street. She didn't favor heels only because of her height, but also to accentuate her calves: That pride in her ballerina days hadn't changed. When she walked off the train, she was gabbing—something about her life, something she still hadn't told Andrew Brewer about herself. The man in the red jacket had to lean down to catch what she was going on about. He wanted to hear it all, didn't want her saying things he couldn't make part of himself. The man in the red jacket loved her, and he was right. Nobody had deserved love as much as Eileen Cahill did.

Malek waited until the next morning, until West 47th Street was teeming with its usual wholesalers, wise guys, thieves, and couples-to-be searching for engagement rings. When he entered the lobby of Cy Green's building, the security man at the front desk jumped up from his coffee and bagel to point him back out to the street. But then the guard hesitated in belated recognition and, though still suspicious, sat back down again and returned to his bagel.

In the elevator up to the fourth floor Malek told himself not to be optimistic or pessimistic about how much Cy Green would advance him for the five opals. But one thing he was going to be adamant about was that the stones weren't top quality and he didn't want any handouts. Not only were they disintegrable like all opals, he rehearsed telling Cy, but three of them were doublets or triplets. The Brazilian Rao might have gotten away with his sophistications on naive customers, Malek was going to say, but neither Cy nor he had been born yesterday.

Secrets

SOME assumed Heyer's rigid routines grew from childhood influences. Either his father had been one of those abrasive Marine captains infatuated with his own sense of discipline, went this supposition, or his mother had been the kind who ironed socks after doing the laundry. In fact, the contrary was the case. Heyer's father had been an itinerant poker player who had confined his salutes to the full houses in his hand and his mother's idea of doing laundry had been to wait for the dryer to come to a stop and then to cry out for everybody to grab what there was for grabbing from the machine. Inevitably, those aware of this background championed the reverse theory that Heyer's routines were protesting his upbringing, as if to say human society consisted of so much of this quality and so much of its opposite and if one generation overindulged in one direction, its successor was preordained to restore a model balance. Heyer didn't believe this mechanistic gibberish. Outside of the likelihood that he would die some day because so many others before him had, the notion that one person's habits should predefine a second person's—in emulation, rebellion, or some blend of the two—dismayed him. No man was an island, as the sages were addicted to saying? He dismissed such a concept as hastily surveyed topography. For himself he had no brief with the solitary. The thing was just getting on with it.

Over the years Heyer had gotten on with quite a few things. A lanky, dark man with deviously vigilant eyes and a sharp nose—a face that suggested a perturbed crow—he would have been the first to admit he hadn't been *born to* anything, as the expression had it. Before reaching his fortieth birthday, he had worked in six countries at six entirely different occupations. The only visible bridges between them were the transportation tickets he kept neatly bundled in a rubber band in the top drawer of his latest desk. There was the freighter ticket that had taken him to Bergen, where he had worked in a fish canning factory; the train ticket to Frankfurt where he had sung in beer halls while flirting with being an entertainer; the highway toll and ferry tickets he had preserved from driving to Dublin where he had made change for the housewives playing the O'Connell Street slot machines every afternoon; the air ticket to Milan where he had edited the Italian edition of *Playboy* magazine; the cruise ship ticket to Montreal where he had produced CD anthologies of European film scores; and the bus ticket to New York where he had bought a restaurant in Tribeca that gained an aura of exclusivity by serving only five tables an evening with a single deluxe entrée at an extraordinarily high fixed price. Those who didn't know Heyer might have concluded that by keeping evidence in his drawer of all his moving around, he had a sentimental streak, that he savored reminders of his travels. In truth, he was wholly absorbed with the neatness of his collection within the rubber band—how whatever adventures the tickets insinuated about his means of transportation, places of relocation, or career pursuits, they were ultimately reducible to the packet he could make of them next to his Swingline staple box, 5000 Standard, Staples No. S.F. - 1.

Heyer's personal relations also reflected the priority he gave to the neat and the compact. Because he had lost his virginity to an Anne and had had his first lengthy relationship with a Bryna, he had made sure not to toy with the clarity of his desires from that point forward, getting involved even for one-night stands only with women who kept him alphabetically on track. (If his first lover had been named Josephine, would he have been so assiduous about it? Heyer didn't waste brain cells on that speculation. His first lover *hadn't* been a Josephine.) His biggest compromise came in Milan, where X was not part of the Italian alphabet. This he resolved (at least to his own thinking) by picking up a bass guitarist named Emilia with the rock quintet Xanadu. If he was deluding himself with her (and maybe on more than one count since she left him after stealing his wallet for a cocaine score), he was nevertheless able to move on to Yvonne with a minimal sense of failure.

Day-to-day practicalities were equally ordered. One morning he used Crest to brush his teeth, the next Colgate. He had learned the hard way that to use either two days in a row left him vulnerable to cavities. For breakfast there was the three-day lineup of cherry, raspberry, and pineapple jams on his English muffin, allowing him to relish daily changes in pairings corresponding to his parallel rotation of Maxwell House and Folgers coffees. Given his aversion to suits, he created another surprise every morning when his ample roster of sports jackets, pants, shirts, and ties produced an unexpected combination. He didn't mind it when he arrived at the restaurant and the elated and stymied looks of the staff betrayed the outcome of the bet on how he would be attired for the day. He even took their attention to his clothing as a compliment (save for a passing worry that someone would lose so heavily on his choices as to be tempted to clean out the till).

An unforeseen product of Heyer's routines was that, while they kept him personally within rigorously defined paths, they simultaneously gave the impression to others that he was a man of incessant whim. Excluded from the internal dynamics of his systems, people not named Heyer acted as though he might say or do anything at all, as witness the staff bets on his clothes. Nothing could have been more untrue, of course. Their limitation was that they didn't share *his* limitation, not realizing that just so many elements were in play for his rituals. Heyer was intrigued by this oversight. Already tinkering with the idea of selling his restaurant and becoming a teacher of philosophical astronomy in Bolivia or some other country closer to the sky, he had the feeling he was on to something more significant than the food business with that semblance of a contradiction. Was it too much to assert that the less variety in life, the more variety there appeared to be?

The question began to tease him through his drill at the restaurant, raising its head with increasing frequency while he checked to make sure that all the suppliers had completed their deliveries, that Antonio the chef had a creative gleam in his eye for preparing the meal of meals, that Isabel had given an extra coil twist to the napkins on the tables, that Sacha had received rum and tequila reinforcements for the bar. Day after day, it continued to nudge him as he greeted his five tables for the evening, once causing him to lose the thread to a conversation and to respond to an observation with what he knew was a dumb smile.

And his dumb smile was hardly the worst of it. The more Heyer gave in to his divagations about life's varieties, the more restless his reservation lists grew. Sitting in his small office next to the kitchen one evening, he had to acknowledge their glare out at him from his laptop. As one of the city's more exclusive restaurateurs, Heyer had been scrupulous about tempering the need for word-of-mouth publicity with care not to estrange his most satisfied customers for months at a time because of the restaurant's limited seating capacity. The challenge of negotiating the fine line between satisfying the wishes of repeat diners and catering to what might become a fatal few was exhausting. But now evidence that he had crossed that line was undeniable. Every single table for the next two weeks had been reserved for a return customer, the unfamiliar names confined to his futures list extending months into the summer. If he wanted to be optimistic, he could view the table guests of the returning hosts as prospects. But he had never had any reason to want to be optimistic. He knew from experience that most guests came only because they wouldn't have to pay; few had the income to play hosts themselves on a subsequent evening. The reservation list confronting him on his screen was a formula for bankruptcy.

Heyer acted. As he had learned in Norway when the whitefish or salmon conveyor belt hit a snarl, his first move was to shut down all that could be shut down, to freeze the crisis in place. In Bergen that had meant shutting off the can dispenser and the sealing compressor; in his office it meant switching his telephone to the message machine before he was interrupted by more return customers making reservations. For the next few hours, trying to control his aggravation with his own short-sightedness, he moved back and forth on both booking lists until he had completed reasonable trades or at least had preserved the good will of the customers who couldn't immediately commit to alternative dates. He wondered what any of them would have said if they realized they didn't have infinity to play with, but only with the dates on the two lists. It struck him as another illustration of people deluding themselves about the varieties of human experience they had at their disposal. Fortunately, he didn't feel any obligation to enlighten them.

* * *

Miranda didn't know what chaos was any more than the ocean knew what wetness was: Observing it externally, even for a second, wouldn't have been Miranda. In gazing around her loft for her white sweat socks, she felt overwhelmed by the number of hiding places she could have wasted the next few minutes investigating. She knew the socks couldn't have gone far because she had tossed them from where she was now sitting on the bed, but they were nowhere in sight. Every piece of clothing and bag on the floor, every sneaker and shoe in front of her, seemed intent on hiding not just one but both. And should she find them? She knew already they would just lead her elsewhere, further than she wanted to go so early in the day. She would rather go around the loft barefoot, risking the splinters on the floor, than deal with the secrets within secrets waiting for her.

Miranda's thirty-odd years could hardly reproach her misgivings. As a nine-year-old, she had wanted to see how much money her father kept in his shirt drawer; the answers were $48 and, according to the document under the bills, he was her step-father, not her father. At 13, she had finally penetrated her mother's evasions to learn that her biological father had been a subway track worker killed by poisonous fumes trapped within a closed well years after an old CIA anti-terrorist experiment. At 17, she had wanted to see how deeply Larry Cohen's dick could penetrate her; the answer had been deeply enough to force them into the embarrassment of being separated in an emergency room. At 23, she had hoped to gain extra insight into her doctoral thesis on Real Appearances by becoming a teaching assistant, only to discover that the professor she had so admired and wanted to work with had been plagiarizing other academics for years. One temp job and one casual affair followed another, each of them contributing to the ultimate secret she had gained nothing by learning—that she didn't want to do anything or know anybody, that she functioned most easily when the money in her jeans stayed merely a few dollars ahead of disaster and the people she came across wanted no more information about her than what she was willing to volunteer.

Getting up from the bed, Miranda stood still for a moment until her head caught up with the rest of her body. She hadn't smoked or drunk all that much before going to sleep, but she seemed to have a running tab with some of her neurons going back years. She gave it a couple of blinks, didn't feel dizzy, then looked down at the glass ashtray on the night table. She decided cleaning it out would be her first chore of the morning. She felt so much better to tie the first knot in her string that she immediately planned the second (making coffee) and third (taking a shower). Or would it kill her to put off making the coffee until after she had taken her shower? Would she enjoy the coffee more if she were clean and in fresh clothes? Wouldn't her stomach bloat if she stepped into the shower immediately *after* her coffee? She didn't like being seized by that kind of doubt. It was just like doubts that had paralyzed her in the past, most recently last night when she had considered getting undressed to put on her nightgown, objected that she had to throw the clothes on her back into the laundry anyway, and ended up compromising by just taking off her socks and flinging them who-knows-where while she got under the covers in her green Mister Magoo T-shirt and black jeans. The only thing she hated more than getting into arguments with other people was getting into one with herself.

Miranda emptied her mind quiet, grabbed the ashtray, and walked it over to the garbage can under the sink. She had long steeled herself for the sight of a cockroach on the counter or in the sink in the morning, to the point that arming herself against the possibility had become practically the same as seeing one. This morning she didn't see any, but released a quiver of disgust anyway. When she had first moved into the loft, she had blamed the wildlife on the restaurant downstairs. Lately she hadn't been so sure. There were roaches in the poshest apartments on Fifth Avenue. They were a fact of New York life. And not to forget, the restaurant could have equally accused her of being the building's roach magnet, and with a lot more invested in its indignation than she had. She didn't want to be indignant, no matter how absurd the accusations against her. The only thing she hated more than spitting contests with herself was a spitting contest with somebody else.

She ran the water for her coffee maker with a thought for the owner of the restaurant, the birdman named Heyer. Whenever they had crossed paths on the street or in front of the restaurant, he had been painstakingly polite, never mentioned a word about cockroaches, but had still made her uneasy with his stare. The gaze was peculiar, not the usual one from a moron wanting to grab her ass. It was as if Heyer were thinking of making an appointment for his lust with her, that it couldn't be right now but that he would try to fit her in eventually. She thought this creepy, but also in its own way . . . *civilized*. Only human beings in an advanced society had the capacity to schedule their pawing in advance. Would that make surrendering to it equally civilized? She had had grubbier hands on her than Heyer's. Maybe she would have felt like a respectable social institution sucking him off.

While she waited for the coffee to percolate, she went to her only street window to look down on the commuters going to the kind of jobs she didn't have. In this latest of her neighborhoods she assumed most of the jobs were media-related—video types, computer whizzes, fashionistas, hotshots starting up advertising firms—or the blue collars and service people that kept the first group going—carpenters constantly redoing storefronts, lumpy women with tape measures around their necks, waiters putting on and taking off penguin shirts and vests. She played her morning game with the parade hurrying along on the sidewalk, wondering how many of the marchers she might have been if she had taken a different turn at any point along the way. For her alternate universe sister, she beamed in on a tall brunette in a rust suit and white pullover. She wouldn't have worn gray heels with the outfit, but then again, she might have done even that in exchange for the brunette's straight shoulders, perfect boobs, and confident gait. So far away, she couldn't make out much detail about the woman's face, but she guessed the thinnest of makeup and lip gloss. The brunette knew who she was, knew where she was going. Where was that, exactly? To an executive's desk? To a receptionist's chair? Or was it to one of those art galleries on the side streets where she did both the decision making and the greeting? How could anyone be that versatile?

Miranda was glad she wasn't down in the street with the brunette. If she had been walking toward her and if the brunette had been accompanied by a boyfriend, she would have been oafish about sizing the woman up to explain to herself how she had attracted the man. In this case, she wouldn't have liked the answer, so she was relieved that she was up at her window and that the brunette didn't have a boyfriend. She scratched at her right shoulder blade. It had been itchy for a couple of days now. At her age was it better to have an allergic rash or a pimple?

In the shower she thought about masturbating, but felt no compelling urge for it. Her stomach felt as heavy after the coffee as she had feared, and she couldn't imagine herself being attractive to anyone. Humiliation might have been a masturbation theme, but she seemed to have already exhausted that with her study of the straight shoulders and the nonexistent boyfriend. She had always felt more humiliated by what she had narrowly avoided than by what had happened to her: It was debasement *plus* not having the wherewithal even for that. As she turned off the shower, she just felt like a schmuck, over and out, and there was nothing erotically inviting about that, even for a few seconds; the most she would have gotten out of coming was having some phantom notice that it was indeed a pimple on her shoulder.

She knew she had chosen wisely when she wrapped the big rose towel around her and stepped out of the shower stall and back into the main room. She was superior to the mess on the floor in front of her. It had stayed as it was while she had been renewing herself. She liked leaving her wet footprints around it. They attested to a mysterious presence in the jungle she hadn't noticed before.

Her satisfaction was gone by the time she had put on her clean underwear. The electronic beep-beep-beep from the truck backing up to the side door of the restaurant downstairs said Heyer was offloading a delivery. He had been coy about how much he charged when she had joked about the subject, but she had to think it was somewhere near a thousand dollars for him to survive on merely five tables every night. But a thousand a table or a thousand a head? If by the table, the nightly income would have been $5,000; if by the head, in the $20,000 range. Either way, it was obscene, at least for her. She was already on Miracle Street having the money for her rent. But for a trendy restaurant in Manhattan? She had no idea how much somebody like Heyer had to take in to make a profit. She wondered if being curious about it made her less of a person.

Once she was dressed, Miranda bundled up anything that looked washable from the floor and the bed and stuffed it into a pillow case. One of the socks turned out to be at the foot of the bed, the other next to her plaid blouse. She was surprised she hadn't been able to see them from the bed, and could only conclude they hadn't been where she found them when she had been looking earlier. Not that she believed a fairy had slipped into the loft and moved them while she had been in the shower; more likely, her perception had blanked out on those two precise spots during her earlier scan so that they really hadn't existed for her. She had been fooled by that kind of reverse mirage before. If she ever stumbled across a magic lantern, she would make sure her first wish to the genie would be to truly erase from reality what had only seemed erased to her.

As soon as she had loaded up the pillow case and deposited it near the elevator door, she went to her desk to get some work done before committing herself to sitting around the laundromat. Too many of her leads were in Central and Pacific time zones so she had to focus on the few she had on the East Coast. She didn't know why they hadn't put their names on the telemarketing block list; she had done it with a minimum of fuss and had rarely been bothered by people like herself.

The first number had a Massachusetts prefix. It was a woman with a screaming tot in the background. She predicted five seconds from her opening before the receiver was slammed down. "Mrs. Warneke?"

"Yes?"

"Hi. I'm Miranda and I'm calling from Certified Plus."

"Not interested."

"You don't know what it is, Mrs. Warneke."

"You just told me. Miranda from Certified Plus. 'Bye now."

She had overestimated her abilities: four seconds, not five. Still, she had introduced herself to wherever in Massachusetts Mrs. Warneke lived. That alone vindicated using her name and not hiding behind some alias the way others doing her job apparently did. It wasn't an Alice or a Katherine now flitting through the New England air, it was Miranda. She liked that. If others were ashamed of how they put a few dollars together, that was their problem, not hers. It hadn't been easy explaining that to her section supervisor Billy when he had told her about the practice of using aliases. (Was that even *his* name?) On the one hand, he sounded as apologetic as any of his minions about pestering people for something else they didn't need; on the other hand, he didn't sound like someone who took his supervisor title lightly. Billy was somebody who wanted credit for every sale by underlings, and that would have been harder if they knew him around the main office as Norman.

But she wasn't Billy. It was Miranda who punched out a number in New Jersey. She could have really used a few hundred dollars. The phone bill had been collecting dust in the middle of the envelopes at her elbow and a double bill was due any day.

✳ ✳ ✳

Heyer's relief at resolving the reservations crisis lasted only until a nightmare stirred him from his sleep a few hours later. It was a particularly unpleasant wakening, as if his dreams had expelled him as unworthy. His one consolation as he reoriented himself to his bedroom in the darkness was that he had held on to the culprit responsible; the suffocating dread from the nightmare hadn't escaped with consciousness. With all his shifting of customers back in his office, had he left one table open? In his sleep he had visualized the deleted names and the space on his laptop screen that hadn't been covered, and the picture remained frozen in his bedroom. He couldn't have made it up in both states of mind.

Heyer got up and stumbled over to his laptop. The screen confirmed his oversight: The fourth table for the next evening had been left unoccupied. Worse, he couldn't expect to fill it on such short notice, certainly not with the theater producer he had already switched off it to another date. One change required diplomacy, two shame, and he had never been good at shame.

Heyer felt outmaneuvered by himself. It wasn't the loss of income; he had more in the bank than he had ever had. It wasn't even the threat to his reputation that would build when the diners at the other four tables wondered about the unused table and started talk that maybe he wasn't doing as well as he had been. None of that mattered. But what did bother him was that he would be responsible for creating the core misunderstanding, the inevitable misinterpretation that he hadn't been able to find somebody for the fifth table. It had been so unnecessary to foment that gossip with his sloppiness. That kind of thing remained gratuitously indelible, no matter how persuasively it was explained away. It was bad enough not to control everyday practicalities, but to be at the mercy of personal inventions was twice as tormenting.

Heyer wished he could wake up someone for sharing his problem. He had found that another person's opinion sometimes cleared his head, if only because he didn't have to do all the talking. But the most logical candidate—Leticia—he had recently broken up with, and not on the friendliest of terms. She would be the last one to appreciate a call at four in the morning to discuss what she had been given to calling his "manic lists."

Since he was too wound up to return to sleep, Heyer went to the refrigerator for the half-grapefruit he hadn't eaten before going to bed. He saw no reason not to count it as part of the new day, as an early breakfast, rather than an extension of the evening.

He hadn't eaten at such an hour since his days at the recording studio in Montreal, and he didn't know if he felt adventurous or nostalgic. But he did take the grapefruit as a sign: with one routine broken, what was to prevent him from breaking others? And one that occurred to him right away was his spotless record in charging for every meal consumed at the restaurant. Not once, not for a holiday or for a staff member's birthday or for some old acquaintance who had come to town, had he served a meal on the house. He didn't think of himself as cheap, simply not in need of creating occasions that couldn't create themselves. But now the grapefruit was so pink and sweet it seemed to encourage him to a baronial generosity. It was almost mocking him: If it could taste so unusually satisfying, why couldn't he do something equally unique? Would there ever be a more convenient time to invite somebody?

Heyer was baffled by his sudden urge. He had learned long ago that the most innocent of generosities on the surface concealed serious feelings of debt below that surface. But what debt? As far as he could tabulate, he didn't owe anybody anything.

✱ ✱ ✱

Miranda hoped the restaurant was called the 5X5 for some better reason than the five tables inside. The question hardly kept her up at night, but it popped into her head every time she saw her reflection in the 5X5's green-tint street window. The birdman Heyer hadn't struck her as so banal. Better would have been if his birthday was May 5, or if the restaurant had had an earlier incarnation at Fifth Avenue and Fifth Street, or if he had always stumbled over the five times table in school. She liked guessing what the source of the name was because she really didn't care what it was and she only had to entertain her speculation when she saw herself in the window. As soon as she moved off from the glass, her curiosity did, too.

Most of the time. But today she continued conjecturing all the way down to the Spin-Fast Laundromat and while she loaded her favorite machine at the far end of the third row. She thought it striking, for instance, that a slim, raven figure like Heyer would give his enterprise a name with the ultimate in squat connotations. It was the reverse of what she would have never had the nerve to do: calling a restaurant of hers The Giraffe. As she slid her bills into the washing machine and it grumbled into motion, she wondered if Heyer had a fat man inside him crying to be liberated. She liked thinking people like that existed somewhere.

"Go ahead. I do it all the time."

Miranda needed a second to take it in that the skinny redhead with the hipbones protruding from her jeans like six-shooters was addressing her. Then she remembered her right hand, the one still holding the liquid soap she had forgotten to add to the wash.

"They always act like you'll break it or something if you don't do things in the right order," the redhead said. "What's the machine going to do if you put the soap in after—block the vent?"

Miranda realized that yes, somewhere in her mind, she had assumed just the danger the redhead was now ridiculing. She didn't like feeling stupid about things she had been stupid enough to believe. "They used to clean things with just water and rocks on the frontier," she said, trying to smile her way through, "so I guess I'll do that today."

"Oh, go ahead. Nothing 'll happen. Really."

Before Miranda could react, the redhead yanked the soap container from her hand, screwed off the cap, and poured the blue liquid into a practiced dose. Miranda wanted to stop her, clung to the thought that just her disapproval *should* have stopped her, but couldn't move. She flinched as the redhead raised one of the lids on the machine and emptied the soap through the hole there. "There you go," the woman said, sounding thrilled with herself. "And look! The machine's still running!"

Miranda had little choice but to smile again as she took back the soap container extended to her. She loathed so many things about the redhead—her assertiveness, her slim body and peek-a-boo belly button, her shrewd blue eyes. But most of all she hated being shown up by the machine's instructions. If they were so worthless, why bother printing them? She didn't care what it cost her in clothes, but she prayed for the machine to break down.

But it didn't. Instead, the window glass was quickly smeared with the soap. She felt as though she were the one smeared.

"The Stepford Wives didn't just happen in Stepford," the redhead winked, taking an old magazine off the table and camping down on one of the plastic seats. "*We're* the Stepford wives! Right?"

Miranda made a point of not winking back. The woman's presumption in knowing something about her, in including her in some fictional world of robots, was beyond galling. "Whatever that means."

Miranda hoped she sounded bitchy enough, and the redhead didn't look particularly happy as she flipped open her magazine, but she didn't trust it. With almost a half-hour to kill before the machine stopped, she couldn't help but remain within conversational distance of the woman if she did her waiting in the laundromat. Before she had the vaguest idea where exactly, she headed back out into the street for a walk. She felt better instantly to be moving nowhere in particular. The weather was warm enough for her windbreaker, but not so warm that she didn't have to button it up over her Mae West T-shirt. The people passing had no weather: They looked like they were late for work and thinking only of excuses.

She stopped in front of a junk shop that called itself an antique store. It was big on Mr. Potato Heads inside bell jars and covered with rhinestones and chains. She had made cuter things from clay in kindergarten, but minus the pasty glitz that probably justified a ludicrous price. To the people she never wanted to meet she added whoever threw away money on such idiocies and considered it kitschy art. She liked not being able to think of someone like that.

"How are you this morning?"

Miranda groaned for thinking she could walk down the street without being hit on. She was already giving the Mr. Potato Heads the stiff nod she did to ward off pains in the ass when she recognized Heyer in the window. She was mortified to bumble out a "fine" when she knew he really wasn't interested in how she was, then made it worse by asking him how he was.

The birdman smiled as if he didn't know, but recovered with the aplomb of somebody who owned a restaurant and dealt with the public every day. "I was just thinking of you," he said, making it sound like the truth. "We keep running into each other on the street and just saying hello. How about I raise the ante and invite you down to the 5X5 this evening?"

Miranda hated not knowing what to say because she didn't know what to think. "That would cost me a month's rent," she managed.

"As my guest. Neighbors should be neighborly. And god knows I've probably cost you a headache here and there with all the deliveries and the coming and going."

Miranda waited for mention of the cockroaches, but Heyer was too busy staring at her in his weird way. He had said all he had intended saying, and it was her turn again. "I couldn't let you do that," she said. "And you really don't owe it to me."

"Oh, c'mon. Bring a friend. Bring two friends. Guaranteed you'll like it. Any allergies? Shellfish? Chocolate?"

The question rattled her; it was as if he had been in the shower with her and noticed the pimple on her shoulder blade. "That's what you're serving tonight—shellfish and chocolate?"

"No," he laughed. "That's just one of the things I ask when people call for a reservation. You'd be amazed how many food allergies are out there. Most places can deal with them. They have big menus. But if I get somebody in and they're allergic to peanuts and we're serving peanut butter that night, well, you can imagine how that might ruin the evening for everybody!"

She smiled, and he was pleased. He had very even teeth for such a raptor. "Somehow I can't see the 5X5 serving peanut butter."

"Not this evening. Promise. So what about it?"

"I really . . ."

"It'll save you coming down some day to borrow a cup of sugar."

Once upon a time, when confronted with appointments she didn't want to make, Miranda made up stories about other commitments. But now she didn't want to do that. Not only would it have rung hollow, but she suddenly didn't want to disappoint the birdman. He gave the appearance of having invested a lot of will power in his invitation. "Do I ask what's actually on the menu or would that be *gauche*?"

"*Gauche* away. I've heard a rumor the cook has ordered a lot of veal."

"Like breaded cutlets?"

"That part of it is a secret."

"I don't like secrets."

It was out before she realized she was saying it—*her* secret, the one she never shared with anyone. But instead of being miffed, he laughed again in his weird, distant way. "Not breaded cutlets. How about we leave the secret at that—half and half?"

There was no way she couldn't leave it at that, not without being completely boorish. Heyer went off up the block toward the restaurant with his half of the secret and she had the rest of the day to dispose of her half the way she wanted. Thoughts of the gauzy black dress from the flea market hanging unworn in her closet for months made her feel outfoxed.

✳ ✳ ✳

Heyer tried not showing his surprise when Miranda walked into the restaurant alone. She had had the whole day to find an escort, and he couldn't imagine her without boyfriends. But alone she was, and in the kind of plain black dress and sling heels that she might have just stepped into on the way to her loft elevator down to the restaurant. The only effort at all she seemed to have made was around her eyes—the liner thicker than he had seen it when they had run into one another in front of the junk shop. He thought she had exaggerated: She already looked too much like a small ball of a woodland creature to risk further comparison with a raccoon. If he hadn't still thought it was a good idea to invite her as his guest for the unoccupied fourth table, he would have thought it a bad idea.

He felt the eyes of the other diners on them as he held her chair for her to sit down. Since he had already steeled himself for some blowzy eruption that would give away what he was up to, he was pleased by her demure smile and impersonal thanks. The unpretentious silver chain bracelet on her wrist might have also been a happy omen if his eyes didn't follow it to her pudgy hand and to where she had been chewing on her nails. "You decide," she said deferentially in the middle of his reading of the wine list. "Your reputation is well known, Mr. Heyer. Anything dry white."

It took Heyer a moment to accept the flattery for what it was. At worst there was a wink-wink in it, no true sarcasm. He was only sorry he waited to let his appreciation show in front of Sacha. The bartender eyed him suspiciously; clearly, Isabel had already spread the word not to expect much of a tip from the fourth table. "Number Three," he said, affecting no reaction to Sacha's look. "Everything okay here?"

The bartender had never been happier, so Heyer returned for another tour of the tables. The pâté was about gone at One and Three, only halfway through at Two and Five. He was tempted to skip it altogether for his upstairs neighbor, but then scolded himself for the thought. Full service for her was more important than keeping the courses at all the tables simultaneous. When he took that decision into the kitchen with some of the dirty pâté plates, Antonio was waiting for him with a beatific smile. "You're not telling us something, Heyer," the chef said in the tone of an uncle who had learned of his nephew's naughty doings.

"What are you talking about?"

"What am I talking about!" The two assistants on for the evening sniggled. "I wonder what that could be!"

Heyer let them wonder. He was diverted anyway by Antonio's latest concoction—sweetly aromatic veal betraying both its mint and sage without either winning the upper hand. He thought it typical of a chef whose genius lay not in a meal as such, but in the articulated measure he gave to all the ingredients that went into it. A pinch more or less of what he used would hardly have polluted his creation, but nor would it have equaled the satisfaction of tasting the absence of that more or less. Heyer always tasted that absence. In the kingdom of Absence, he had thought more than once, Antonio sat on the throne.

✳ ✳ ✳

Miranda could have used a book. The room was too dark for actual reading, and she would have probably come off to the other diners as a lonely nerd, but she wouldn't have minded some smart novel about preppies committing mass suicide in Aruba as a prop. As it was, she felt exposed to have nothing between her and the two near tables but the glass of wine the bartender had brought. How could she look straight ahead without seeming to be snooping on those at the two tables? The bald man at the table to the left had already smiled at her—one of those awkward smiles that wanted to say hello and I-know-you're-looking-at-me and I-wish-you-would-stop-staring-at-me all at once. At least he was more practiced in deflecting idle eyes than his Botox blonde, who had to keep catching herself from returning the stare and making up endlessly banal conversation for her Sugar Daddy so she would know where to direct her look. Miranda decided that the two of them hadn't made it with Baldie on top in years and that Blondie had long given up complaining about it.

The Twenty-Somethings at the right table were more grating because they were even more obviously fragile in their chitchat. All four of them kept buoying one another into laughter over their Wall Street office tales. The two overfed frat boys looked like they had been fitted out in their blue suits with their MBAs and hadn't bothered going back to their tailor for a tune-up since graduation. The women kept laughing a half-second too late, as if still feeling their way toward all the right moves. She took them for assistants picking up pointers before climbing over the frat boys up the office ladder. She couldn't imagine any other reason for them to be paired off or quadrupled off or whatever they were. Fully dressed, they were the setup scene for a porn movie.

Miranda took a sip of wine, reminding herself to behave. She owed it to the birdman for giving her something different to do for the evening. Why he had given it to her didn't seem as important as being able to eat something besides her own cooking, and gratis at that. If all he was after was getting laid, she could deal with that one way or the other when the time came. Her serious doubt was in her thought that she might find out if he usually charged by the table or by the customer. She didn't want to know which it was; it was part of the secrets of his business, and finding out which it was would lead only to trouble. But beyond coming alone, so that the table price and the customer price had to be the same, she didn't know how else to head him off from volunteering the information. Even kissing people to shut them up didn't guarantee what would be said as soon as the kissing stopped.

She hadn't made up her mind about the vampire-looking waitress named Isabel who brought her pâté. Either Heyer and Isabel went prowling on the same piers for the same necks after closing the restaurant or they bit and scratched each other to a bloody mess once they were alone together. Miranda had never understood the attraction of Isabels to men. They had bodies like pencils and minds like erasers that had nothing interesting to erase. Whatever her mirror said, she was developing stretch marks sexier than that. Where was the fascination for somebody like the birdman? She might ask him just that because his answer was unlikely to involve any secret; she was sure he didn't have the slightest idea why Vampyra turned him on. Plus, it would get him talking about something besides his tables.

The bartender was refilling her glass before she had swallowed her first piece of pâté. She had an impish urge to ask him if the wine was supposed to cover up the pâté or the pâté the wine, but again felt stifled by whatever contract she had willy-nilly entered into with Heyer. She hadn't asked him for his generosity, but now it was weighing on her. Didn't that make it less than generosity?

Real things always appeared more real than they were. She had the doctoral thesis to prove it.

✼ ✼ ✼

Normally, Heyer would have ranked the evening in his Top Ten. There had been nothing forced in the compliments from the four tables. Antonio had scored again—with the pâté, with the veal, with the sautéed vegetables, even with the coffee mousse that Heyer himself thought leaned a centimeter too close to the thick. Sacha and Isabel had been impressed with their tips, Table Three had insisted Antonio come out of the kitchen for a bow. But the triumph was not total because of his own condescension. It had lasted mere seconds and Heyer hadn't shared it with anyone, but he hadn't missed his smugness: His mark of a successful service had been the enthusiasm from his four paying tables; only their reactions counted. He had all but tut-tutted Miranda's opinion because, whatever her announced delight with everything, she hadn't been a routine customer. He didn't like himself for that snobbery.

When he invited her to stay behind the other diners to have a sambuca with him, she replied with a wince of a smile that said she had expected him to make the offer. Isabel had thrown him the same knowing look on her way out the door, and, though he couldn't make it out, he was sure the tune Sacha was mutter-humming behind the bar as he cleaned up had *double-entendre* lyrics aimed at him and his designs on Miranda. For Heyer, it was another vivid example of how the narrowest of purposes—in this case, apology—could be misconstrued as adventure. Yes, he hadn't seen Leticia in almost a month, yes, he was due to move on to an M, and yes, he felt his pulse beating more rapidly at the thought of going upstairs with Miranda and slowly stripping her of her black dress and the black bra he had glimpsed under it. But there was still the meal in the middle, and it made him feel more like a host than a lover. How could he give or take anything when he was still asking if everything had been satisfactory? As they sat and sipped their sambucas, he needed more than her turgid lead for clarity.

"So this is what you do down here every night!" she seemed to say for the third or fourth time.

"Five nights. You must've noticed we're closed weekends."

"Isn't that supposed to be the best time for a restaurant?"

"For those that depend on the calendar. We depend on the menu." The woodland creature she most reminded him of was a chipmunk. She didn't have buck teeth, but her prominent upper lip put them there in their absence. As with Antonio's measurement of ingredients, the secret was in what wasn't there. "You haven't shown much curiosity about why I invited you this evening."

She feigned innocence. "I haven't?"

"No."

She pretended to think about it. "You told me this morning. You wanted to be more neighborly."

"True. But there was also another reason."

She scrunched her nose and leaned more heavily on her elbows to raise her glass to her lips. "Don't spoil it."

He was sorry; he had counted on telling her about the reservation list, on being candid with her. But the more he seemed to lean toward her, the further she receded from him. "Something else, then."

"Something else what?"

"That I can tell you and will sweep you off your feet."

He grinned before she had to study how serious he was. But it hadn't been necessary. She was suddenly all seriousness as she asked: "Tell me something that won't cost either of us."

He thought he knew what she meant, then realized he didn't. She wasn't talking about the amnesias of one-night stands, but about a much more final insignificance. "I'd have to know you better to know what that is," he heard himself reply.

She thought about it, then nodded. "Yes, I suppose so."

"You can't know what's absent unless you know what's present. So tell me something about yourself. Anything. Then I'll have a better idea of what might cost you."

"Everything costs everybody."

"We're talking only about you."

"I really don't like talking about me."

"Make an exception."

"Why?"

Heyer knew that answer. "Because as soon as you finish that sambuca, you'll get up and go upstairs and I won't matter to you anymore. Your secret will be safe."

Her skepticism said she had heard that one before, and not with the promised results. But she didn't flee from the idea, either. "I could say anything. I could lie."

"But you wouldn't. Because you know you're just one of the many women I invite down here so I can go to bed with them afterward, and no one of them is more important to me than the next one. You count on that and I count on it, too."

✳ ✳ ✳

Miranda admired the way he kept a straight face. She couldn't recall the last time such an appearance had felt so real to her. "We've gotten a little mixed up, haven't we? I thought you were the one who was supposed to say something to knock me off my feet. But now it's suddenly on me."

His birdman stare didn't falter. "I'll make it up to you."

She didn't know if he would or not, but she wanted to believe he would. "Okay," she decided. "Some secret that won't cost either of us?"

"Right."

She had never said it before, but she had never had such an ideal opportunity for saying it, either. Not only would they go upstairs and screw or not go upstairs and screw, but he owned a restaurant, and restaurants went out of business every week. "My real name isn't Miranda," she said, feeling hot at her ears just saying it. "I took that from Shakespeare because it sounded romantic. My real name is Alice Katherine."

✳ ✳ ✳

Heyer thought instantly of the rocker Emilia in Milan. Had Xanadu *really* counted?

JOHNNY ON THE SPOT

WE called him Johnny, but that isn't what his mother and father called him. Back when they were drippin' the holy water on his skull, he was known as Michel Grossard. Not a French name I'd run across before, but who knows with the French and the Germans and the way they've always been jumpin' back and forth in Alsace? That's where he told everybody he was from—Alsace. I couldn't swear to it. When you don't want people knowin' where you're from, you pick some place that's got a new flag flyin' over it every few years. Makes it harder to look up the birth records if that's what you want to be doin'. This one's from Transylvania and that one's from Croatia, that kind of thing, and who's the wiser? You got Alsace in the same category. "Why does Grandfather always sing those strange songs?" you ask your mother. And she says, "Shut up and get those peas out of the pod. You'll understand after the next invasion." If you follow what I'm sayin'.

But anyways, knowin' the man, I'd have to say he wasn't lyin' about where he came from. If he said he was from Alsace, he was from Alsace. If you're goin' to lie about somethin', sayin' you're from Alsace wouldn't be at the top of any list of mine. We never really knew him as Michel Grossard, though. To us he was Johnny, like in Johnny On the Spot. We called him that because he was never on the spot except for when he was and didn't know it. A gentle sarcasm, like, but with a grain of truth in it. In all your life you never met a correspondent who missed more street cats runnin' past him. There was this one afternoon, for instance, when he was workin' in Algiers and he gets a call from his paper askin' about a rumor the Algerian President has been overthrown in one of your bloodless coups. Johnny is past all annoyance at the call because he's in his livin' room with yours truly drinkin' the scotch the Algerians don't like seein' bein' drunk on the streets. But just to do a favor to this editor on the phone, he agrees to leave me alone with his bottle for a half-hour, gets on his motorbike, and scoots across the city to the presidential palace to get an official denial of the rumor. When he arrives in front of the palace gate, he unfurls the local slang that's made him popular with waiters and market vendors. This guard he knows, name of Akbar, says he don't know what coup Johnny's talkin' about, there's been no trouble at the palace. Now doubly annoyed he's been forced to leave his guest—meself—stranded in his home with his scotch, Johnny scoots back home, tells me what happened, and calls his editor to pass along the nonsense of the rumor. He's still bein' connected to the paper when CNN comes on to report Akbar must have left his sentry booth to take a whizz for a few minutes that mornin' while the new president was seizin' power.

It was after that episode people really started callin' Grossard Johnny On the Spot. Say this for the man: They wouldn't have had anythin' to smirk at if he hadn't been the first to go around tellin' the story on himself. Nobody roared more than Johnny did when one of the other boys allowed as how Akbar might not have been the best news source in Algiers. A good one was a good one where Johnny was concerned, and if it was on him, that was all right, too. When his wife scolded him for playin' the fool, he comes back to her like simplicity itself: "What, play?" he says to her. "I *was* a fool!"

The wife Felicia, you have to understand, was of the sensitive sort. One of your tall, raven-haired beauties that seems to rise out of the sea and with the divine temper of Galatea to match. I always connected her beauty to her knees. With most women their knees are their least attractive feature. Even the ones who aren't attractive elsewhere are *more* unattractive in their knees. They're always too knobby or not knobby enough. When the skin's not foldin' down on them, the bone is all out of shape. The way I see it, you shouldn't have creases in your knees and they shouldn't be lookin' like sharp elbows, neither. But Felicia Grossard didn't have those flaws. She was blessed as perfection itself in that department, just the right amount protrudin' out. When you matched that up with the rest of her, you knew it was no accident, that the creation deities had given her a second good shakin' to make sure she'd stand out in any crowd of knees you see goin' down your public thoroughfares. When she'd throw her long legs over you, you didn't feel no awkward impingin' around the waist, if you follow me. It was all smooth from her pubes down to her ankles.

But that's another story. What I was sayin' was that Felicia didn't like Johnny actin' what she considered the idjut. The way she looked at it, his wont to be so calm before his own foibles was also a criticism of herself. What did it say about her that they'd been together for 15 years on what suddenly felt to her like the most superficial of surfaces, above another level where some seriously agitated Johnny lived all private and locked away from her? For meself, I never got any whiff of this lower level, of Johnny boilin' downstairs under the amiable lad up top I saw all the time. But you couldn't convince Felicia of that. For her, there had to be another Johnny who was hidin' down in the depths from her and refusin' to admit episodes like the one with Akbar disturbed him. And mind, that was only the spool of her thinkin'. Reel it out and what she got was that if he couldn't be honest about an Akbar, how many other deceits was he playin' on her day in and day out? There was no secret to her suspicions, either. She'd given great ponderin' to them in this syndicated advice column she wrote and invited him to comment on her conclusion. Johnny? The way she told it to me later, just a shrug of his big shoulders, a whistle through the pipe stem he was cleanin' out at the time, and a "Could be, Felicia. You see these things better than I do."

For Felicia that reaction just confirmed her worst fears. Nobody could be *that* untroubled by strikin' other people as a horse's arse. Now your base thinkers might jump to the idea she was thinkin' only of herself, how Johnny's pratfalls might reflect on her and slow down sellin' the books she got out of her advice columns or keep her from bein' invited to the next hoity-toity cocktail party. All that social calculation guff. But that wasn't Felicia. The truth of it was she was genuinely bothered that Johnny's behavior was a telltale criticism of their marriage, of their honesty with one another. How else to say it but that she loved the man and was payin' one of your insecurity fees when you get into that condition? Sure, she liked her little romantic adventures, and some of us were grateful she did. But so did Johnny follow the feedbag out of the stable every now and then and he wasn't more or less of a horse's arse for it than he would've been otherwise. That wasn't what they call the issue. First and last, the issue for her was their marriage.

For a while, Felicia kept rein on her apprehensions. And she had some help with the task. Between her columns and her books, she was a busy woman, tellin' this one what to do and that one to stop doin' it. And you'll also notice that whenever there's some uneasiness in life waitin' to become full-blown strife, you always get your fill of ironies hoverin' about. Wasn't Shakespeare that made that up. With Johnny and Felicia you found your ironies exactly in him bein' the horse's arse he was. Because he was given to screwin' up where he was sent by his paper, you see, he rarely lasted long in any one city or even with the same employer. So he was forever settin' up quarters in some new foreign capital for this paper or that magazine. And, funny to say it, that's exactly what kept the blanket on Felicia's jitters! They were always havin' new adventures together, discoverin' new people and new cultures, findin' out about new problems in another part of the world, movin' in to new apartments and findin' exotic things to eat in the markets and restaurants. As Felicia said in one of her books, there was always a stint of makin' love thinkin' that the Johnny learnin' about the Tuaregs wasn't the Johnny learnin' about the Armenians, like she could look forward to havin' breakfast with him thinkin' that the Johnny readin' up on the Zulus wasn't the same one readin' up on the Lapps. And for an extra payoff, there were always these new local customs she could learn to approve and disapprove of for her newspaper and book readers! Because of always havin' to find a new job, there were lots of Johnnies and lots of Felicias to go around. Come up with a better irony than that one!

But then they go to Istanbul. It just so happened I was there, doin' my usual. I'm not sayin' it was fate that brought us together again. I'm always uncomfortable throwin' that word around. I can't help thinkin' you mock another's religious creeds by borrowin' a principle like fate to explain what coincidence has ordained. But forget about yours truly. The point is, I can attest to what happened. If there was a closer witness to the events in Turkey, it had wings, a halo, and one of those little portable harps.

Now I've told you how Johnny was always losin' his jobs. What I've yet to mention is how come there was always some new employer to come along and hire him again. How come they all kept missin' that track record of his? You had your theories, of course. Some said it was because he could learn any language under the sun after a few days. I don't dispute that helped. You got wise men in your universities with an alphabet of letters after their names who could learn a thing from him in that department. And he wasn't one who looked down on his surroundin's, neither. Nobody went native, as they say, faster than Johnny On the Spot. Most correspondents took a year to build up the local contacts he did in a week or two. Plus, he wasn't known as the worst writer on the planet. There was some said you could take a blindfold test with his dispatches and always know who'd written them. I don't know who actually did that, I can't say I ever tried, but that's what they said. And let's not forget the benefits Felicia brought. You could've had whole religions concocted out of desires for that creature, and it didn't make no difference if you worshiped in them wearin' a burnoose, a crucifix, or a yarmulke. You'd invite Johnny to your temple or mosque just to have Felicia sashayin' her fine rear quarters down the aisle with him.

No question these were all factors. But as important as all those things were, Johnny also had another asset that kept him employed: He was just a nice man. Thought no harm against anybody. One second you're meetin' him for the first time, the next second he's charmed his way around you like your favorite publican. *Engagin'* is what your dictionary would say. Which is another way of sayin' I was as taken with him as everybody else. It took me a long time to figure out what the secret of that charm was. The stories he told were all right, but they weren't better than the next man's. He never skipped a round, but you had to be a special skinflint to do that and you'd never be allowed to forget it if you did. So what did I find so engagin' about him? How could he be so nice? Why did all these employers seem to line up to hire him after another one had given him the boot? Then one day it came to me: Johnny was so engagin' because *he was happy!*

You heard right. Your usual lot of foreign press club slugs, their idea of happiness is the smart repartee, the tart crack as an antidote to their boredom. They're all just cynical bastards who jot down the sufferin' and depravities where they're assigned like shopkeepers takin' down the delivery order on the phone. They've got hearts like my ATM machine—you need a code to open 'em and even then you won't get rich. But did you ever stop to think there's also a reason why the lot of them go around actin' like there can't ever be anythin' under the sun they haven't already seen? The reason is because they don't *want* anythin' new to happen. They're too busy hidin' the fact they once *did* believe in somethin' more than what they're doin' and they sold it out to the first pimp in the marketplace who gave them a passable wage and put them up in a good apartment. If they can act like the world's never goin' to change, they've got themselves an alibi for their own lack of spine. They're just doin' what's been done since the cavemen were doin' it so don't get it into your head to go criticizin' *them* for all the sorriness around.

Johnny wasn't like that. He never had anythin' to sell so he never had reason to cover himself up by soundin' cynical. Maybe it was bein' born in a waftin' balloon of a place like Alsace, but he never grew up clingin' to one belief more than another. He was always a lark bouncin' from tree limb to tree limb, pleased to meet whatever roots were waitin' for him. Anything you said to him was as important as what the next one said and all of it, minus your hangover here and there, made for chirpin'. And because he had that outlook he wasn't ripe for a pimp to come along in the marketplace and offer him untold tomorrows if he'd just give up what he'd been holdin' on to for dear life. He was the farthest from your cynicism you could find outside some blind waif singin' the *Ave Maria* on Assumption Day, and even that kind you have to keep an eye on.

Now look at it from the point of view of the editors and publishers who kept hirin' him. Men and women with their own bitterness for bein' what they call successful at their trade. Themselves, some of them, former foreign correspondents who knew all about the ways of the cynical marketplace. Experts on everythin' and believers in nothin'. You got those who envied a lad like Johnny for bein' what they could never be. You got others who liked the idea of throwin' him in the middle of some charnel house to see him admittin' defeat and comin' down to their level. Maybe you even had a couple who looked to Johnny for givin' them back the innocence they'd lost along the way. So what if he gets a little fact wrong here and there? They could cover that over by stealin' from the news agencies or CNN. Facts were always in what they call your public domain. But you associate your paper or your magazine with Johnny On the Spot and you got a chance at a lot more than that. *You might get to be as happy as he was!*

Mind, I sound a lot firmer about all this now than when I was back in Turkey. Back then, I still wasn't a hundred percent positive happiness had been the key to his success and failure. But I had to know, for me own peace of mind. So when we all met up again in Istanbul, I decided to put it to them to see if I've hit on the secret. I'm not proud of it, not after what happened, but I did it, first with Johnny at the hotel bar one evening. He just stares at me like I've found out water is wet. Why *shouldn't* he be happy, he asks. He's married to a beautiful woman, he's been all around the world, he's in good health, and he only misses the meals he wants to miss. What bothers him is the assumption behind me question, that I'm the one who's less than happy. I assure him I mean no such thing, and he believes me because he's always givin' people the benefit of the doubt, but I know to meself he's put his finger on somethin' I'd rather not have him fiddlin' around. I'm so busy coverin' up me flanks that I lose sight of how odd his response is compared to your normal run of mortals. Here's a lad who's not only happy, but he has no trouble sayin' so! Who'd you ever meet more than a week after the honeymoon who's up for the likes of matchin' that natural-as-you-please? Shouldn't the jinx factor alone have left him more evasive?

I'm ready to drop the whole subject then and there, but a few nights later, with Johnny off to Izmir on an assignment, here's Felicia calmin' herself down in me bed and me over me nicotine habit gettin' the brilliant notion to fill the catarrh void with thoughts on Johnny's happiness. At first she gives me the same look of marvelin' Johnny had. But whereas he thought me question funny because I should've known the answer, she thinks it's funny because only a crazy man could have me thoughts. She's not even sure she's heard me clearly. So what do you do? You could try to get her excited again, but what's that goin' to lead to but a lot of mechanical motion when the last excitement still has you left empty? Right you are. I insist on repeatin' what I said about Johnny and his happiness.

Well, let me tell you! The deeper it sinks in I'm bein' serious, the less she likes it. I tell her I don't know what she's so upset about. If Johnny's so happy, I remind her, a lot of that must be because of her. Fifteen years and he's still bouncin' around like he's got the lease to the Garden of Eden? There's not a Turk outside walkin' the streets who wouldn't want to trade places with Johnny. But she doesn't see it that way. She's gettin' madder and madder, pacin' up and down around the bed in her godly flesh. Then finally she gets it out: "Happiness is more than my husband! It has to be!"

When she yelled that out, you could've knocked me off a cliff with a feather. For once I didn't know what to say—a miracle me good mother had been waitin' for since the day I was born. Is Felicia so wound up in her advice columns, tellin' others how to reach happiness, that she's ashamed she herself didn't recognize it right next to her for 15 years? Or is she of a philosophical frame of mind, takin' it for granted happiness is in the strivin', not in the arrival, so Johnny bein' the epitome of happiness sort of blurs her aim on where she should be puttin' her dainty toes next? Whichever, it's enough for her to grab all her clothes off the floor and dress like she wants to be out of the buildin' before it burns to the ground. She's through the door before I can even offer to call a cab for her. A teensy-weensy flea in me ear says that's all for the better because I don't want any taxi driver tellin' the police she came from my place in goin' off to shoot Johnny. You don't like petty thoughts, but that don't keep them from comin'.

I wake up the next mornin' and turn on the radio for news from Izmir. It's all just blather about the Turks and Greeks facin' off in Cyprus and how the Turks are sendin' reinforcements across the Aegean to keep the Greeks in their place. What else was I expectin'? Edgy I was, like the next worst thing to sayin' you're happy is pointin' out to others they are. You feel like you're breakin' the spell for them. I go through the rest of the day doin' the usual and expectin' the phone to ring any second with news I don't want to hear. Finally, the clock gets to five and I go down to this café in the Stambul quarter where the boys always gather. And who's sittin' in the middle of them all but Johnny, back from Izmir! To my eyes he's as gloomy as a crow, but at that point I wasn't trustin' much of what I was seein'. What they call the guilt factor. I'm even on the verge of apologizin' to him for my loose talk to Felicia. The way I see it, it's one irony too much when talk of happiness makes you unhappy. Then one of the others says somethin' that shuts me up.

It turns out Johnny's gotten himself fired again. The way he tells it, he was seein' off the last of the Turks for Cyprus when a photographer comes along and asks for a picture of him and the crew of a tank waitin' to get loaded on the ship. Johnny figures the tank crew just wants some record of their sail they can share later with their wives and families. So he gets up on the tank where the Turks are all happy to see him, everybody smiles, and the photographer snaps away. It's all thank-you-very-much and the tank sets sail to blast away at the Greeks. It's only a few hours later in Istanbul he hears how all hell's broke loose. His editor calls to tell him the Greeks are runnin' the picture of him on the tank all over the world as proof the press isn't bein' objective about the doin's in Cyprus, that here's one of their correspondents bein' pally-wally with the Turks. The paper can't afford that kind of criticism in such a delicate international crisis, the editor tells Johnny, so the paper's puttin' out an announcement he's bein' given the axe for his bad judgment to mollify the Greeks.

Me? I'm thinkin' it could've been worse if all the gloom I'd made out was about Felicia demandin' to know what he was so happy about. Takin' the long view, wasn't it more important the lovebirds don't break up because of this one's loose mouth than because the Greeks had their little hemorrhage over a picture? But that's just the opinion of yours truly. Johnny, meanwhile, he's tryin' to be the good sport while the others go on raggin' him. He's all sincerity when he says he didn't know the photographer was a Greek spy and he would have done the same thing for the Greeks if he had been in Athens instead of Izmir. I'm sorry some Greeks aren't there to eavesdrop when he says it. But as I'm dwellin' in that wish, here comes Felicia stompin' down the street, her black leather boots all the way up her calves and emphasizin' the beauty of her knees. She don't care if there's a stadium of witnesses for what she's about to accuse him of. And the needles she throws me says she won't mind throwin' me into the fire while she's at it. "So we have to move again?" she starts out.

Professional that he is, Johnny wants to know the sources of her information. "How do you think I know?" she says, snatchin' his glass from the table and swallowin' half the scotch in it. "They called to confirm our address for sending the severance check."

So now he had no choice but to explain the whole tank business to her, and this in front of all of us who don't need to hear all the details of the story again. But we kept our patience. There were war clouds over Felicia's head, and it wasn't for us to be thickenin' them more. Then Johnny finally finishes his tale and, out of words as he is, he just gives her a little shrug—not like some defeated warrior, mind you, but more like that cartoon rabbit with his That's All, Folks. And she who's been ignorin' all this time a chair that's been pushed out for her to park, she looks around at us all with this expression that says we're not by any stretch of the imagination the witnesses she would want but it's too late for her to fly in any others. Then she makes the big announcement. "Johnny," she says, "I want a divorce."

Speakin' for meself, I'm mortified. I don't like being dragged into personal business. As my good mother used to say, that's why they invented walls. But then I get over those scruples fast when, thanks to Johnny, I'm made part of the most beautiful thing I've ever had to witness. "Great," he says. "So we'll be free to marry again."

She doesn't give up the lines in her forehead so easy. She asks him what he means, already not trustin' what he'll answer, and he simply repeats what he said. The breath goes out of the table, startin' with yours truly. Have the great poets ever had such a sentiment in such a situation? She certainly can't think of one who has. She stands flabbergasted and wantin' to keep her fury. Here she's been givin' advice to people from New York to Djakarta, but she don't know what to say to herself! And then Johnny puts a dollop of fine cream on it all by reaching' into his pocket and comin' out with a phone number for some magazine in Copenhagen that wants to hire him as its foreign correspondent. Not only that, he tells her, but they could have their new honeymoon in Patagonia because that's where the Danes want to send him on a first assignment. How many times have they talked about goin' down there? Isn't she still interested in knowin' what the Patagonians should be doin' and not doin'?

She all but collapses into the chair that's been waitin' for her. I had no doubt then and there that the chance to go to Patagonia was part of her fast calculations. But I also see they weren't the most important part. Her eyes were too swollen to be envisionin' only blessed penguins. "Why are you so happy, Johnny?" she finally comes out with it, and in a voice so tender the angels would have been leanin' over to be sure they were hearin' it. "Is it something I've done?"

Johnny bein' Johnny, he don't understand the mystery. He even looks at me to be the one to laugh along with him. I don't have the titters in me. There's cruelty and then there's cruelty, and I've contributed more than enough of it to this particular imbroglio to be addin' still more. Seein' he's on his own, Johnny goes back to her and has to say, "It's *everything* you've done," he says, his voice risin' as though it should be obvious. "Why can't you see that?"

The tragedy of it, as Shakespeare and the old Greeks before him might have said, was that Felicia *did* see it. And didn't want to see it. "Patagonia is the end of the world, Johnny" she gets out with more lumps than the Andes in her throat. "There'd be nothing after that. So no, I won't go with you. And yes, I really want a divorce."

We were all what they call frozen. She's up on her fine boots again and she's walkin' away from the table so that we can't even see her fine knees. Beethoven symphonies don't have as much finality to them in the last movement. And Johnny knows it, too. He watches after her for a long moment, then back at the piece of paper he's tried to use to win her over. I'm ready to put meself on the bottom of somebody's shoe because I get this sudden expectation that he's finally been brought low like the worst of us and I'll be as relieved for it as the most cynical bastard up in some nest of a newspaper office. You don't like discoverin' your own nature through another's destruction.

"She'll change her mind," he says, pocketin' his assignment from the Danes. "Patagonia isn't the end of the world."

Somebody objects that, at least judgin' from your average atlas, it's pretty close to it. Johnny flags down our waiter Hakim and orders a round for everybody to celebrate his new assignment. "There's more world than there is me," he laughs. "And Felicia knows that."

You may not take it from me as your most reliable source. I won't deny that. But he was right.

Till's Piano Lesson

"YOU'RE early, Till. I told you never come early."

"Sorry. I guess my watch is off."

"Buy a new one."

Klein refit the crutches under his armpits and swung his crabbed legs back toward the studio, leaving Till to enter the living room for himself. Till didn't like living rooms. He thought them banal in their predictable assembly of tables, chairs, lamps, and rugs. What he wanted to see was a living room with people who dropped dead as soon as they put a foot outside it. Living rooms should have been what they claimed to be.

Klein's pupil in the studio seemed to be trying to erase his presence through sheer aggression. Had Mozart started that way? Till didn't think so. If Mozart had chafed his tiny fingers the way the student had to be doing, grazing the wood of the adjoining note every time he aimed at the ivory, Wolfgang wouldn't have had anything left for picking his nose. Genius simply wasn't nourished under the wing of Edgar Klein.

Which was all right with Till. He had no love affair with Genius and wasn't even on first-name terms with Talent. What Till liked about music was that he was totally disarmed before it. He knew the names of tunes, but in the best of cases recalled only a line or two from any particular one. Theories about music bored him; on-and-off attempts to penetrate them had lasted only a few pages before his retreat to hunting magazines. As for musicians, he knew the names of every first violin who had ever cowed under Toscanini, of every drummer who had ever sat in with Miles Davis, and of every actor who had ever played Porgy, but he knew that was sycophancy, not music. But it was also precisely because he couldn't appreciate music technically, intellectually, or vicariously that he was drawn to it. It was an area so impervious to him it merited his attention for this fact alone. Its exclusivity made *him* exclusive. By being rejected so absolutely he became music's equal—a status he had no intention of losing. In short, as he sat in Klein's living room waiting for the start of his lesson, Till had the world on a string, was sittin' on a rainbow, had the string 'round his finger, but no more than that. Lucky Till, he wasn't in love. He only had to worry about Klein not running out of patience and himself not running out of cash for paying the old grouch twice a week.

Till picked up a small glass ashtray from the coffee table. At the center of the tray was the name of an Atlantic City hotel surrounded by a circle of smiling fish. Being a non-smoker, Till considered ashtrays useless; not being a collector of the past, he thought them oppressive in their reminders of bygone entertainment and petty thievery. But standing up from the couch and taking a closer look around, he saw that Klein was of another opinion, having an apparent fetish for ashtrays from far and farther places. There was a Montreal hotel, a Des Moines hotel, a German brandy, an Italian beer, even a Danish mermaid hovering over an ashtray-matchbox. Till thought the collection depressing, suggesting that the old man had ventured over two continents when he had still been able to walk and was now resigned to covering all that with ashes.

Till had an impulse. Switching his keys to the handkerchief pocket of his jacket, he swooped up the smaller trays and put them in his side pockets. The larger mermaid stumped him until he decided it was warm enough to shed his jacket altogether. He worked rapidly in his shirtsleeves, sticking the Atlantic City fish and the mermaid inside the jacket, then trying smooth ways of walking with the coat under his arm. After a couple of tries he was confident he could carry the jacket into the studio, lay it on a side chair, take his lesson, then leave without arousing Klein's suspicion.

He was still congratulating himself for his ingenuity when the clatter from the next room ceased and Klein started thudding around on his crutches. Till returned to his perch on the couch, his jacket a ball under his arm, his eyes trying to be nonchalant about watching the doorway to the hall. His pose almost came undone when Klein, instead of following his routine of accompanying students to the front door, suddenly just loomed up in the doorway while the boy continued his way out alone. "All right,

Till. I'm ready for you." Till cackled nervously. "I say something funny?"

"No."

Klein dropped his leeriness to the ball of a jacket. "You treat your clothes the way you treat my instrument."

"Needs a pressing anyway."

"My piano don't. Come on. Let's get this over with."

Till clutched his jacket tightly, imploring the ashtrays not to click together, as he entered the dim lights and faded upholstery of the studio. Every time he entered the hot room, he thought not so much of beginners learning scales as of exhausted old pianists returning in their dotage to give back the basics they no longer needed.

"Put that heap in that chair there. Cat'll like it."

Till did what he was told as Klein dropped himself into the recliner that had been pushed up next to the piano bench. "I was thinking about you today, Till," he said. "Don't take it as a compliment. I think about things all the time. I think about paying bills. I think about walking into a room on my own feet like you just did. Thinking counts for shit."

"No point being maudlin."

"No point being a cripple, either. What the hell you doing there?"

"Just trying to make the cat comfortable." He meant it, too: He didn't need the cat jumping up on the chair and pawing at unexpected lumps in his jacket.

"You surprise me, Till."

"I like cats."

"Guess so. If you had half a brain, you'd hang it over the back instead of spreading it out like that."

Till was alarmed by the old man's suddenly shrewd look—the more so because he was simultaneously removing a cigarette and matches from his pocket. Klein's stare remained fixed on him as he slid on to the piano bench and made a show of closing the exercise book left by the student before him. "Ready to start."

"On one condition."

"Condition?"

Klein tossed his burning match into another school of happy Atlantic City fish on the arm of the piano. "You tell me what you're getting out of all this."

"Out of what?"

"What you come here for, what else?"

"The music, naturally."

Klein looked incredulous. "I put on the radio, I hear music. What we spend your money and my time on here is your money and my time."

It was the conversation Till had been dreading, but tonight it came as a relief: At least they had gotten off his jacket. "I'm a slow beginner. I told you that the first day."

"There's slow and there's slow. At five, most kids know they have ten fingers. At ten, they stop trying to poke them into wall sockets. At your age, they shake my hand and thank me for not wasting more of their money."

"That's not what you told me when I first came."

Klein exhaled his smoke with a sigh. Not for the first time, Till thought the man's broad, granite face and overdeveloped shoulders belonged as a bust atop the piano. "Okay, it isn't your hands," he said. "A snowman with mittens will pick out notes if he keeps at it."

"Then what's the problem?"

Without moving his eyes, the old man tapped an ash onto the keyboard. "What do you see?"

"Ashes on a piano."

"And what did you hear when I flicked them there?"

"Hear?"

"I heard something. You didn't? Listen again."

Till watched in bewilderment as Klein took a long drag on his cigarette, then tapped the new ash onto the back of his other hand. The old man smiled at the tiny start he gave. "Hear it then?"

"I don't hear anything."

"Pain, Till! Pain is what you heard!"

"Oh."

"Maybe not screamed to the rooftops. I'm not young anymore. The skin hardens. But still pain. And you should also hear it when I tap ashes onto the keyboard . . . Don't believe it? Of course, you don't. That's why you'll never be a pianist. You don't respect your instrument, Till. You don't want it to communicate with you. When you sit on this bench, you're a would-be conqueror. No dialogue, just monologue. You don't play, you dictate. Granted you're not even competent at that yet, but some day practice could make perfect. Only you won't practice with me. I refuse to be your accomplice."

Till was still taking in the outburst as the old man sat back in his recliner and glanced over at the jacket. "In all the time you've been coming here, I've seen you make a gesture towards something outside yourself only once. Know when? Just now. Everybody needs something to care about, and with you it seems to be a cat. For that flea-tree you showed consideration. If I had a pet shop, you'd be welcome here every night. But I don't have a pet shop. I'm trying to save you money, you understand?"

"It's my money."

"But my time. Want I be more brutal? I don't throw away my money training for the four-minute mile, you shouldn't throw away yours coming here twice a week."

A giddiness washed over Till until he had to turn away. He thought about thundering out a melodramatic chord, but the realization he couldn't manage it after months of lessons only fed his convulsion. He'd known more about the piano before he'd ever heard of Edgar Klein!

"You've taken everything I can give you, Till. Use it for whatever it's worth."

"Including your advice?" he asked, calming himself.

Klein got to his feet as he usually did—first testing the waters, then grabbing his crutches and locking them under his arms. "A waste of time sulking. On me because I won't change my mind. On yourself because you're probably already working out how to spend your time instead of coming here. I don't say that as an insult. You look like a bullshitter who'll never stay down long. You're resilient, Till. Now hold on a minute while I get the money for the lessons you've paid for in advance."

As Klein started out, Till had an impulse to call after him, to tell him the money would cover the ashtrays. But he said nothing. To get kicked out was one thing, to quit another. He wanted every penny back for what he had paid but not received.

At the front door, Klein was still disapproving of the way Till carried his jacket. "No respect. It shows even in how you treat your clothes."

"That's what tailors are for, right?"

"So shoot yourself. That's what undertakers are for, right?"

"Mind if I ask something?"

"What?"

"Ever been to Europe or Canada?"

"No. Why?"

"What about the Midwest? Around Des Moines?"

"What the hell should I go to Des Moines for?"

"Change of pace. A vacation, maybe."

Klein began swinging the door closed. "For a vacation I sit on my brother-in-law's porch in Atlantic City watching *schmuks* walking in the sand. I like seeing how they labor along. That answer your question?"

"In part."

"Take what you can get. Good Night, Till."

IN CONCERT

PEYROT was a difficult man, and he would have been the last to deny it. Although he had gained considerable professional recognition by his 60th year, it hardly tickled the literary satisfactions he had envisioned as a young writer. As a journalist in Rome, he had fought constantly with editors, deadlines, and the transient impact of daily newspapers. As a critic in books and periodicals, he had quarreled remorselessly with the painters, novelists, and filmmakers who had consumed his time with trendy or solipsistic concoctions. As a guest on television discussion shows, he had inquired querulously about an industry that demanded reporting to a makeup room as a prerequisite for delivering the fruits of the mind and about his own receptivity to playing the game. Rarely did he feel a word or thought as other than a commitment to some banal embroilment—or as other than an obligation to denounce it as such. The only significant variable was in the when and where of the denunciation, this usually depending on how much money he needed and how quickly.

Physically, Peyrot radiated a robustness that belied his pinched surveillance of humankind. Standing almost six feet tall at a trim 175 pounds, his full waves of white hair and glowing color transcended health regimen calculations to a genetic self-confidence. His father, a book binder in Siena, had lived without hospital stays to the age of 93, and his father's father had withdrawn from the same family business because of diminishing eyesight only at 89. His mother's family boasted equal endurance. She had outlived his father by three years, and her parents had been looking forward to a joint 80th birthday when they had been killed by Allied bombers during World War II. Peyrot being Peyrot, so much longevity on both sides bemused him as the sentence of a sardonic judge. Would he have enough bile to see him through?

Paola, Peyrot's wife of 31 years, felt little need to reassure him. She had grown so used to the cycle of his rages against the Philistines, self-lacerations, and more rages against the Philistines that she had adopted it as a protective cover for her own misanthropies. *They* were making her husband miserable so *he* was making her miserable so all of *them*—him included—were a daily misery she wouldn't have minded seeing ended by a bolt of lightning striking him, her, or them, whoever happened to be walking closest to the tree. Having once had her own aspirations as a sculptress, Paola brought a chiseled envy of mind to the substantial library of outsized art books they had accumulated over the years. On the one hand, she conceded Peyrot had always earned enough to afford such expensive items and that he had known enough artists personally to fill the living room shelves with first editions, signed copies, and rare portfolios. On the other hand, she refused to forget he had never achieved the financial independence that would have allowed her to set up a studio and work all morning instead of having to sit at the kitchen table double-checking the totals from the supermarket bill.

The inevitable fractiousness in the Peyrot household was the least of it. As anyone exposed to them for the length of a meal could have attested, there was a tartness in Paola that often made Peyrot come off as the warmer side of the couple. Where even his most fervid attacks on the institution of the moment usually left a small pocket for judging his own complicity with it, she had little patience with self-deprecation. If *they* wanted her to turn into a bubbly, carefree personality, if *they* wanted her to see more than crooks in the prime minister's office, more than hypocrites in the Vatican, and more than empty cynics in movie theaters and on television, let *them* give her an incentive. Lacking that, she saw no reason to feel as guilty as they should have felt for cretinizing life with their petty greeds. But it was also this caustic spirit that, between the arguments coloring just about every meal and every attempt at a Sunday afternoon outing, continued to make Paola attractive to Peyrot. At least *she* wasn't always banality. When she wasn't impressing him as despicable, he still saw the verve of the chunky Roman brunette who had once accosted him at a cocktail party to ask if he realized he was wearing one blue sock and one black sock. Vice versa, she knew that, even 30 pounds overweight and given to increasingly painful arthritic sieges, she maintained a sexual command in his eyes. It was an asset she did not squander when, two or three times a month, he fell into the shoulder rubbing that served as a ritualistic prelude to making love. Even when she couldn't tolerate the predictability of his advances, she usually went along with the consolation of at least enjoying the shoulder rub.

The three Peyrot children who grew up on this energy field learned at an early age they were better off not acknowledging the high-tension lines all around them. But the older that daughters Miranda and Silvana and son Lucca grew, the harder this became and the more regularly their actions (or lack of them) became the ignition for setting Peyrot and Paola against one another, the consumer society, and the other opiates of the masses. Where each child had been doted on by both parents until 11 or 12 as a retreat of joy and sanity within a smarmy world, the teenage years brought smellier relations with smellier clothes. Their adolescence was an invasion not only because they turned snippy, impenetrable, and exhausting, but also because, one after another, the children demonstrated there were no genuine retreats from the crassness of the world at large. All their sexual, drinking, and driving episodes, their academic languors, and their precocious ennuis fell as the relentless drops of a disenchantment that ultimately swamped Peyrot and Paola. More than they had been aware of desiring it, they found in their children confirmation that their normal contentiousness was the best guide to getting through the day, blood pressure readings be damned.

Over the years, Peyrot's gruffness cut progressively deeper into the bone of his relationships. A 40-year friendship dating back to his school days in Tuscany ended abruptly over the telephone when he heard one endorsement too many of another United States military adventure in the Near East. Disagreements over the Mafia's control of a state utility company claimed a second friend, disputes over Roberto Benigni's talents a third. Eventually, the Peyrot circle was one of professional acquaintances and immediate family and nobody else. This was borne home vividly one Sunday when Miranda insisted her parents accept an invitation to visit the Parioli apartment of her fiancé's family. For close to two hours, Peyrot and Paola drank a cheap liqueur and nibbled on aniseed biscuits in a stuffy, brown-lit sitting room while they politely shook their heads at Miranda's future father-in-law's problems operating a lingerie boutique and wondered what had happened to the Sunday jaunts into the hills that had sometimes required three and four cars for accommodating their old crowd. Driving home that chilly day, Peyrot realized he was lonely.

But this didn't make him more sociable. On the contrary, rather than risk a repeat of the experience with the lingerie store bore, he resorted to any and all excuses for remaining within his own walls. Except for professional engagements and constitutionals in neighborhoods where he was unlikely to come across acquaintances, he directed most of his energies to the path between his computer and the shelves of his favorite old books. Miranda regarded it as a wearying triumph when he managed to be cordial through her civil wedding at City Hall and at the reception afterward. For her part, younger daughter Silvana avoided the stresses of formalities altogether by moving in with an art restorer. As much as he disliked Miranda's heir to the lingerie business on Via Cavour, Peyrot liked the art restorer, welcoming him for dinners a couple of times a month so he could hear tales about bureaucrats more concerned with keeping the doors of museums open than having something on the walls for tourists to see. Not that he was any more disposed to visiting Silvana's apartment than he was Miranda's, however. When there weren't last-second deadlines interfering with the dinner invitations of his daughters, there were colds, allergies, or flu bugs that would have made him an unappreciative guest for their elaborate meals. Another time, thank you.

At first, Paola made little of Peyrot's growing reclusiveness, even tried convincing herself it had its beneficial side. She was no longer exclusively responsible, for instance, for banging on Lucca's door at noon to wake him up for a university class or for his job at a neighborhood cafe. She was also able to indulge a warm memory or two before his renewed passion to share with her and her alone perspectives gained from his latest rereading of Dante, Balzac, or Joyce. But these were passing moments, and the more his conversation ran to the past, the ancient, and the dead, the more Paola resented his assumption that she wanted to be sentenced to them as meekly as he did. She hadn't let *them* overwhelm her coming through the front door and she wasn't going to fall prey to them from the back door, either.

The spring for acting came when Paola read an item in the paper about an imminent convention of political cartoonists in Rome. She knew one of those in attendance would be Carlo Luzzi—the Tuscan schoolmate Peyrot had sentenced to oblivion on the phone for his mild evaluation of American foreign policy. Seven years had elapsed since that breakup, and she knew it was the relationship Peyrot most regretted severing. While she herself had always distrusted Luzzi's Tuscan irony, thought the man too elusive both personally and politically, she didn't need a caption for the dismissive "Boh!" Peyrot emitted whenever he looked at the cartoons of some lesser draftsman in the morning paper. She had also noticed how the two collections of Luzzi's cartoons had somehow drifted down from exile in the far corner of the top shelf of the library to an eye-level space with the computer. That suspicious convenience was reason enough one day for steering the conversation around to Luzzi and suggesting Peyrot drop his stubbornness and call the cartoonist in Siena. The icy silence of an answer had discouraged a second urging.

But then she read about the convention and decided she had put up with enough childish feuding between two men speeding toward senility. Even giving the worst of her thoughts to Luzzi, she couldn't imagine him still being so mealy-mouthed about America, not after the chaos in Iraq. Giving the worst of them to her husband, she couldn't see him rejecting an opportunity to crow to Luzzi about how right he had been about the Americans before the two of them got back to squabbling about which of their teachers had been a pedophile. But she didn't want to think about worst cases. She needed some fresh air in the house, and fast. The fact was, Peyrot had begun sounding eerie with his drifting monologues about Florences, Parises, and Dublins that had not existed in centuries. On a work level, his interests had grown steadily more arid and obstinate: academic journals that paid nothing, were read by four professors, and were barely organized enough to send him a copy of what he had written for them. In their narrowest financial straits, she had never thought twice about opening her bag for the children, but Silvana's sudden request for a 1,000-euro loan toward a car had left her sputtering before she had finally written a check. Whatever her own reservations about the man, Carlo Luzzi had become a path back toward a normality she had once hated thinking of as one.

The cartoonist took her call mere minutes before setting off from Siena for Rome. She had been so intent on delivering a composed speech—half-hectoring, half-pleading—that she needed a moment to relax before the easy laughter in her ear. "I was thinking the same thing, Paola," Luzzi said. "We're not getting any younger, so why act like we are? I'll call him as soon as I get to Rome tonight."

"Don't let him say no, Carlo. Please."

"Don't worry."

Because Peyrot's isolation tactics had included letting the telephone ring until she answered it or the machine picked up, Paola made sure she was visiting Signora Borgato next door at the time Luzzi promised to call; before leaving, she also disconnected the machine. When she returned to the apartment an hour later, she found Peyrot sitting in his living room lounger savoring a cognac. "You'll never guess who just called," he said, wonder still etched on his face. Paola didn't guess, merely absorbed the announcement that he would be going into the city center the following evening for dinner. She took it as a good sign that he didn't say anything about Luzzi coming to his senses or make any other reference to the old argument. America, Iraq, and Mars were secondary: Seeing an old friend was the priority.

✳ ✳ ✳

Peyrot's astonishment at Carlo Luzzi's call made it impossible for him to work the next day, to concentrate on anything but the dinner. He was irritated Paola found it funny he was going for a haircut; it wasn't the first time he had gone to the barber twice in three weeks. He also could have done without her martyr's moan about needing his best blue shirt from the laundry; she knew how to turn on the washer and dryer by now, didn't she? On the other hand, he had no need of the car. He had never sat down to a restaurant meal with Luzzi when the two of them hadn't consumed at least two liters of wine, and he was getting too old to chance driving home at night after one of those sessions. The bus would do fine; more than that, it would impose a curfew since the last one left the terminus at midnight.

Paola tried to stay out of Peyrot's way until he left for the *Centro*. She knew she was being ridiculous, but she felt as scattered as the day Miranda had gotten married. She always seemed to be mislaying something or standing in the wrong room. When Silvana called to say she was in the neighborhood and wanted to show off her new car, Paola said she wouldn't be home and hung up without explaining her edginess. Lucca, she all but threw out the door to his job before he sniffed too much and let loose with his insolent questions. When Peyrot was finally ready to leave— his hair as neat as a cardinal's, his blue shirt elegantly assertive, his silver watch gleaming, she couldn't resist kissing him on the cheek. "What was that for?" he asked, not knowing whether to be pleased or annoyed. "I want you to have a good time," she said. "If you don't, don't bother coming home."

On the bus going down to the Piazza del Popolo, Peyrot hoped Luzzi wouldn't insist on some grand reconciliation hug. A, he disliked big gestures for small things. B, it would have been suspiciously atypical of Luzzi, still known in certain streets of Siena as Rinculo Luzzi for the way he had always recoiled at kisses from girls. C, he wouldn't know there *was* a true reconciliation until he renewed his measure of the man.

He needn't have fretted. Already seated at a sidewalk table in a piazza cafe, Rinculo Luzzi, glasses across his forehead, his hair still too black for it to be natural and his face still mottled with dark freckles, looked up from a mound of daily newspapers in front of him and barked: "Still drink that Campari shit before dinner?" Peyrot didn't like the idea he had probably been under the man's watch across the piazza, but that seemed like the lesser evil to having to make a show of embracing him prematurely. "Mineral water," he snapped back. "If that's all right with you."

Luzzi had no objections. And as soon as the waiter went off for the water, he dispensed with the seven years, too. "You look older, I look older, and the world's more of a shit hole," he said, shuffling his newspapers in search of something. "Anything else I missed?"

"You wouldn't look half as old if you'd stop dying your hair. Who's that for? The American girls seeing the Palio?"

"They have a vision of the world."

"I know. Spider Man and invasions. Which one are you?"

"Here," Luzzi said, finding what he had been looking for. "Tell me how you print something like that."

Peyrot found himself looking at an editorial cartoon he had already seen that morning. It was of the Italian prime minister dressed as Julius Caesar and being stabbed in the Senate by John Bull, Marianne, and other European national symbols. The draftsmanship was crude, not all that removed from stick figures. "Boh!"

"Forget *Boh*," Luzzi demanded, his eyes dilating in anger. "When I used that motif 40 years ago, it was about the Christian Democrats betraying Aldo Moro. A real betrayal! Moro ended up dead! But this shit? The rest of Europe doesn't agree with this conman about some finance bill, so he's been betrayed? I don't think so."

Peyrot couldn't resist. "But at least the artwork's polished."

Luzzi snatched back the newspaper and contemplated the cartoon again somberly. "Tell me I'm better than this," he muttered after a moment.

"You know you are." But Luzzi kept staring at the drawing; he had been seeking more than a mechanical reassurance. "You're comparing yourself to hacks these days?"

"Absolutely," the other nodded, still no humor in his eyes. "If they're what the market is, how can I avoid it?"

"They've always been the market."

A smile finally slid across his lips. "But I had my illusions. Now I don't have them anymore."

Peyrot remembered his impatience with the man the last time they had spoken; then it had been about Iran and Afghanistan— something that suddenly seemed, by comparison, respectably intellectual. "Born-again Luzzi! We should have a toast! Where's that waiter? Forget the mineral water. We need scotch to celebrate Luzzi's great awakening!"

"And you, no? You're still sleeping and happy to stay unconscious?"

"When I'm unconscious, I do better than that garbage."

"How do you know? Paola tell you?"

"Even you do better. Whatever your American friends tell you."

"I don't have American friends."

"Then they're just squatting in your brain. Call a cop and get them thrown out."

"Cops aren't the answer to anything. Or have you changed your mind about that?"

"I haven't changed my mind about anything. Why should I?"

"I don't know. See how the rest of the world does it, maybe?"

Peyrot said nothing as the waiter brought his water and glass. He knew if he looked over the boy's elbow he would see Luzzi staring at him, daring him to smile. He wasn't won over so easily. Nobody had ever accused *him* of being Mister Recoil.

✳ ✳ ✳

When Lucca returned home and learned where Peyrot had gone, he nodded in approval. Paola was glad for his reaction—but only up to a point, up to where the condescension started. "All I said was, it was a stupid argument in the first place." "Were you there? Were you eavesdropping? How do you know what the argument was about?" "Okay, Mama, whatever it was, I'm sure it was something epic. Whether the Americans should give guns to the Kurds or something." "Don't be fresh."

As soon as Lucca banged his bedroom door closed, Paola turned on the television. Whatever he was muttering about her, she told herself, he would think twice about being flippant with his father. She kept pressing the remote-control buttons until she realized she was looking for something she wouldn't find: the dinner with Luzzi. She was dismayed by her curiosity, then not so dismayed. What she was counting on Luzzi to dispel was not reclusiveness or 24-hour-a-day irascibility, but simple age. More than anything else, Peyrot's withdrawal had been that of a prematurely old man—somebody bent on defying his own bloodlines to crawl faster into a grave. And so where did that leave her? It left her frightened, that was where. Peyrot had been performing the small miracle of simultaneously boring and terrifying her. Was she to be the ward of her own children before her time? Peyrot might have found it fascinating to hear about the varnishes used to preserve a Donatello, but the last thing she needed was Silvana's art restorer telling her which place was hers at the dinner table. She would find her bolt of lightning first.

Instead of Luzzi she found the six 40-year-old American imbeciles who lived together and kept jumping in and out of each other's beds. Sometimes they made her laugh despite herself. She also knew the tall blonde one was going to have hips twice as big in a few years.

✳ ✳ ✳

Midway through their first liter, Peyrot had the whole story. Some of Luzzi's freckles weren't freckles, and he was due to have them removed the day after he returned home from the convention. "But look at the bright side," he told the cartoonist. "Even if they're malignant and they kill you, you should still have a couple of weeks to do a few more drawings."

"*'fanculo.*"

"You don't want to be a pessimist."

"Let them take them off *your* face."

"If it'll give you another week, give me one of them."

Luzzi lowered his smile into his plate. "Maybe I'd do shit work in that week," he said, searching for a mussel shell with something in it. "Maybe it wouldn't be worth it."

"The pope says miracles happen every day."

The cartoonist speared a mussel with a grunt. "I remember every single one of them," he said. "Most of them I wish I couldn't, but I do. The pencil I used, where I was sitting, who I was doing it for, how good or shitty it looked in the paper the next day. That happen to you, too?"

"I don't look back anymore. Half the stuff is embarrassing and shouldn't have been accepted by anybody. The other half is intimidating. For sure *I* can't write like that today. So I'm worse than I was except when I'm better than I was. Why do I want to know that?"

"Maybe you're the one who's always been a hack, Peyrot."

"Another possibility."

"Look into it."

Peyrot refilled their glasses to give his hands something to do; he didn't need any more repartee. "It's the first time," he realized aloud.

"What is?"

"We have mortality sitting with us."

Luzzi nodded. "I was thinking that, too."

"So tell me something about it."

"I'm the expert?"

"You know it better than I do. I've just been taunting it. Running up to the door, knocking, and then running off again to hide. Making Paola and the children crazy. And I know why."

"Why?"

He was vaguely disappointed Luzzi didn't know why. "Because I don't *feel* mortal, idiot. Because that'll still be something *I* decide. So I play with it. I tease it. I'm so invulnerable I stick out my tongue at it."

"*Beato te.*"

"So the wisdom—where is it? I want to hear from somebody who's quaking in his boots. What do I have in store for me?"

Luzzi wiped his fingers off on the napkin over his lap; he gazed without reaction at a chic blonde in a shiny black mandarin blouse at the next table. "You might not like the answer."

"Of course, I won't!"

The impish smile returned. "No, I mean because it involves your favorite people—the Americans."

"Jesus Christ! Have they redefined mortality, too?"

"Frank Sinatra. Remember a few years ago, when he was dying? Went on for weeks, all these cryptic bulletins. I thought to myself, what is that man thinking as he lies there dying?"

"Mastroianni died a few years ago, too. Fellini. Pinco Paolino. A thousand Pinco Paolinos. Only you would think of Frank Sinatra."

"Do you want to hear or just go on feeling immortal?"

"*Avanti, avanti!*"

"So there is Sinatra dying," he said, toasting the memory with his wine. "This great idol of America and the gangsters and the women and the musicians. All the people he was vicious with, got into fights with. And what is he thinking as he's dying? Only one possible thing—that he can't do Frank Sinatra anymore."

"So?"

"You're not listening, Peyrot. He's not thinking, 'Oh, I'm so sorry for all the things I've done.' And he's not thinking, 'Oh, I'm so sorry I didn't get to do that.' He doesn't care what he's done. There hasn't been anything he wanted to do he didn't do. His only sense of loss is he can't do himself anymore. I can't think of a richer way to confront your own mortality than that, can you?"

"And that's what your pimples make you think of?"

"*Scemo!* That's what I *wish* I could say. Just no more Luzzi doing Luzzi things. Nothing more than that. But I can't say that. There are a thousand things I wish I'd done and a thousand I wish I hadn't."

"Because you're not this Frank Sinatra??!!"

"Or at least my idea of him."

Peyrot didn't know where to start; his anger swelled on too many fronts at the same time. "You're talking about *your* life, Carlo. Not this singer with his gangster friends . . ."

"He was a good actor, too."

He lost his thread. He had been wrong about their argument seven years ago, he realized. It wasn't even smugness he was looking at; it was absolute bliss!

"Well? You don't think he was a good actor?"

Peyrot watched the elegant blonde pick up the smallest morsel of steak with her fork. Because she used her fork backward, her bottom teeth alone seemed to receive the meat onto her tongue. Was the meat lured into a false sense of security before her upper teeth came down on it? "Whatever he was good at," he heard himself saying, "he can't chew anymore."

Luzzi looked perplexed.

They went through the rest of their meal without talking about death or mortality. After seven years there were too many other plots and connivances to be covered. Gradually, Peyrot slipped inside layers of familiar places where not just seven years, but whole decades, felt renewed. There was ugliness in some of the details (cowardices by friends, debacles by the well-meaning, perfidies at home and abroad), but Luzzi was as on guard against romanticizing it as he was, and by the time the waiter laid the bill on the table, his main doubt was whether he could forgive himself for having shut out the man for so long. Cowardice, debacle, and perfidy all seemed to be named Peyrot.

Luzzi wanted no debate over the bill. "You've forgotten the whore's life, Peyrot. *Money*. That's what makes it all worth it."

"You lie."

"About what?"

"Poor, humble Carlo Luzzi. The common man. Not being a Frank Sinatra with nothing to regret on his deathbed."

Luzzi nodded for the waiter to keep the change. "Part of the strategy of the conquered people is to always make the occupiers feel like they're loved, envied, and admired. It keeps them off their guard."

"And in the meantime—the long meantime—everybody drinks Pepsi-Cola, eats hamburgers, and swoons over all the actors named Tom."

He looked as happy as one of his bumbling cartoon creatures. "So stay vigilant, Peyrot. Beware of quislings like Carlo Luzzi. Confront us in the streets and go, 'Shame! Shame! You've surrendered so easily!'"

"I will."

"I count on it, *amico*. It's what they have left us with, and we must have more than the past between us."

✳ ✳ ✳

Paola grabbed at the phone on the bed table before it rang a second time. She felt stupid watching it slide immediately out of her hand lotion onto the carpet next to the bed. "What the hell is going on there!" Peyrot demanded from the floor.

She retrieved the phone using her fingers as pincers; she wouldn't have minded grabbing his neck veins the same way. "I dropped the phone, all right? And why are you calling? Don't tell me you had another argument with Luzzi and left him at the table. I don't want to hear it."

She was taken aback by his soft chuckle. "No argument. We've finished dinner and are going to take walk."

Something tense dissolved in her chest; she hadn't known it was there until it was breaking up. "I didn't ask for a detailed report. You sound like you've been drinking."

"That's good, Paola. You're a regular detective!"

As long as he wasn't there to see it, she didn't mind smiling. "What do you want, Peyrot? Want me to pick you up?"

"Don't be an idiot. I'll get the bus. I just wanted . . ."

"What?"

She knew his wine sniffles; they always came when he was about to blame himself for *them*. "I'm glad Carlo called. That's all."

"Good. Why don't you stay in the *Centro* tonight? Luzzi can put you up in his hotel room."

There was no more sniffling. "What for? I told you, I'll get the bus. What kind of imbecile stays in a hotel in his own city?"

"I didn't know that was a rule."

"As a matter of fact, it is. You don't feel at home and you don't feel like a visitor. Why should I do that?"

"I don't know, Peyrot."

"I know you don't because there's no sense to it."

"Are we finished now?"

"I just thought you'd want to know everything's gone all right."

"Thank you. I'm glad to hear it."

"And if you dropped the phone because of that damn cream again, could you clean it off the plastic? It sticks there for weeks."

Paola liked herself for hanging up without a rejoinder. She didn't even mind grabbing a tissue from the night table and rubbing down the phone. For once, he had been right about something.

* * *

From the restaurant Peyrot and Luzzi strolled through the mild night in the general direction of the bus terminus in Piazza Augusto Imperatore. Every bar they passed, Peyrot thought about suggesting a nightcap to extend the evening, then thought better of it, fearing that would have abbreviated things because then they would have had to part company as soon as they had finished their drink. He didn't want to impose concrete deadlines. So instead, they exchanged inventories over what they could see through screened shop windows—a frames store reminding Luzzi of a mounted collection of his cartoons given to him at an awards dinner, a lingerie boutique returning Peyrot to Miranda's deadly husband and in-laws, a cellphone franchise goading Luzzi into a tirade against pedestrians and drivers who went around with electronics attached to their ears. A bookstore stalled them for five minutes because of a prominently displayed best seller by a Siena mystery writer. Peyrot had liked the book because it had evoked the city for him, Luzzi decided Peyrot had been away from the city too long. They agreed Peyrot would make up for that failing by visiting with Paola as soon as the skin cancer doctors had turned off their laser guns.

For all their ambling, Peyrot still had a feeling of arriving too soon when they reached the bus stop. But with a bus already idling at the curb, there was no reason to keep Luzzi waiting. He didn't think of their hug as a reconciliation, only one more good-bye over a half-century of goodbyes.

"What was it about, Peyrot?" Luzzi asked, his eyes searching even as his mouth prepared for glibness. "That last conversation about America?"

Peyrot knew, though it hadn't occurred to him so clearly before. "What else? The waiting. It's always obvious what's going to happen, but what do we do about it? We just sit around waiting for it. We have no urgency, no outrage. We save all that for when it's too late."

He ended up sitting on the bus for a quarter-hour before the driver closed the doors and started off. He spent the time speculating about the lives of the people sitting around him. The two Filipino women were maids going home from their hotel jobs. The young couple had seen some caramel film that had allowed them to hold hands. The primly dressed bank clerk had just paid for it with a woman, a man, or a Lego toy. The old gentleman with the morning newspaper sticking out of his pocket . . . wasn't so old! Peyrot laughed. Since when had *old gentlemen* grown younger than he was??!! Since when had everybody in the bus glanced at *him* as the old gentleman?

He shook his head out at the lights glistening off the Tiber. If he had more of a gift for slapstick, he could have been a circus clown. As it was, he seemed to go around often enough with a big red nose and an exploding cigar in his mouth. Was it any wonder he seemed to breed only stagnation, even literally? The best student in her class all through the university, but Miranda had settled for somebody whose conversation died after markup ranges on nightgowns! The liveliest ball-breaker of the three, but would Silvana ever see Giotto as more than an avenue to the latest DVD? And in what century would Lucca pay enough attention to his bar job to make a drinkable cappuccino? Thank God they were all healthy and could put their right feet before their left feet going down the street, and he certainly hadn't counted on them turning out as the Bachs, but Jesus Christ! . . .

The bus slowed down, then stopped altogether. Traffic was backed up all the way along the overpass to the stadium; it might have been six o'clock rather than eleven-thirty. "Concert," the driver said before anyone asked. "They're just getting out."

Peyrot had thought the word *concert* inappropriate for anything but Beethoven and Wagner. Even when he and Paola had gone to the stadium to see the Rolling Stones and the ABBA Swedes, it hadn't been appropriate. Concerts should have been only what he had grown up thinking of as concerts; beyond that, another word should have been coined. A true concert was of music heard centuries after its composition without regard to how it was selling at the corner store. What he and Paola had attended was something else. But what was the right word, exactly? None came immediately to mind.

"Britney Spears," the young boy said to the driver.

"What?"

"Spears, the American," the boy replied. "We tried to get tickets, but they were sold out."

"The one with the navel?" the driver asked through his rearview mirror. "Little skinny one?"

"Her," the boy nodded.

The driver's contemptuous hiss annoyed Peyrot. So did the car honking behind the bus. The driver leaned out his window and shouted something back to the moron. The not-so-old gentleman took the morning paper from his pocket and settled down to read what the entire day had aged; he looked resigned to waiting for hours for the traffic to clear up. The Filipino women couldn't have cared less; they continued talking in Tagalog about some topic they had brought onto the bus with them. The bank teller tried not to be transparent about eavesdropping on them, wanting to make some sense of their language. None of them helped Peyrot get any closer to a better word than *concert* for what had just happened at the stadium.

A traffic cop came sauntering toward the bus; he seemed to have even more time on his hands than the one reading the old paper. The driver leaned out his window to hear what the cop had to say. Peyrot knew what it was—wait. Ten minutes, fifteen minutes, a half-hour—who cared how much time as long as the American with the belly button had her crowd? "At least 15 minutes," the driver turned back to announce. "So just relax. Nothing we can do about it."

Peyrot hated that lament—*nothing we can do about it*. Even just moving for the sake of moving was better than doing nothing about it. And if he needed any more encouragement, there was the teenage girl taking out a cellphone and punching up a number to recount to some friend the magnificent adventure she was having in a traffic jam. "I'll get off here," he said, going up to the driver.

"Get off where? We're in the middle of the overpass!"

"There's room to walk. And Christ knows nothing's moving."

"Too dangerous, Signore. I can't be responsible for that."

Peyrot raised his voice to include all the passengers. "They're your witnesses. I insisted I get off because I'll get home walking before you move another yard. You won't be responsible for anything."

The driver looked back uncertainly at the others. The young boy nodded and the gentleman with the newspaper shrugged. That was all it took to wear down the driver. "Why can't you wait like everybody else?" he asked, already releasing the door. "Make sure you stay near the railing until you get to the other side."

"Promise."

Peyrot felt a surge of doubt as he stepped down into the narrow space between the bus and the overpass railing. The air that had been mild back in the *Centro* streets felt suffocatingly humid closer to the sky. Telling himself it was the fumes from the stalled cars, he set off toward the stadium. Ten minutes across and another twenty minutes after that and he would be home, he figured. He paid no attention to the odd looks he received from the people in the cars he passed. They were waiters, and if he had taken his car to meet Luzzi, he would have been stuck with them.

But he had another doubt about the wisdom of his move as he neared the end of the overpass and came to the cars streaming out of the stadium onto the avenue. The two traffic cops on duty might have been standing in the middle of a speedway for all the good they were doing. Shoulder to shoulder, they were just watching the cars approach, then hurry past, no need for them even to raise their arms to keep things moving. If they noticed him standing on the small patch of grass at the foot of the overpass, they gave no sign of it. He had forgotten to attach a steering wheel to his chest.

Peyrot cautioned himself against even thinking about trying to cross before the cops saw him and stopped the traffic for him. None of those going by looked like the kind who would have respected his right to match his father's age. And he still had a lot to do, as Luzzi had reminded him. Frank Sinatra or no Frank Sinatra, Luzzi had been right: The ideal at the end was being able to say only that he couldn't do any more Peyrot, not that Peyrot was sorry he had done this or hadn't done that. That was something he had to start working on in the morning.

There was a horrendous squealing of brakes just around the curve on the stadium access road. Peyrot saw nothing, and was comforted to see the cops searching the middle distance as vainly as he was. "*Viva l'Italia!*" one of them bellowed sarcastically.

Peyrot laughed. Buffoonery still trumped wit. Then, even as one of the cops was telling his partner to stay put while he investigated, a red sports car shot around the curve, pretending there was nothing in front of him. Two, three drivers yanked right to get out of the way. A fourth didn't, and the sports car veered diagonally before smashing into it. The cops stood frozen before the roar of the engine and the madman gunning it. Peyrot watched the car coming toward him, wondering what the odds were that it would hit one of the road cones, flip completely over his head, and allow him to breathe on in the Peyrot tradition. They were slim, of course, but not entirely non-existent. He hadn't thought of himself as a romantic for so many years for nothing.

✳ ✳ ✳

Paola didn't understand why the shaking was going on outside her as well as inside her head. When she finally opened her eyes to see Lucca, the shaking stopped. "Mama, the police are here!"

She didn't like her son looking so frantic; even his insolence was better. She also didn't like the tightness in her shoulders. She wished Peyrot would finish arguing with Luzzi about what the Americans had or hadn't done and get back to take out her kinks. All the *theys* he was always ready to accept in his angry way could wait another day.

STill Life

THE clotting aerosol of the nursing home lobby made Shelley feel bloodless. The murmurings and dumb silences from the ancient people sitting around with their middle-aged children reduced her to a mechanical time-server: She had buried her grandmother, she had buried her mother, she would soon be burying her aunt, and one day she would be buried. The natural had never felt so unnatural.

In the elevator she blamed her mood on her last class. She had been going along fine until Stockton had raised his hand and, in his usual disenchanted way, had asked: "But isn't it true artists aren't men or women, just artists?" The question had instantly thrown everyone into poses. Marta Moreno had snickered into her notebook. Beth Hallman had told Stockton to work it out for himself. Hassan had shouted for everyone to shut up so the class could get back to the subject. Howe had shouted back that maybe Stockton's question *was* the subject. Standing at the blackboard, Shelley had felt overwhelmed by disparate, predictable noises— each a center of rival understanding, maybe perfectly sensible on individual terms but absolutely imbecilic within the whole. She hadn't counted on having to preside over so much chaos.

From the elevator she followed the toes of her boots to Room 306. If it was true she wasn't going to see Victoria after today, as Doctor Musselman had all but said on the phone, she didn't want to share a second with the other old people vegetating in their rooms. Her gleaming black boots were her alone for Victoria.

"I'm not dead yet, dear."

Victoria was covered up to the neck by a perfectly folded green sheet and citron blanket, looking totally serene within the room's ridiculous pink walls. The oxygen tank Musselman had insinuated had been in full use was up against a far wall. "Must be this damn room," she said, kissing the old woman's cold, bony cheek and taking the straight-backed chair next to the bed. "It'd scare anybody to death."

"I told Mrs. Robb, she's the night nurse, that if this is the place ladies come to die, there must be other rooms painted blue for men."

"And she didn't think that was funny."

"When you talk about dying, nurses always think you're questioning their ability. Believe me."

Shelley did and didn't. Her aunt had been a nurse for more than 40 years, so must have known what she was talking about. On the other hand, she couldn't imagine Victoria Kern letting any remark get to her.

"Tell me about your work so we can get it out of the way."

Shelley smiled gratefully. On the way over she had told herself that any discussion of her work would have been inappropriate, but then had immediately jumped to the other side—that not bringing up the subject would have made their time together artificial. Victoria's flip command absolved her of self-importance. So she started with her awkward class, then moved on to her book about women artists and how it was weathering galleys on its way to one of the smaller book clubs.

Victoria dabbed at her nose with a tissue. "I wouldn't think there would be that much interest in lady painters."

Shelley welcomed the dig as home territory. Like her mother, her aunt had never come to terms with the baffling tastes of a younger world, but could accept them if her niece had been bright enough to exploit them. The big difference from her mother—visible again five feet away—was that Victoria always regretted letting her feelings out. "Oh, don't listen to me. I stopped making sense a long time ago."

"Really? I missed that."

The old woman tightened her smile, then winced as she tried to reposition her head on the pillow.

"Let me help you."

"No, no."

"Victoria . . ."

"Shh, Shelley. Shelley, shush. Shh, Shelley. Shh, shush."

Shelley sat back, wondering how her aunt could still quote the kiddie nonsense she herself had long ago stopped being charmed *or* irritated by.

"We have to talk about something, dear."

"Not the will again! I feel like a vulture when you start that."

"Not the will. Your father." Her abruptly severe stare seemed like an accusation. "Your mother was a proud woman, Shelley."

"Pig-headed."

"Yes, she could be infuriating."

"You've had your moments, too."

Victoria tried to look patient. "We all do things we're ashamed of, dear. Like when your mother told you about your father's accident and I kept quiet."

Shelley wished she had some grass. She had almost always had a joint in her hand when she had told of wandering in from the backyard one morning and finding her mother angrily cracking pea pods over a colander on the kitchen table. The grass had made her feel blasé when she had described the tiny shocks rippling through her that day in the kitchen while trying to picture a white-and-blue Pontiac smashing through a guardrail outside Las Vegas, leaving her father too burned even to have a funeral. And she had also usually been smoking while recounting how, a few weeks later, she had gone to the library in search of photography books on Nevada. She had never found any pictures of highway guardrails, only of open desert highways, but that didn't mean Nevada was without guardrails. All her friends and lovers had been firm on that point: Guardrails were as common in deserts as on mountain roads.

"Do you hear what I'm saying, Shelley? Your father was never killed in any accident. He just never came back from one of his trips."

Shelley had no place to lay her eyes. The pink paint on the walls was truly unbearable. It was the same shade her mother had used in her bedroom because Carla Sardi across the alley had that color.

"Before your mother died I told myself it was up to her to tell you, it wasn't my place. I begged her a hundred times to tell you the truth, but she kept saying it was so long ago, better leave it alone. Last month when you brought me that boozy cake for my birthday I almost convinced myself I was tipsy enough to tell you. But I couldn't."

The odds were incredible, Shelley thought. On one side, all her friends going back years; on the other, merely two picture books from the library that she had looked at for less than a half-hour. But the picture books had been right: Nevada *didn't* have highway guardrails in the desert!

". . . They were having their troubles. Your father was never a family man. Didn't like New York, either. That's why he was always driving trucks. He came from farmers or something in the South . . ."

"Please stop, Aunt Victoria."

Her aunt did, but looked mystified.

"Why tell me this now? Would another couple of . . .?" She caught herself too late. "I'm sorry."

Victoria shook her head. "You're right," she said evenly. "Another couple of days and it would be in the grave with me. I'd like thinking I'm right not to let that happen."

Shelley heard the appeal, but didn't know why she had to be the one to be kind. "Mother's pride."

"She loved you very much, Shelley."

"Because I never found out? Because she never gave me a chance to be mad at her asinine lie?"

"She thought she was protecting you. I'm not saying she was right, but that's how she was."

Shelley stood up to get away from so much belated reasonableness. At least Victoria's hideous pink room had a window over a trimmed lawn and lemon trees; from her own pink bedroom—that her mother, not her father, had painted—she had been able to see only the rain gutter on the second floor of Carla Sardi's house.

"You suspected, didn't you?"

What was the answer to that question? Tricklings of fantasy now and then? Furies against her mother about something in particular so furies against her about absolutely everything? When had suspicion ever been anything more than a substitute for acting on it? When had it ever been more than an avenger's hope?

"Isn't there something you want to ask, dear?"

"For god sake, Victoria, I'm still taking it in!"

"Of course. Forgive me."

But there *was* an obvious question—the one she had run from her entire life. If her father hadn't burned to death going through a Nevada guardrail, how *had* he died?

Victoria was dismayed; her watery eyes moved futilely in the shaft of sun coming through the window. "I guess I'm not explaining myself, dear," she said finally. "I don't even know if he is dead."

Shelley listened to a car engine start up somewhere behind the lemon trees. It seemed ridiculous that from where she was standing she couldn't see something making so much noise.

✳ ✳ ✳

Thanks to Victoria's planning, Shelley had little to do at the wake but order her own flowers and make small talk for a few hours with a dozen strangers. Her most awkward moment came the morning of the funeral when, just before the sealing of the casket, the undertaker left her alone in the parlor for a final prayer to a visible Victoria. As soon as the man walked out of the room, she imagined the other mourners in the vestibule timing her grief. What was a one-minute stay worth compared to a two-minute show of respect? Even the carpeted floor behind her sounded judgmental in resettling itself with a loud crack.

Then there was the idiotic banjo tune that had been in her head since Victoria had mentioned the letter her mother had once received from an Alabama lawyer announcing divorce proceedings. That made sense, according to Victoria, because her father had spoken several times about friends with a pig farm somewhere in Alabama. A detail, but all but useless by itself. The name of the lawyer? The city where he had been practicing? Exactly which mountain in Alabama had her father been comin' 'round, a banjo on his knee? It didn't seem like much of a farewell prayer to be saying goodbye to her aunt in the reminder that neither of them, the living or the dead, had a clue about the past or present whereabouts of Jimmy Carpenter.

Shelley went directly from the cemetery to the library. She began by listing the addresses for all the dailies in Alabama's five biggest cities—Birmingham, Mobile, Huntsville, Montgomery, and Tuscaloosa. Even in her own hand the list seemed to be the work of another person. She knew Tuscaloosa as the office of an arts magazine she had once subscribed to and Birmingham and Montgomery as the sites of civil rights marches, but little else. Did Jimmy Carpenter read magazines; had he? Was he a redneck in the KKK; had he been? And even assuming he was still alive, did he read any of the papers she was listing—or, on the wild chance that he did, bother with the personals that were probably stashed on a back page with ads for second-hand pickup trucks?

There were so many daunting questions she knew she had to ignore them and concentrate on the practicalities. Wording the personal took most of an afternoon in her campus office. The long-distance phone calls for placing the notices took another afternoon on her office phone and a Saturday morning at home. She was grateful to the Mobile *Press* for refusing credit card payment because that made it necessary to get on a line for a money order and then again for a registered delivery. And then there were the daily mechanics of not having to think about Alabama at all—of preparing and conducting her classes, of finishing her galleys, of feeding and washing herself, of doing the shopping and the laundry, of attending an anniversary party for a faculty member. Only after all these duties had been acquitted was she alone again, staring at her answering machine for a message that, even when she accepted it as a possibility, made hope and dread the same thing.

After a week of silence from Birmingham, Mobile, Huntsville, Montgomery, and Tuscaloosa, she began to consider her B list of Decatur, Auburn, and Selma. Hal told her no, to be more patient, even to pay for another week of ads in the A list cities. Francesca told her yes—partly because Hal had told her no, but also with the reasoning that smaller cities implied smaller, more thoroughly read newspapers. Shelley appreciated both perspectives, and procrastinated between them long enough that she made it through another week of silence. Then the call came.

She was watching the news on the portable TV she had taken from Victoria's apartment and set atop the refrigerator for eating company; Brian Williams was talking about a train that had hopped a track in Tennessee. As she reached for the wall phone, she wondered why crashes—of planes, trains, even cars—had rarely figured as the theme of major paintings. She decided it was because no matter how many people were killed or maimed in them, accidents were not quite tragedy.

"I'm answerin' your advertisement?"

She was so surprised by the raspy voice she thought it was a genuine question. "Yes, you might be."

In the sudden quiet on the line she heard her superciliousness only too clearly; for all the ways she had imagined answering such a call, she had never foreseen being offensive. "I'm sorry," she tried again. "I was in the middle of something. You're calling from Birmingham?"

"Mobile," the voice, stronger in indignation, said.

"Oh, the Mobile *Press*."

"*Register*. Don't read the *Press*. You the one put in this ad lookin' for James Carpenter?"

She blotted out straw hats and bib overalls. "That's right."

"So what do you want?"

Shelley looked over at Brian Williams; he had left Tennessee for Belfast. Nobody—not Hal, not Francesca, not anybody she had told about her ad—had asked the question so starkly. "You're James Carpenter?"

"My name."

"But I'm not sure . . ."

"I'm the right one? I appreciate that. Six of us here in the Mobile book. But you tell me your name and what you're lookin' for and we'll see where we're at."

At least once, Shelley told herself, she had to put him off to gain time for more control. "You a farmer, Mr. Carpenter?"

There was more rasp in his chuckle. "Don't turn up your cards too soon, do you, Miss? Okay, I appreciate that. Though I don't see what you can be afraid of up there. This is New York, right?"

She stretched the phone cord over to the table and sat down. She knew she was talking to the right James Carpenter; not the dead one, but the divorced one. "How did you know?"

The laugh was easier. "No military secret. There's a whole list of prefixes here in the book. But yeah, I have a little land. Do I pass your test?"

"This is Shelley," she announced before she had to hear more stupid questions. "Sheila's daughter."

It was so easy to picture his astonishment she was sorry he had wasted the call. If she had left it at her imagination, couldn't he have saved himself the long-distance charge and she the broadening burn in her chest?

"Shelley."

She had never felt so sentenced to her name—and by nobody with more authority to do it. James Carpenter had had as much of a say in it as her mother. Had "Shelley" even originated with some 19th-century woman who had spent her waning years rocking on a Mobile porch?

"I guess both of us are a little off guard here," the raspy voice came back—filled with dismay, but also a strength she hadn't counted on. "I'm not sure what I should be sayin' to you . . . Shelley."

Her best shot in 30 years, and she hadn't floored anybody. "You are my father?"

"I think that's right."

"Think?"

"Yes, I am."

"I thought you were dead all these years. Victoria told me the truth just a couple of weeks ago."

"Yes," he said, making it sound as though agreeing with her was the point. "How's Victoria?"

"She died. She told me just before."

"Oh."

There was more silence. Then she realized it wasn't about her or Victoria. "Mother's dead, too. Almost six years."

"I'm sorry to hear that."

"Saved you asking, right?"

That was her best shot, and James Carpenter admitted it—almost. "I don't expect you to understand, but it was a long time ago," he said. "It wasn't like your mother and I kept in touch. I'm sorry to hear she's passed."

"I didn't call for an apology . . ."

"I know."

"What do you know?"

"You," he said, sounding like her rising anger was beside the point. "I've thought about you a lot, Shelley. I imagined . . ."

"I'm here. You don't have to imagine."

He backed off. "And you're doin' all right for yourself?"

"Sure. Why not?"

"You married?"

"No." Her anger was suddenly so full blown she wanted to slam down the phone. No, she wasn't married. No, she wasn't a dike. No, she wasn't condemned to the life of an old maid like Victoria or to one of abandonment like her mother. And absolutely none of it was his business.

"Maybe we could write to one another?" he asked.

As soon as he said it, with just the right amount of tentativeness, she realized it was exactly what she wanted. "Yes, I would like that," she said, wondering if she would ever feel easy adding Father or Daddy or Dad.

* * *

For a few days, Shelley stared at James Carpenter's name and address in her notebook—sometimes with the page in front of her eyes. She told Hal she might respond if a letter came, told Francesca she doubted she would reply even then. Neither of them acted surprised when she told them she had decided not to wait at all, that because she had started everything by taking out the ad in the *Register*, it was right she also be the one to initiate the correspondence. For once Hal's lawyerly cautions and Francesca's astrological extravagances were in accord—in warnings that she was setting herself up for a fall.

For a week after dropping her letter in the mailbox, Shelley thought of herself as an overzealous postmaster. Whether teaching, wrangling with her editor, or cleaning out a closet of old canvasses, she kept assiduous watch over the progress of her letter. She followed it into the post office, accompanied it out to LaGuardia Airport, flew with it down to Birmingham, boarded a train with it to Mobile, sneaked into the right zip code pigeonhole with it in Mobile, then waited with it until James Carpenter's mailman came along to load it into his bag, drive out to a dirt road, and drop it into a tin, gray box with a red flag in front of a white clapboard house with dark screens all around the porch.

Even then she didn't leave it. She escorted the letter into James Carpenter's rough hands, watched his weather-beaten face as he scanned her *curriculum vitae*, matched his glum smile as he came to her closing line about how she probably hadn't been very personal, still being unsure if they really wanted to know all that much about one another. Finally, she settled down with the letter in his head, debating with him all the reasons he should be stirred to reply, reassuring him she wasn't an English teacher, would have been satisfied with crayoned block letters if they told her something about James Carpenter and his daughter.

The answer came without crayoned lettering, without even cursive except for *Dear Shelley* and *Your Father, James Carpenter*. It was two pages of single-spaced typing—with little regard for a right margin and with a heavy stroke in the middle of every line, but also with the feel of somebody who had spooled out his thoughts on typewriter keys before. Telling herself *she* was the only stereotype in the Carpenter family, Shelley sprawled out with the letter—first on the living room couch, her windbreaker still zippered to the top and her frozen yogurt melting in the bag on the coffee table; then at the kitchen table while the water boiled for her pasta; then in bed, the sound of the TV atop her dresser muted. Only after her second reading in bed did she hazard an estimate of how much the letter's dutiful tone owed to an exaggerated respect for ancient correspondence rules and how much to somebody who believed he had to insinuate a sense of paternity; it was 50-50, she decided.

She responded around the kernels of his information. She made no reference to the fact that he had been married again for 21 years, that he had no other children, that he had a modest holding for growing strawberries and blueberries, or that he hadn't been out of Alabama since a Super Bowl trip to New Orleans 10 years ago. It was his attitudes she took on: his disappointment he had never gotten along with Victoria; an admiration, but also an intimidation, before her mother's toughness; his dislike of apartment house neighbors in New York who had to be forced into saying hello; his conclusion, painful as it might have been, that she and her mother would have been better off without him around. About these details she had opinions, as she didn't have about marrying the daughter of a Mobile Baptist minister named Katherine or growing strawberries. Yes, Victoria had put off a lot of people. And yes, her mother's bluntness had sometimes seemed like merely the top layer of a profound coldness. And nobody despaired more than she did over the constitutional grumpiness of New Yorkers. And as for his decision to leave, she was hardly in a position after such a long time to say what might have gotten better or worse, but . . .

Hal was amazed. "You didn't know what the *but* was?"

"Or even if there was one," she said, her head on his lap on the couch the night after she had mailed her second letter to Alabama. "I was really going to give it to him, ask him where he got the nerve to say the things he did. But the things that came out made me sound like I agreed with him."

"You're angrier than that, Shelley."

"Am I? Yes, I thought I was."

She didn't pursue her second letter south as scrupulously as she had the first one. Instead, she looked forward to an extended holiday weekend as an opportunity to forget about teaching and to begin work on a new canvas. She had been excited to clear her closet of the various Shelleys who had used her oils over the years. There had been the Morisot Shelley, the Frankenthaler Shelley, the Hartigan Shelley, even the Marisol Shelley. Now all but empty, the closet dared her to fill it up with the Shelley.

The subject? She thought of fathers. Then she thought of fathers and daughters, fathers clad in bib overalls and holding boxes of blueberries, irresponsible drifter-fathers, icy women in nurses' uniforms, and other icy women who sat with their backs to windows shucking peas. Francesca and Hal helped her get over these inspirations—Francesca by getting giggly drunk with her one night and Hal by making love to her twice in the same week with the intensity of someone afraid of losing what he had gotten used to. She was grateful for both their instincts.

And not at all exasperated when the holiday weekend and then another week went by with nothing to show for her eagerness but a nestling self-confidence that she was ready for the kind of work she had been postponing for a very long time.

✳ ✳ ✳

James Carpenter's second letter was a page longer than the first and had the same penned greeting and signature framing his sprawling typing. He told her it was his mother (a new grandmother, she thought) who had taught him to type. He was pretty sure Shelley would have gotten along with his mother, at least to judge from her letters and their phone conversation: the two of them dry-eyed and strong, but not calculating in any cold way. That was one of the things he had never figured out about her mother—the purpose of so much edginess. Even Victoria, who as a nurse had seen so much sickness and death, had been understandable by comparison. But Sheila had seemed to value her wariness for itself, directed at anybody and everybody, like it was in the natural order of things. Had that been partly his fault? Would a more responsible husband have penetrated that facade? *Was* it a facade? The truth of the matter was, he had never been altogether convinced it was.

Shelley didn't need a second reading to detect the difference between the first and second letters. What had been James Carpenter's attitudes had evolved into her father's opinions. Had she asked for them—the compliments *or* the criticisms? She assumed she had, so that when she wrote back she was careful not to criticize him in kind, instead going into detail about the promise of some of her students as art historians, the energy she felt about undertaking a new painting, and her suspicion that she had been too easy on herself lately, slipping into work and relationships that were attractive precisely to the extent that they weren't challenging. She hoped she was making sense to him.

He said she was—sort of. In his third letter he confessed to knowing nothing about painting or art history or what it was like for a single woman to be living in New York. But what was familiar to him was the sadness he had detected between the lines of her letters. That bothered him, made him wonder if he too hadn't been easier on himself than he should have been. What was he trying to say, exactly? Maybe this: If there had been one thing that had allowed him to think about her over the years without much guilt, it was the idea that she had grown into a happy woman, that instead of having him around, she had benefited from the presence of some caring stepfather and she was what they called "adjusted." But now she was making him worry, and he could only hope the melancholy of her letters was due to her jumbled feelings about him, not something she felt about life in general.

By the time she received the third letter, Shelley was immersed in her still life. It was Stockton, her perpetually fatigued pupil in the back row, who had opened her eyes to it. Taking in one of his teasing questions one morning, she had been struck by how his black T-shirt contributed to a jagged field that also included Beth Hallman's black-and-white print dress to his right and Susan Behr's white cardigan to his left. It was a tableau of asymmetrical parts—or maybe just the elements that had fallen from a tableau and were looking to be restored to some coherent arrangement. And then, turning around to the blackboard to illustrate the answer Stockton might or might not have deserved, she had suddenly fixed on the chalk in her hand. Rather than writing out forms on the slate, she had watched the chalk nick it with the weakest, most transient graffiti. It occurred to her that the blackboard was *all* black symmetrical field, not only able to accommodate the slight white vertical and horizontal marks she was bringing to it, but to overwhelm them in the bargain. It seemed like an impression worth preserving.

"Looks like a homage to masking tape," Francesca said, uncovering the easel in the living room a few evenings later.

Shelley kept chopping away at the celery in the kitchen; she had learned to ration her remonstrances to one for every three of Francesca's invasions. "You're not supposed to look at that."

"Tell me it's unfinished."

"I've barely started."

"Thank god."

"Screw you."

"Yes, how *is* my favorite lawyer Hal Barclay these days?"

Hal didn't like the last letter from Mobile; he hadn't thought too much of the first two, either. "What're you saying to him that he feels so free to write that crap back to you?" he asked one night on the phone.

"He's entitled to his opinions, Hal."

"Sure. About everything but you."

"He's not being critical."

"What? Considerate?"

"Yes."

"Better late than never."

"I'd really rather not talk about this."

"Shelley! That's *all* you want to talk about lately!"

"I didn't know it was oppressing you so much."

"It's not oppressing me, it's oppressing you."

"Thanks for the warning. I'll look into it."

"What I mean is, it's oppressing *us*."

"Us."

"You know—you and me?"

"I want to get back to work, Hal."

"Don't run off like this!"

"I'm not running off, I'm working."

"I think he's hurting you, Shel."

"I thought it was us."

She thought Hal meant well in his lawyerly way, then thought he didn't, then thought she shouldn't have been left in a position to have to guess one way or the other. When she went back to her easel that night, she lightened her black field until it looked more accommodating than overwhelming for the perpendicular nick she had in her eye. The next day she wrote to her father and, after reassuring him he was reading too much into her letters, felt bold about being the first to propose they meet in person. Mobile, New York, or anywhere in between, she said, trying to head off any practical objection he might have hid behind in the name of his strawberries and blueberries.

✳ ✳ ✳

There was no fourth letter—not for three weeks. To Shelley it seemed all of a piece, as though Mercury, Pluto, and the other horoscope gods Francesca claimed to be on intimate terms with had tumbled into her house bent on demolishing it. Beth Hallman, one of her brightest students, was killed in a car accident on her way home from a weekend party on Long Island. Her book club editor informed her that her study of women painters was being put off six months because the club had developed unexpected financial problems. Claiming added stress from buying out his law partner, Hal moved even further away from where she was used to his being. Whatever the oil tubes asserted, the nicks on her still life kept coming out more gray than white, and she had to put the canvas aside. Daily grit had never seemed less like its own reward.

She refused to tolerate it. On the 22nd day without a letter from Alabama, she tossed a heap of junk mail on the kitchen table, picked up the phone before she thought her way out of it, and punched out the area prefix and number she had been carrying around in her head for days. There were three low buzzes, then a click and a woman's cheerful hello. She realized she should have expected something of the sort, that the second Mrs. Carpenter would certainly have to be the opposite of her mother.

"Who do you say?"

"Shelley."

There was a pause, and she could imagine the woman reminding herself to be tactful about a situation over which she had no control. But then the silence—and the cheeriness—ended. "Why you doin' this to us?" came the accusation. "Why can't you leave us be?"

"Mrs. Carpenter . . ."

"You said it—*Mrs.* Carpenter. And you've been upsettin' my Jimmy for weeks now. What is it you want, young woman?"

"Just to talk to my father."

"Right. To get him to go to New York or some damn thing. Don't you have any decency at all? How do we even know you're not some blackmailer or somethin'?"

"If I could talk to my father . . ."

"He don't want to talk to you. You've upset him enough."

There was something like an echo on the line, and she knew what it was: the second Mrs. Carpenter holding the receiver away so that her voice could boom more authoritatively around her Mobile kitchen or living room or whatever. And she also knew with a dull certainty that Mrs. Carpenter's second intended target was her father.

". . . All this time you don't exist, then you suddenly come along to ruin a person's life . . ."

Shelley felt her control returning. The second Mrs. Carpenter wasn't the opposite of anything: with every word her Alabama rage grew more familiar, sounded more like the fury children heard when they made the mistake of leaving their pink bedrooms at the wrong moment. "Mrs. Carpenter," she interrupted calmly, "would you please put my father on?"

"He's not here. He's . . ."

"I know he's there, lady. Just put him on."

There was another silence, and she pictured the anxious looks between the two of them. But so what? She was long past the days of *Shh, Shelley, Shelley, shush, shh, Shelley, shh, shush,* wasn't she?

"Shelley?" he finally came on to ask.

She rushed into it; she didn't want his embarrassment—or her part in it—drawn out. "I didn't mean to upset your wife. If you don't want to see me or write me again, fine. But I must know one way or the other and that it's your decision, not hers."

"Things have always been my decision," he said promptly.

That seemed to answer one more—and one less—question than she had asked. She waited him out, to get back to her point.

"You got to understand, Shelley," he relented. "It's been a big shock to me. Maybe it didn't set in altogether at first, but it's been kind of sneakin' up on me."

She told herself to see Mr. and Mrs. James Carpenter as merely two more of her students at odds with one another. The worst move would have been to insinuate herself between them, as in "Well, what kind of a shock do you think it's been to *me*?"

"You see that, don't you?"

"Okay, I won't bother you anymore."

"I'm not talkin' about botherin' me, Shelley. I just need some time to take it all in. Help Katherine take it all in. You understand?"

Hanging up, Shelley knew several more things. She knew the second Mrs. Carpenter was a Katherine, not a Kate or a Kath. She knew her mother must have given James Carpenter a strong push out the door to his "decision" to run off. And she knew the only pieces of mail she was likely to receive from Mobile in the future were Christmas cards for show and (should Katherine Carpenter outlive him) an obituary notice one day from the *Register* announcing that James Carpenter, grower of strawberries and blueberries, had passed away.

Francesca doubted Katherine Carpenter would even be up for the obituary notice; Shelley said she didn't care. Hal said he was glad the whole thing was over, saying it as though he had just heard about an armistice in some African civil war; Shelley *really* didn't care about that. But what did bedevil her was how her still life continued to elude her. What was proportional was never solid. What was solid was never personal. What was personal never seemed to be *her* person. It was as if she were still out in her asymmetrical field collecting all the pieces that had fallen out of their arrangement, putting them into a shoulder bag, and then realizing too late they had been falling right through the bottom of the bag, forcing her to start from scratch again.

Then one night, after getting off the phone with Hal and hearing his relief too that they had slipped easily into little more than catch-up calls every couple of weeks, she found herself doodling on a legal pad. The more heavily she retraced what looked like a double-decked curve on the edge of the pad, the more rattled she became. Finally, she got up from the kitchen table, put a fresh canvas on her easel, and copied the doodle as faithfully as possible. For once the white that responded more as gray seemed right: It *was* more confining than the blankness in the middle of the canvas. As she had done on the pad, she went over the right-margin form repeatedly until it looked heavy enough to tip off the easel altogether. Only when she stepped back a few feet to take in the emptiness of three-quarters of the canvas did she see she had gotten the Nevada guardrail right.

It felt like a good start.

A Shaggy Monkey Story

YOU probably didn't know Bert Akins. No great loss. Akins fancied himself a lot of things he wasn't, startin' with tellin' people he just met he owned one of those hydraulics supplies store. The truth of it is the man only managed the place for the real owner—a ne'er-do-well who called in from his yacht once a month to be sure nobody had nipped his tank balls. I suppose some people 'd say that's the ideal way to put bread on the table, no daily bother from the higher-ups, but that wasn't good enough for Bert Akins. He never passed up the chance to say he'd made the bread, the oven where it was baked, and the grain out in the field. What nobody was the wiser to was all his. He also had this annoyin' way of talkin' to you like you were blind. "Well, as you can tell from the pen I'm holdin' here in my hand . . ." That kind of thing. He had to take care of his blind mother for 25 years and he never got over it. I don't know how his wife and kid put up with it every day. I would've thrown a chair at him. How long can you be told what you can see for yourself? But that was his family's lookout, not mine. If they can deal with it every day, I tells meself, I can put up with it on the odd now and thens I run into the man.

Anyways, one day Akins says to me he's thinkin' about buyin' a piano. I says why do that, he's no piano player. He says I got ten fingers and I got two ears here, Doherty, so you'd have to say I'm well along on the road to bein' good at it, wouldn't you? I laugh because I can't believe he's serious. He turns to a beet. You don't like to see that because if there's one thing Akins likes to believe about his horseshite, it's that others take his word as gospel as much as he does. When he sees they don't, you get more whingein' than any five-year-old will give you. Woes about everythin' from havin' had to take care of his old blind mother to how he can't visit people without them expectin' him to give a look at their toilet for any necessary repairs. Anythin' at all, you see, to get off the subject of bein' caught in one of his little farcicals. You never hear the end of it. So I right the ship as fast as I can. Life's short, and Bert Akins whinin' don't make it any longer. Couldn't agree with you more, Bert, I says, you got the rudiments right there, so why not take the next step and get yourself that piano?

Too bad for me he don't recognize diplomacy when he hears it and he's got an answer. Because I don't have money to buy one, Doherty, he says. You send a kid to school nowadays and they want money for computers because that's the only way they teach the fuckin' alphabet. When I said to them I never needed a computer to learn the alphabet, I get this down-your-nose look that says right you are, and that accounts for the letters you never learned how to use. But don't get me off the point, Doherty. It's a favor I'm askin' you. Uh, oh. I know an alarm bell when it goes off. Oh, no, I says, not carin' if he turns red as the sun itself, I'm in no position to start lendin' out the cost of pianos! No, no, he says, I just want to borrow Rudy for a few days.

This, believe me, was a stumper. Rudy was this little monkey I'd been takin' care of for somebody who left me stranded with the bloody thing. One favor too many, if you ask me. But that's another tale. The gist of it is I've got this cheeterin' creature at home and every day is a treasure hunt except it's not gold I get up in the mornin' to search for, but the turds and piss Rudy's left around somewhere durin' the night. You want to make a few coin, open a school for trainin' monkeys to look after theirselves. You'll be a millionaire inside a few months.

But what I'm sayin' is that it's Rudy the monkey, not money, Akins wants me to give him in the interests of gettin' his piano. Be damned if I could figure out what one had to do with the other, but right off I didn't care all that much. Rudy had his entertainin' moments, there was no denyin' that, but they weren't near as many as the hours I could've done without. Between the smelly filth and the knockin' over things all over the apartment, he was a dozen handfuls. Just openin' the front door to go out meant plannin' NATO maneuvers so he wouldn't go dartin' through the door and down the steps into the street. Don't ask me why I ever agreed to keep an eye on him. The only sensible answer would be I'd had a few jars at the time. That wasn't the fact of the matter, but I like thinkin' it was. You take sense where you find it.

Anyways, as soon as Akins says he'd like to borrow Rudy, me first objection isn't to what he wants to use Rudy for, but—and never say crassness isn't always upon us—it's why he has to be talkin' of *borrowin'* him instead of takin' him outright. I don't blurt that out, of course. It's shame enough to be thinkin' it with people dependin' on me to watch over Rudy. Besides, it'd undermine me negotiatin' position. I kind of shrug, like as to say lendin' the animal out isn't all that thrillin' a prospect unless he can throw in a little more of what they call allure. Well, first Akins starts with how much of a favor he's doin' for me since I'd complained more than once in his presence about Rudy. I pretend not to hear word one. He finally reads the signals and says, okay, he's got a scheme for makin' a few coin with Rudy that he'd put against the price for a piano. Would I oppose takin' some of the profit from the scheme seein' as how I'd contributed to it with the monkey?

Well, I got to admit it: Pounds, euros, dollars, drachmas—the teller's window in me pocket is always open for deposits. Akins says he wants to take Rudy on a little trip to the countryside for a few days. Truth to tell, it was a lovely vision—Akins in his old car and Rudy jumpin' up and down in the back, over the front seats, all over his face to pick at his mustache as he's drivin' along, Akins endin' up in a ditch. Put some of your piano music to *that* little scene, I think to meself. But then the practicalness of it all spoils my little picture. What, he's goin' to close the store while he's off gallivantin' with Rudy? What's His Nibs sailin' out on the Mediterranean goin' to say about that? What about his wife and kid? And where does he want to take the animal, anyways? Not to some travelers who need a monkey for their carnival, I hope. I don't need the damn creature wreckin' me apartment every day, but I did promise to keep an eye on him until the owner gets back. A Doherty promise is a Doherty promise. No, no, says Akins, not to worry. He'll bring Rudy back. Nobody will know he was ever gone. But if I wouldn't mind, he'd prefer not hexin' his scheme and tell me about it only when he gets back. And I'll have a little more coin for my trouble.

That much I understand. You got a lot of superstitious people in the world and they don't want to say they've shagged the cute little waitress with the mole on her chest until everyone's shower-in' off afterwards. You have to respect people's fears even if they don't belong to one of your organized religions. And then there's Rudy. The truth is I wouldn't have minded a few days without havin' to step into his product. They say a woman's work is never done, my mother certainly always said that even though she never did much of anythin', but it's also true if you're the male of the species and you got one of your pet simians around. What's the word I'm lookin' for here? *Monotony.* That's what it was—*monotony.* So all right. I'm ready for a little break. If he can get the leash around the creature and promises to bring him back, I tells Akins, he can borrow Rudy for three days. And how much is my blind trust in him worth? You can imagine the hemmin' and hawin'! He's got his great scheme, he's got his paws around me monkey, and it's all goin' to lead to a windfall, but don't press him on particulars like an exact figure. Jeezus, no. I can rest easy, he assures me. He's sure he's goin' to make a few pennies and that means I will, too.

Well, the short of it is I let him have Rudy without more conditions. The least it gets me, I figure, is the time to clean up me place and maybe shoot one of your deodorizers in all the corners. You don't want to do that when you got an animal in the house because you don't know how it'll react to all those chemicals in the spray. You read about these things killin' humans with the cancer and that lot, but imagine what it's like for creatures with smaller rib cages. Their resistance can't be half of what ours is. Be worth lookin' a little more into that instead of into what bra size your latest actress takes. But that's not for me to say. Anyways, over comes Akins one mornin', I throw in showin' him how the leash works, and off the two of them go. Rudy's already on Akins's head as they go down the stairs. And let's give him credit—Akins isn't mad, he seems to like it! The thought occurs to me that even with his wife and kid and customers at the store, he must be a lonely man. What other sort thinks of startin' to play the piano at his age and probably with no talent for it outside his fingers and ears?

For the next three days I hear nothin' but the radio in the flat. Then on the fourth day there's a knock at me door. Rudy's sittin' there in the hall perched on Akins's shoulder and lookin' none the worse for wear. He's even got a little red beret Akins bought for him. He gives me a big cheet-cheet and hops over to my shoulder, but then he's right back on Akins. I know right away I've lost a little authority with the bugger. As for Akins, you never saw a rooster so proud of himself as he steps inside. Flops down on me rockin' chair so hard I thought he'd go through the floor with it.

It's all a little too violent for Rudy so he goes scamperin' off his shoulder out to where he remembers his bowl is in the kitchen. At least *that* much loyalty I still have from the animal. You wouldn't believe it, Doherty, Akins says. And to back it up, he pulls out two wads of notes you could prop under a cathedral to keep it standin' straight. I got a lot of money here, he says to me, and for once I don't mind him tellin' me what I can see. I don't even have to ask for what he promised. I'm still gapin' at all the bills when he peels off a chunk of them from one of the wads and tosses it in me lap. Jeezus, I say, where did you get all that? And he tells me.

He left the city with Rudy, you see, and he drove and drove. Finally, he finds the right village, gets into the right conversations, and goes into the right local a coupla hours before closin'. Well, you can imagine how the regulars take notice of Rudy. And here Akins runs true to form—tellin' them how Rudy is his. The man couldn't pay for a ticket to a filim without claimin' he made the picture he was goin' in to see. But none of the locals in the pub know Akins as well as I do, so they don't dispute his farcicals and everyone has a grand time watchin' Rudy cavortin' here and there. Suddenly Akins is their friend and they're his, and the rounds go back and forth. If I'm tendin' the counter, I'll tell you, I might not be so happy seein' Rudy wavin' his tail 'round all the glasses and bottles, and that's without mentionin' what he probably broke. But I didn't get into that. Akins was too full of himself talkin' about his triumphs to dwell on a monkey's arse dippin' into your pint. Anyways, as he tells it, in the middle of all the festivities, there's a word here and there about the dog fights they have behind the establishment after closin'. Akins says, oh, really? And he asks more about it. Well, believe me, Rudy never left more turds 'round my apartment than this *oh, really?* Akins's whole scheme, you see, was based on knowin' this little fact before he ever left the city. Seems one of his customers at the hydraulics store had talked about it and that's what got the idea racin' in Akins's skull for buyin' his piano in the first place.

Be clear here I'm not defendin' these dog fights. Personally, I've seen only one in me lifetime and there'll be more lifetimes before there's another one. You got your pit bulls and your shepherds and your mastiffs and your other big monsters and all they want to do is get down in the pit and rip out the belly of the other one. Say what you want about your professional sports, but you can't ever feel half as dirty after watchin' one of them as you have to feel after seein' these dogs go at it. But that's what some people do anyway to make money. Like they say, the only race you never bet on is the human race because you'll always come out a loser.

Anyways, with all this talk in the pub, Akins springs his scheme. My monkey Rudy, he announces to one and all, will defeat any dog in the village. Well, of course they all have a big laugh at this. At least until Akins convinces 'em he's serious. And down on the counter goes the money he's absconded with from the hydraulics store. They want to go on laughin' at him or they want to take his punt? You know the answer to that one. Rudy might've entertained them for an hour or so, but the money they could win seein' some Rottweiler chew his head off could buy them all the entertainment they wanted for a lot of hours. So here goes the money down so fast the barman needs a calculator to keep track of it. And not a single one of the locals bet on Rudy, it's all on whatever the local champion dog was. And as Akins is tellin' me this, I have to admit feelin' sorry I wasn't there. Maybe it's just because Rudy is out in me kitchen pullin' stuff out of the closet droppin' it all over the floor and I know he survived the night at the pub, but I had this teensy twinge of havin' missed somethin'. I guess it's always a fairy tale knowin' the endin' to somethin' before you get there.

The short of it, though, is that Akins follows them all out to the back where they got a zoo of growlin' beasts tied up in a shed. As soon as he walks into the shed, he says to me, he had some real doubts about what he'd gotten himself into. His scheme looked marvelous when he was thinkin' about it, even when he was drivin' along with Rudy in the car, but now he's in this dim shack smellin' of smoke and old kegs, all his money from the store in the grubby fist of the barman, and, to make it even worse, Rudy's lookin' far more interested in goin' back inside the pub to slurp the heads off more pints than to get into the circle with one of these beasts. But there's no time for dallyin'. One of the locals unhooks his mastiff and brings him into the circle and everyone's yellin' for Akins to get Rudy in there with him. Rudy lets out some of those annoyin' cheets of his at the sight of the mastiff and runs up Akins's arm. This gets a big laugh from everybody. Everybody except Akins, anyways. You can imagine how he must've felt the weight of the world and the cash he'd nipped from the hydraulics store on his shoulders.

But he snaps to. He hasn't come that far to see all the store's money lost on a bluff over a pint. He reaches into his pocket and comes out with the little toy he's been practicin' with all day with Rudy. It's one of your small hammers you use to bang things back to shape inside your toilet tank. Hard as any hammer, mind, but small enough so you can squeeze your hand inside all those little pipes. Rudy grabs the hammer like he's been handlin' it all his life, jumps off Akins, and hops into the circle. The one holdin' the mastiff lets it go, and the dog goes straight for Rudy. But Rudy's nothin' if he's not a monkey, so he jumps up out of the dog's charge and ends up right on the dog's shoulders. And there he is, right from there—bang, bang, bang! Right on the growler's noggin! The dog is down in three seconds flat!

Akins sat there in me place glowin' with relivin' the moment. He said he'd never heard a more religious silence in his life. The mastiff was down on the ground unconscious and even Rudy shut up his cheeterin' for a minute to study what he'd done. The locals? They seemed to need to summon up nerve just to gape at one another, like maybe what they'd just seen hadn't really happened except in their own heads and would stay there if they didn't see their neighbor next to them confirmin' it was all true. But it *was* all true, and the barman bein' an honest sort, he handed Akins his money. The way he tells it, Akins gives back just enough for a round for everyone, then tries to look as casual as he can as he edges out with Rudy on his shoulder. A coupla them are shoutin' after him for another bout, and there's one or two who're wondering if what they just saw was legal, but Akins pays them no mind, thinkin' only about getting' to his car before they stop worryin' about what's legal and just come after him with their own hammers. And he makes it, not sure to that day, he says, if it was his own wheels kickin' up gravel in front of the pub or if they were startin' to throw stones after him.

Well, that was just the beginnin'. For the next two days Akins and Rudy keep drivin', as far away from their first fight as they could get, and find another village, another pub, and another fight. Then a third one. And by the time he gets around to bringin' Rudy back to me, he's got all the money I mentioned before. Buy a piano? He could've bought a blessed orchestra!

And there you might close a happy enough tale except for one thing and another. Akins never got over so much success with

Rudy, so there was no more talk of usin' his winnin's to buy a piano. The only thing he was suddenly keen to play was Rudy against these monster dogs all over the country. He already had his next trip planned, he says. Well, I disabused him of that notion quick. Sure, it was good to have the extra cash and to have the apartment smellin' some nice cherry deodorant for a change. But I had me responsibilities to Rudy and his owner, I reminded Akins. There was no way I was goin' to have to explain one day that I couldn't give Rudy back because he hadn't swung his hammer fast enough.

Think that discouraged Bert Akins? Not on your life. The man turned into an addict. You got your alcoholics and your sex fiends, but with old Bert Akins it was matchin' up a monkey against wild dogs. When he finally stops tryin' to wheedle Rudy out of me, what does he do? Jeezus if he don't go out and buy his own little creature! And that leads to more trouble because his wife don't want the damn thing in their house so he's forced to keep it in the store. You can imagine! The bright and early customer who wants to be first to buy tubes that don't leave his bathroom a cesspool ends up walkin' in the door and steppin' into what he's trying to clean up in his own place. Not the ideal way to conduct your business. Word gets back to His Nibs on his yacht, and Akins gets an ultimatum: Lose the monkey or lose your job. That's like sayin' to a junkie another dose or a good book to read. Akins never hesitates. He tells the ne'er-do-well what to do with his job because he can make more money on a coupla trips than he would sellin' basins and the like for a whole year.

About that he turned out to be right because he went on to make it hand over fist with his little tours. But the tragedies kept comin'. His Missus is scandalized by the change that's come over her husband. She wants him to go back to the hydraulics store and make a respectable livin'. The boy says other kids at school are mockin' him as the Son of the Monkey Man. He wants his Da to be like all the other fathers with their suits and ties and shirts and the rest of it. Akins starts stayin' away for weeks and then months at a time. When he comes back, he's always got more cash for the Missus and the boy, but it's like some peddler droppin' by every so often. And believe me, he don't get to sharpen his knife in the house, either. The wife wants nothin' more to do with him, the son is embarrassed whenever he's seen in the neighborhood. You had some talk of how the son tried to kill Clarence—that was what Akins called his pet—but I never put too much stock in it. I mean, there was a logic to it, no denyin' that, but that's also the reason to doubt it. The main thing was that Akins and Clarence became unwelcome around the hearth. He finally got the message and settled for sendin' his winning's home by the post. Nobody ever saw him in these parts again, though there were plenty of tales. Most said he'd become so notorious he had to go abroad to ply his trade with Clarence. You had your variations on that tale, too, one of them sayin' it wasn't Clarence, but a Clarence II or even a Clarence III. Meself, I never really knew for sure.

Don't get the idea, though, that Akins leavin' was the end of it. His wife had the money he sent regularly, but she couldn't come to terms with livin' off just the proceeds from dead canines. She got herself a job as a receptionist for a doctor, and one day some excitable patient with a poor prognosis—some kind of tumor, the papers said—decided to take the whole waitin' room off with him for company. He killed four or five before turnin' his gun on himself. The boy talked a lot about suicide as he was growin' up. Seems he got over that, but not his mother's obsession with someone in the family earnin' a stable livin'. They say he turned into an accountant for one of your bigger companies.

I'd be lyin' if I said Akins's little adventures with Rudy didn't have its effect on me, too. For a while there, Rudy couldn't see a dog through the street window without hoppin' off the sill and runnin' to the hall closet where he knew I kept me toolbox. He'd screech and screech to get inside, but I wouldn't open the door for him. Broke me heart frustratin' the creature, but I wasn't about to let him go through the window to attack every dog that passed by. After a bit he seemed to get over it, though he'd throw me a glance every so often like as to see if I'd changed me mind about givin' him me hammer. Ended up havin' the creature for two years. The owner didn't come back for him, and, truth be told, I was glad. Bawled me eyes out when he got an infection and died on me.

And there you have the story of Bert Akins and him wantin' to play the piano because he had ten fingers and two ears. Except for one thing that I carry around to this day. Only a suspicion, mind. No provin' it because Rudy could never talk about it and I never even met any of the Clarences. But you know how they say we all descend from apes? Well, I've always had the thought that Rudy and the Clarences, that they had one of those primitive gene hands in all that happened. Sometimes, when he was still livin' with me of course, I'd look across the room to Rudy on the sill watchin' for the dogs to pass, and I could feel some secret knowledge there. Like me and Bert Akins and his family were the last to know what Rudy had known from the start. The thought made me sad for the human race. How long do you have to be told what you can see for yourself?

Three Black Sweaters

WHEN Keenan graduated from law school, his father rewarded him with a one-month tour of Europe. Strolling by the Rome train station one evening, vaguely bored by what had promised to be an adventure, he was accosted for some change by the Gypsies Danka and George. Keenan guessed Danka to be about 25; she had short blonde hair and a small tight face, and wore a blue polo shirt, jeans, and tan sandals that seemed a size too big for her. George looked older, in his mid-30s, with shaggy black hair and a few days growth on his face; he smoked heavily and, July or not, wore a checked flannel shirt that made Keenan hotter just looking at it. One word led to another, and Keenan, tired of his own company after three weeks of museum tours in four countries, invited the two of them to dinner at a nearby *trattoria*. They seemed to exchange a dictionary of eye signals before saying yes.

Keenan hadn't known about Polish Gypsies, had associated Gypsies strictly with Hungary and Romania. George and Danka enlightened him, telling him about tinker traditions in Ireland, circus traditions in Poland, and bear traditions in India. The palm reading came after dinner. Since they couldn't pay for their meal, George insisted, they were honor-bound to give Keenan's hand a free look.

Danka did the reading, with George sitting back with his wine to supervise. Keenan felt squeamish, wishing he'd gone to the bathroom to clean his nails. His palm showed four things, Danka said as George nodded gravely. The first was that Keenan would live a long life and enjoy success in his profession. Keenan smiled at this, knowing every fortune teller had to say something of the kind. The second thing, according to Danka, was that Keenan would meet the love of his life underground. This brought another solemn nod from George, but Keenan couldn't resist a crack about having to spend more time on the subways when he returned to New York.

Two children, one boy and one girl, Danka then declared, and Keenan was disappointed by her lack of imagination. Why not 23 boys and 46 girls? Or one boy, one girl, and something from another gender?

"And I also see three black sweaters."

Keenan waited for more, but Danka just smiled and folded down his fingers, signaling the end of the reading. There had been nothing arch or ominous about her pronouncement: She had seen three black sweaters in his hand as casually as she might have seen them in a shop window, then had turned to George with her empty glass and motioned for him to share out what wine he had left.

"Three black sweaters?" Keenan asked, wondering if the problem was Danka's English, fluent as it was.

"Sweaters. They exist in America, yes?"

"But why black?"

"Black, yellow, green," she shrugged. "Your palm says black. Don't you like black sweaters?"

Keenan never saw Danka or George again after that evening. The black sweaters didn't go away so easily. Even after returning home and shelving them in the same memory drawer as his visits to the Tower of London and the Vatican Museum, he was kept aware of them. The slightest provocation—somebody wearing a black sweater, a tambourine that called Gypsies to mind, some movie where Poland was mentioned—was enough to send his thoughts back to Danka and George. There were ceasefires with his memory, too, such as the birthday he received a black cardigan from his fiancée. Keenan decided *this* was the meaning of Danka's reading—that the black sweaters (for surely there would be two more at some point) symbolized Donna Sardi's love for him.

Keenan went on with his life. At his father's firm he quickly mastered the personal and professional nuances needed to ensure that another generation of Keenans remained the neighborhood's most effective legal hand for resolving real estate problems. Beyond that he parlayed conversations at neighborhood association functions into profitable contacts with county and city politicians. By the age of 30 Keenan had amassed six-figure savings in two banks and had little reason to doubt Danka's forecast that he would be successful.

The Gypsies also proved to be right about his family. Although he had known Donna as the daughter of the local undertaker, Joe Sardi, most of his life, Keenan had never thought of her romantically until they were thrown together one night at a neighborhood association meeting. True to Danka's prediction of a meeting "underground," the encounter took place in the basement of the parish church. A month later Keenan and Donna went to bed together for the first time; seven months after that they were wed in the upstairs part of the church. Their children came smartly—Jennifer within 10 months, James a year and two weeks later. Neither Keenan nor Donna wanted more, but even when he thought about the Gypsies, he reassured himself, as he had back at the Rome *trattoria*, that there was nothing exceptional about having two children.

But then one evening, with Jennifer and James already of school age, Keenan and Donna came home from the annual association dinner where he had been given an award and, tipsy giggly from wine and brandy, left her diaphragm in the medicine cabinet while making love on the bedroom rug. Keenan felt an eerie relief in the news a few weeks later that Donna was pregnant; he had refuted the Gypsies in a crucial way. But then he lost that relief—and more—with Donna's miscarriage. Amid comforting her in the emergency room he was struck by the stark idea that if the prospect of another child had released him from Danka and George, Donna's miscarriage had left him even more subject to their predictions.

It took Keenan some time to ascribe this notion to the symmetries of his legalistic mind and to refocus on more concrete tasks. Between his 33rd and 37th birthdays he enlarged his (now deceased) father's firm by bringing in Beth Wynton and law school classmate Teddy Barclay as his junior partners. In his 13th year of marriage he had an affair with Beth, a pencil-thin brunette who wore her hair in bangs. The affair lasted more briefly than their procrastination about starting it and ended after a night in a Manhattan hotel room when they had lain together for a half-hour just staring at one another, wondering if they would ever again desire one another as ardently as they just had, both waiting for the other to be the first to propose they try. Finally, Beth kissed him on the chest, got up from the bed, and padded into the bathroom. Three weeks later she resigned from the firm and moved out to San Francisco.

With Beth Wynton's departure Keenan again began thinking about the black sweaters, this time not so much as an unfulfilled prophecy as a symbol of some personal irresponsibility. Everything else the Gypsies had said had come true, so why not the sweaters? What had he done or not done? The fact was, he admitted to himself one morning at his desk, he not only needed the three black sweaters visibly in his life, he *wanted* to need them. Their appearance would confirm the powers of Danka and George, clinch that, down to his smallest satisfactions and most humiliating failures, he was part of something that had to be accounted for on some level outside himself.

As if his energy alone would force the sweaters to reveal themselves, Keenan threw himself into his work with a fervor interrupted only by liquid lunches and frequent stops at Gregory's Tavern before returning home in the evening. Rarely did he walk through his front door at eight or nine without having oiled the day with scotch or wine. He had never drunk so much in his life, nor had alcohol argue its harmlessness to him so strenuously. Was he the same man who had once scoffed at Teddy Barclay's boast about an ability to attract clients over three-martini lunches? Keenan decided there was no contradiction: Somewhere along the line, he told himself, he had acquired a flexibility that allowed him to circle all the other Keenans there had ever been.

Then, on the second night of his mother's wake at the Sardi Funeral Home, the accident happened.

After seeing off the last of his cousins, Keenan spent a final moment alone before the casket, then crossed the street to Gregory's to meet up with other neighborhood association members for a nightcap. They had already gone home, but he had his nightcap anyway—two of them, in fact, before the depressing stale beer odor and muttered bar conversations pushed him out the door and back over to Sardi's parking lot to retrieve his car. He was two blocks from home when he was hit.

At least that was his immediate impression—that some heavy object had come flying off a rooftop and landed on his fender. Even in acknowledging the form of a man that had been in the front of his car a mini-second before, it didn't occur to him that he had done the hitting. As he got out from behind the wheel, he still felt like a bystander, peering over the grillwork to take in the motionless body sprawled out in the street. He was only dimly aware of the people on the sidewalk. His eyes locked on the rips and stains on the raincoat of the man under his wheels and on the tattered shopping bag sitting in the gutter a few yards away. Only when a voice said the word *cop* did it dawn on him he had run over a vagrant.

Then the man moaned and turned over. In the reflected light from the supermarket behind him Keenan saw there was a second layer of clothing under the raincoat, that it was a black pullover, and that there were at least two other layers under the pullover—all of them grazing the frayed collar of the man's yellow shirt.

A voice from the sidewalk warned him not to touch anything, but he felt the base of the vagrant's throat anyway, asking himself what was wrong, then realizing it was the lack of breathing, that the man wasn't expelling any hot air. He swallowed deliberately before flicking back the top pullover to see what was underneath. The corpse—and that was what it was, he realized—didn't move.

There were questions to answer, sobriety tests to pass, statements to sign. The detective who invited Keenan around to the precinct for a second round of questions after his mother's funeral acted nonchalant, and was still nonchalant the next afternoon. Keenan knew leaving the police station there wouldn't be a third meeting.

He expected to be tormented by the accident, but there were no nightmares, no sudden sweats. What did nag at him were questions. Had the two sweaters beneath the black pullover also been black? Had any of them been black, or had all three been blue and merely looked black in the light from the supermarket? Donna wanted no part of such conversations; after a couple of weeks, she behaved as though the accident had happened to other people in other places. But Keenan also saw something else in her eyes, something he hadn't detected even during her strongest suspicions about Beth Wynton—a judgment that he had failed her in some defining way.

What he took for disapproval soon made it impossible for Keenan to look at Donna, or to keep living under the same roof with her. After months of tears in the bathroom and behind other closed doors, of a far too cheerful Jennifer coming home from Yale without warning, and of a morose James announcing he wanted to switch from NYU to an out-of-town university, Keenan moved from the house to a studio apartment a few blocks away. To Teddy

Barclay and others who suggested he seek professional help, Keenan confessed he felt more relieved than distraught, that for all the sorrows of breaking up his family, he had also gained the compensation of feeling out on his own for the first time in his life.

And then the sorrows and the compensation evaporated—replaced by a giddy feel of drift not even Danka and George had prepared him for. A year after moving out of the house Keenan sold the firm to Teddy Barclay, set up trusts for Donna, Jennifer, and James, and flew to Paris. He had no specific itinerary, and didn't even indulge too often the fantasy of coming across Danka and George after so long; at bottom, the Gypsies had become irrelevant. As it turned out, he didn't run across anybody at all in Paris; if anything, his solitary wanderings from the Louvre to Harry's Bar to the Eiffel Tower and back to Harry's Bar were like a delayed replay of his first European trip after law school. On his fifth day he ambled into a train station to see if some destination on the big Arrivals and Departures board called to him. None did, so he bought a ticket for the next train to leave.

He went as far as Bagnols, got off, toured the town, then took a room at the Hotel Chevalier. He liked everything about the Hotel Chevalier—the young couple operating it, the food in the six-table dining room, the bright red and blue squares of the bedclothes. He stayed a week, then a second and a third, spending his days on walks out to the countryside and his evenings in leisurely meals at the hotel or at one of several nearby restaurants. By the end of the third week he had become a familiar presence for the card players at the Paris Cafe and the petaque players behind it. The hotel owners, Arnaud and Yvette, agreed quickly when he broached the idea of renting his room monthly at a lower rate.

As soon as Keenan committed himself to the Hotel Chevalier for a second month, everybody in the district seemed to move over a little to squeeze him into the town's daily routines. He showed his gratitude by buying a small piece of land two kilometers west of Bagnols and by hosting an all-day party to celebrate his new rustic status. More than two dozen people showed up, many of them remaining until after midnight.

The morning after the party, still on the hunt for wine glasses left in the darkest corners of his new home, Keenan was assailed by the worst toothache in his life—except that it radiated out from his mouth to what felt like every inch of membrane covering his skull. He was already on the tile floor when he realized he was going to die. Fifty-six didn't seem that old. Maybe he had wasted too much time worrying about those three black sweaters? He had to laugh at himself with the strength that was leaving him. Suppose the vagrant *had* been wearing blue instead of black, after all? So what? When all was said and done, Danka and George hadn't even interpreted his lifeline accurately: He hadn't lived the long life they had predicted, he had lived a longer one.

All The Aliens In The Neighborhood

THE silver-red shadows dragged after the sun like chains. As he jogged past the empty park benches toward them, Mahan felt a yearning that usually seized him only when he was near fresh water. The glare of the unwarm sun posed the same deceitful perfection as the muscled stream of a faucet or the glassy placidness of a lake: It was drawing him closer, inviting him inside (into the mysteries of twilights and revolutions around the heavens) while it was alerting him James Mahan would never penetrate far enough. It was Nature as Tantalization.

His yearning abated only after the sun had dropped down over New Jersey and a further part of the sky that also looked like New Jersey. The rapid purpling of the clouds made Mahan think instead of the skin peeling off the face of a burn victim—specifically off the face of John Kerner, to whom he had administered the last rites three days ago. Now too, in the final minutes before nightfall, there seemed to be only an exasperated survival in what remained.

As Mahan came up out of the park, the flow to his head came faster. Trotting up to the schoolyard, he squeezed out a shiver for the Spaldine he had once watched attain its apogee over his head and then start down again toward his outstretched hands. He remembered how he had wanted that ball to stay in the sky forever, never to reach the point where he had to hear it whipping down to find him and he had to see the growing black marks from scuffing and lettering. The fact that he had caught the scuffing, the lettering, and all the rest of the ball had made no difference then and made no difference today, 21 years later. He had been scared that day in the schoolyard, and he knew he would never forget he had been.

Mahan wiped his face with the towel hanging from his neck and jogged forward. The accumulating saliva in his mouth told him he was almost gone, would need help for the final blocks. He asked for it from the neighborhood stores, imagining them as a human lifeline along which he was progressing one hand after another. Gregory's saloon, Sumter's video store, Havermayer's deli, Tedesco's fruits and vegetables—he pictured each of the owners standing in his doorway extending a hand toward him as he labored on. They too, he told himself, had a stake in his finishing the course. To himself he blessed them all by name.

The mowed lawn and wider sidewalk space of the church on the block ahead reminded him of the act of humility his run could be if he ended it without applauding his own stamina. Across the darkening sky he strung out Gene McMillan's advice:

MAKE BELIEVE YOU'RE HURRYING BY ALL THE SENSES THAT MIGHT HAVE LIMITED YOU.

MAKE BELIEVE YOU ARE LOSING THE WEIGHT OF ALL THE DISTRACTIONS THAT MIGHT HAVE STAGGERED YOU.

MAKE BELIEVE JAMES MAHAN IS THE MAN YOU WANT HIM TO BE.

✳ ✳ ✳

Mahan took the staircase three steps at a time. McMillan was emerging from his second-floor bedroom; he looked smaller, knobbier, and more red-eyed than he had in the morning.

"No better?"

McMillan sputtered dismissively and, clutching his robe closed with one hand and kneading a handkerchief with the other, shuffled down the corridor to the bathroom. Mahan watched him go without moving from the stairpost. He thought about ignoring the old man's stubbornness and going back downstairs to call Rubenstein. Most people who vomited and toileted their insides out for two weeks at least admitted to the flu; only Gene McMillan had "nothing."

Deciding to wait until after supper to raise the subject of the doctor again, he padded down to his room across the hall from the bathroom. As often as he had covered the same 15 yards in 11 years, past the nondescript landscape of some New England coast on one wall and an equally anonymous triptych of the Ascension on the other, he was struck anew every day by how much the odor of the corridor reminded him of the bungalow his parents had rented on the Connecticut shore for summer vacations. It was a smell of the old, the rotten, the salty, the recently shaven, and, more than anything, the impermanent. Had such a suggestion been deliberate in the rectory's construction—an admonition to the tenants not to forget why they were living where they were?

Mahan closed his bedroom door on the hacking coughing from the bathroom and went directly to the last funnel of daylight streaming through his window. Evening had begun to swallow up the neighborhood—the clouds losing their shapes and colors, lights taking effect in the houses that were backed up around the fence closing off the rectory yard. For all his years back in the neighborhood as a priest he still knew the windows on the far side of the fence better than he knew the rectory yard. In the yard the grass was manicured, the azaleas blossomed, and the blue jays whistled; with its trimmed hedges, two granite benches, and facsimile of a pond, it was truly a sanctuary. But sanctuaries were also artificial, while there was nothing artificial about the two- and three-family houses outside the fence. Instead of walking lanes and colorful birds, the people on the other side of the fence, the ones now sitting at kitchen and dining room tables for supper, had to rely on one another for respites. They didn't have his luxury of living solely to be faithful.

Mahan roped back the last thought, rolled it over for evidence of doubt, found nothing serious, and let it run off again. He lowered his shade on the evening anyway. The bookmark sticking out of his desk encyclopedia was an irksome reminder that he was bogged down midway through the letter *O* on his latest self-improvement scheme. But he was feeling hungrier than guilty. Rather than risk embarrassing McMillan by hovering around until he could take a shower, he gave his armpits a passing grade, slapped some cologne on his clammy face and neck, and ran a comb through his hair. The pale Irishman with the leery blue eyes who returned his look from the mirror said he was acceptable, but also warned him to expect some clucking from Sara Dobbins for eating in sweats.

The Irishman was right. "No rush, Father," Sara Dobbins said pointedly, laying celery and carrot sticks next to the only place setting in the dining room. "I can hold things if you want to change."

"I don't want to bother Father McMillan in the bathroom."

Mahan waited for the reminder that there was more than one shower in the house. But instead Sara said: "He's had that awful cold, all right."

"I'm calling Rubenstein after I eat."

"Oh, Father McMillan's a tough one. He'll get by without a doctor. You shouldn't worry yourself, Father."

"I am worried. The coughing's getting worse. He's not being tough, just thick."

He didn't realize how peremptory he sounded until Sara had marched most of the way back to the kitchen. He started to call after her, then stopped. For one reason or another he had been apologizing to the batty woman since she had agreed to fill in as the housekeeper during Della Robinson's visit to Ireland. He apologized to her for the kitchen budget. He apologized to her for his allergies to shellfish. He apologized to her for wanting only an apple or pear for lunch. Apologizing for criticizing McMillan seemed like the least of it.

Mahan snapped off a piece of carrot and listened to Sara Dobbins rattling pots and pans in the kitchen. The absurd thing about his awkwardness was that she should have been the fidgety one after their crazy conversation. It had been 11 years, but he still recalled her nutty prattle almost verbatim. He had returned from the seminary the previous evening and had spent the night at his mother's. On his way to the parish house the next morning he had tried to show how casual he was about everything by dropping off his mother's shopping list at Tedesco's grocery. It had been in Tedesco's that Sara, looking grayer and beakier than he had remembered, had accosted him and suggested they walk toward the church together. He hadn't wanted to, preferring to be alone to take in the subtle changes in the neighborhood since he had been away. But with the church on the path to Sara's house there had been no way out of her company. And then she had started talking about Jackie Gleason, astronauts, and aliens.

"He was on one of those interview shows the other night. Jackie Gleason."

Mahan had nodded, but had been distracted by how unexpectedly cosmopolitan Havermayer's seemed. It was the same assortment of slaws, salads, and sausages that Havermayer had always sold, but passing the deli that morning, he had suddenly been excited to think there was so much more in his neighborhood—more Culture, more Sophistication, more Experience—than he had noticed before.

"And the man who asked the questions, he asked Jackie Gleason how it was playing golf with Nixon and Ford and all those presidents. So Jackie Gleason started to tell stories. That's when he mentioned the airfield business."

"Airfield?"

"The airfield in Germany. The one with the astronauts and the space ship!"

His astonishment was superfluous, Mahan had told himself; he had to get right to the nitty-gritty; why a German airport, say, instead of a Finnish one?

"I know that sounds funny, Father."

He hadn't liked remembering that the same frumpy woman with the black cloth coat and agitated eyes next to him had once tipped him a dollar for throwing out some old cushions and drapes for her. "I'm sorry, Mrs. Dobbins," he had replied, admiring his calm tone, "but how would some TV comedian like Jackie Gleason know such things?"

"The presidents told him on the golf course! Nixon and Ford know these things, Father. When a famous astronaut like Neil Armstrong says he saw an alien ship on a German airfield, a president will find out pretty fast."

"Neil Armstrong says he saw one of these things?"

"And he told some general. The general told the president, then the president told Jackie Gleason. And you know the oddest part, Father?"

"What's that, Mrs. Dobbins?"

"There wasn't a word about it in the papers. You have a big television comedian, an astronaut, and presidents—all of them famous. And you have them all saying aliens are around us. But not a single word in the papers. I think that's queer. Not that Jackie Gleason didn't expect it. He says nobody wants to talk about aliens because you'd be upsetting all the apple carts. But I still don't know what they think they'll gain not telling us. Some things you can't just keep quiet forever."

Wrong, Mahan thought, tapping some salt on his celery: Some things you could. He'd kept quiet about her craziness that morning for 11 years, hadn't he? Had he even brought it up when Della Robinson had proposed Sara as her replacement? Sometimes keeping quiet wasn't a conspiracy, just an act of charity.

By the time Sara returned with his steak and potato he had filled up on enough self-righteousness about her to feel a new attack of awkwardness coming over him. He opened his mouth anyway. "Could smell it through the door."

She looked cross. "The only time you smell a steak is when it's burning."

"No, I didn't mean . . ."

Sara Dobbins laughed; mirthlessly. "Oh, don't worry about what you mean, Father. Eat while it's hot."

"You know, Sara, one of these days I'm going to stop trying to compliment you and you'll miss it."

She did something like wince before pivoting away from the table and hurrying back into the kitchen.

✳ ✳ ✳

Leading rosaries at Sardi's funeral home wasn't Mahan's favorite pastoral task. At least twice a week he found himself standing in one of the over-lighted parlors waiting for one—just one—of the scores of strangers taking his measure to reject his call for prayer, to tell him openly that he and his beads were about as relevant to their grief as the city buses going past Sardi's on the avenue. That the challenge had never been issued had done nothing to ease his apprehension. On the contrary, every time another unfamiliar mourner meekly made the Sign of the Cross or huffed and puffed to get down on his knees, he felt a further tautening of a catapult that he was positive would snap one day and hurl an unprecedented scorn in his direction.

"Father Mahan?"

The 40ish redhead at the door of Sardi's Marlborough Room extended a hairy hand; the note left at the rectory had been signed by a Charles Hoag. "Mister Hoag?"

"Right. I appreciate your coming."

Mahan glanced at the matronly figure in the casket. Once upon a time he would have faked knowing whom he had come to pray over; now that seemed idiotic "I hope it was easy."

"Ticker," Hoag nodded. "There's worse ways to go. You can say we were lucky."

"Leave the comparison charts to others, Mister Hoag. There're no worse ways than the ones you suffer, especially where a parent is involved. It's important for your family's peace of mind not to forget that."

Hoag tilted his head so far back on his shoulders he seemed in danger of toppling over. "Yes," he said finally. "See what you mean."

Mahan took in the other mourners. Those not grouped at the door had improvised circles with their chairs, reducing Sardi's orderly rows to chaos. The only people he knew at all were Sara Dobbins, Mary Kennedy, Miles Harkleroad, and a couple of the other Sardi ghouls. The way Sara avoided his eyes said she was still mad at him for calling Rubenstein after supper.

Hoag introduced him to more Hoags, none of them looking like they would challenge the usefulness of his rosary. The last was the man's sister Barbara, a tall woman with short dark hair and pale skin who reached up from her seat to shake his hand reluctantly; she looked genuinely annoyed to be interrupted opening a tube of mints. "I'm sorry for your trouble, Ms. Hoag."

"Thank you." She placed a mint neatly on her tongue, then meticulously folded the torn paper over the next one in the roll. Her hands were small for a woman so tall; they also looked like they were always cold.

"Father Mahan will be saying the rosary."

Barbara Hoag nodded indifferently. Her brother's sigh had years of complaint behind it.

"May I have one of those?"

She flushed before an overlooked rudeness. "Of course," she said, extending the tube as Charles Hoag seized the opportunity to wander off. "Excuse me."

"So who's the missing one?"

"I don't understand."

"There's always one missing. The friend who can't be found at an old address. The cousin off on a cruise."

"Oh, I see what you mean."

"But sometimes there's compensation. The unexpected arrival."

He sounded too wake-weary even to himself, but Barbara Hoag nodded immediately toward a heavyset blond in his 60s who was sitting alone near the coat rack and looking around for somebody to talk to. "John Luttinger. He was a neighbor of ours 20 years ago. I can't imagine how he heard about it. The notice won't be in the paper until tomorrow."

"Maybe your brother told him."

She gave something like a shrug; she was more interested in studying John Luttinger than listening to James Mahan.

"Why not ask him?"

"Maybe some things are best left alone."

"Yes. Including our imaginations now and then."

She forced a smile. "I've been sitting here wondering about it," she said, studying her small knuckles. "The good thought is that maybe, just maybe, John and Mother made each other happy for a while. The bad thought is my father was alive 20 years ago and would have known about it. My father never said much of anything, but he always knew what was going on. He was a news-paper editor. For the old *Tribune*." She looked up quickly. "My father."

"Your father."

She smiled sweetly. "Father."

Mahan wished he felt as comfortable as she seemed to as-sume he was.

"Don't you give me points for calling you Father? Most fallen away types I know figure they're making a soulful compromise if they don't call you anything."

He knew what she meant, but had never expected to hear such a direct admission about it from anyone. "The compromise being?"

"Well, on the one hand, if you say Father, you're recognizing the man's position. But if you call him Bert or Bob or . . ."

"Jim."

"Jim. Call him Jim, and you're being clumsy and defensive."

"Maybe even presumptuous."

"That, too," she nodded solemnly. "So the safest thing is not to refer to you at all. That's the soulful compromise."

"Like I didn't exist."

"If you want to take it that far."

Mahan didn't; he didn't even know why he had uttered such a ridiculous remark.

"I don't get so serious about it. I think of it as just another of the little truces we declare with ourselves every day."

"That's easy for you to say."

She laughed; graciously. "Granted."

He swallowed the last mint chip on his tongue and looked over to where Charles Hoag was greeting a young woman. Without warning he felt lifted by a mean satisfaction in comparing the new arrival—with her muscular calves, deep-toned skin, and bright green eyes—to the fretful, lazy-boned Barbara Hoag.

"Why is it I think I know you?" she asked.

"Saw me on the street, maybe."

"No. Mother only moved here a few years ago, and I didn't visit all that much."

"More of your vivid imagination, then."

"Maybe you lived somewhere else?"

"No. Except for my years at the seminary I've always lived around here."

She narrowed her eyes—one last chance for him to come up with a sounder explanation for her feeling—and then, as though on cue, lifted her chin at the precise moment Charles Hoag walked up and went into the introduction of the new woman from the door. The woman's face didn't promise an atom of Barbara Hoag's intelligence.

Mahan reached into his pants pocket for his rosary. For once he didn't mind going up to the front of the room and asking everybody to join him in prayers for the deceased.

✳ ✳ ✳

The sunlight from the hospital window made the empty bed next to McMillan's look ominous.

"Don't look so happy to see me, Jimmy."

"There's been some thought I wouldn't be seeing you at all."

McMillan laughed, but without energy. Covered up to the chin with a blue sheet, his head propped against a mound of matching pillowcases, he seemed too colorless for the big bed. "The devil you say."

Mahan made extra work of lifting the Formica chair from the bottom of the bed to bring it closer. He wanted to be as steeled as possible for his first good look at the man's face. "Don't you talk to Rubenstein?"

"He talks to me. In a manner of speaking."

"What's he told you?"

"That's not his manner."

"He must've told you what they're testing for."

"I suppose. And we'll go over the wrong answers when he's finished grading my papers. I can wait."

When he had run out of moves with the chair, McMillan was waiting for his eye with a smile verging on a leer. "Good, Jimmy. Now that we've taken care of my lack of comprehension and your excess of apprehension, let's move on to baseball and to Sara's odd ideas about what goes into a hamburger."

"I'm just not used to seeing you laid up."

McMillan raised his eyes to the ceiling. Sweat slicks on his forehead, neck, and under the jaw made his normally brutish face look like a Halloween mask near to dissolving. "Not that used to it myself. It was a lot more fun running to the bathroom to cough up my lungs. Gave me a sense of mobility. You were right about that, kid. Sorry I acted like a mule."

"You have to do what they tell you. No Father McMillan Knows Best."

Instead of conceding the point, McMillan looked abruptly concerned. "If you're in need of help, call the diocese."

"We can handle a couple of weeks."

"Sure?"

"Positive."

McMillan shook his head. "May be longer than that. I think I got cancer. Bronchitis on top, but something else's peeking out on the X-rays."

Mahan let the announcement hang: McMillan was no more of an expert on such things than he was, he reminded himself.

"About a half-hour ago one of them comes in and asks if I have a dog. A dog! I tell him I don't have a dog and don't plan to get me one, and he says, 'Too bad, Father, because every once in a while the thing that showed up on your X-ray is a cyst caused by a dog.'"

"There's no point anticipating . . ."

"Remember the Hearns? Lived above Gregory's saloon?"

"The mailman?"

"Him. When they were moving away, the wife wanted me to take a puppy. You know what it was? A goddamn borzoi! Can't you see it? Me running after one of those monsters? You need a coal shovel for their shit!"

Mahan laughed. He didn't really remember the Hearns; he had mixed them up with another mailman's family.

"Know what, Jimmy? I wish I'd taken their borzoi."

"They want to do a biopsy?"

"They do. I don't."

"In for a penny, in for . . ."

He heard his oafishness even before McMillan turned freezing eyes on him. "I hope that's not your usual pep talk. Lacks something in the sensitivity department. Not to mention it's not your goddamn penny."

"There's always a chance it's nothing," he stammered.

McMillan thought about saying something, then just whistled and gazed back up at the ceiling. "Don't listen to me. I just got the news."

"But you suspected it."

"Fear and mediocrity, they seem to go hand-in-hand," he nodded. "In my case the fearful mind wed to the mediocre esophagus. If you've got a prayer, I'd appreciate it."

Mahan closed his eyes to see it better. He didn't try for anything original: It was McMillan, not he, who had the imagination. One reason he had never minded hospital visits was that the sick were the easiest to please—most of them ready to embrace any words at all for solace. But McMillan wasn't that ill, not yet anyway, meaning he would be far more critical.

"No need to invent the language, Jimmy."

"Bless us, O Lord, we who are ailing," he said hurriedly. There was a sound he took for approval, and the rest of the words were suddenly before him. "Bless those of us who are aware of our illnesses and those of us who aren't. Bless us who must make decisions as painful as they are vital and us who have put off decisions too long. Bless in particular your devoted son Eugene McMillan and help him turn a moment of trial into a moment of resolution. Let him benefit from that resolution . . ."

"Amen. Thank you, Jimmy."

Mahan opened his eyes back to the man in the bed. He had wanted to say more. He saw no special gratitude, either. And was instantly ashamed he had sought one.

✳ ✳ ✳

Mahan was reluctant to accept the practical implications of McMillan's sickness. Distracted by the novelty of a McMillan who had to be helped out of beds, lifted into wheelchairs, and laid out on cold, unfriendly tables, he felt at a remove from the seniority and administrative skills that made him the logical substitute for the old man. If his new responsibilities impressed anything upon him, in fact, it was that he wanted them on a permanent basis even less than he had realized. Conversations about ambition dating back to his seminary days returned to mind just to be deflated of significance. Past McMillan allusions about having his own parish someday felt as empty to him as they had probably always been to McMillan. But he didn't want the parish crumbling into disarray on his temporary watch, either, so he reached out for the systematic, the scheduled, and the routine. Whereas before a typical day had been loosely described by Mass in the morning, religious or marriage instruction in the afternoon, jogging and personal study in the evening, and Sardi's or Benediction later, now he filled out his waking hours to a more minutely constant degree. Instead of rotating the weekday Masses with Ed Lloyd and Mike Ballinger, he persuaded them to give him the Six O'clock as a daily assignment. And since he celebrated Mass at the same hour every morning, it was only logical, all but mechanical, for Sara Dobbins to have his breakfast on the table at the same time as well.

From there the rest of his day fell into line snappily. Administrative tasks, visits to the neighborhood hospitals and nursing homes, catechism classes at the parish school, the teen circle, the rosaries at Sardi's, the funerals—all these obligations proved as easy to acquit at an appointed time every day as they were to acquit at all. His time took on a clarity he hadn't thought possible. No longer did he feel, as he had with some regularity before McMillan's illness, that he was just bumping along from one task to the next, with only sacramental responsibilities keeping him pointed in a vaguely forward direction. For all his reservations about replacing McMillan, his one-slot-after-another approach let him feel he was in command of his day.

He also understood the appeal of so much orderliness. The longer McMillan stayed in the hospital, being subjected to this machine and diluted with that chemical, the more the old man's eventual return would mean walking into a specific part of the James Mahan Schedule. More than a light in the window, he liked thinking, his system was a neon sign flashing over the rectory door.

And what the sign said in letters was YOU KNOW WHERE I AM.

✳ ✳ ✳

When McMillan did return, it was at dinner—in the hour that Mahan and Sara Dobbins had established for Lloyd, Ballinger, and himself to sit around the dining room table. Lloyd, whose 6'7" made it difficult for Mahan to imagine him as an ex-Marine, was relating one of Mary Kennedy's crazed theories about the perpetrator of a recent series of purse snatchings in the church. Mahan listened aloofly, conceding that the Kennedy woman's malapropisms and Neanderthal prejudices merited all the condescension they received, but also remembering how Lloyd had been so dismayed at his last confession to be asked if he regarded himself as cruel in any way.

". . . I'm sure the thief's one of your young urbanite Protestants who're always hanging around, Father,' she says. 'You know the ones I mean. The television calls them Yuppies.'" Ballinger rolled his eyes. "Word of honor. So I said to her, 'Mrs. Kennedy, it's not young urbanite Protestants, it's young urban professionals. Doctors, lawyers, things like that.' Guess what she says."

Ballinger guessed. "Only Jews are doctors?"

"No. She says, 'Well, there you are, Father. There's got to be a lot of these doctors and lawyers who're Protestants.'"

"All of them sucking the life out of you!"

Twisting around to the specter in the kitchen doorway, Mahan was conscious of doing stupid things—gaping, letting his soup spoon dangle from his hand, bunching up the tablecloth between his thighs. "I didn't know you were coming, Gene."

McMillan stepped into the room with the rooster strut he hadn't sported since he had begun slopping around in pajamas and slippers. "Either did the doctors," he said in a whoop. "How's it going, Mike?"

It wasn't until McMillan passed the stunned Ballinger with a poke on the arm that Mahan saw his decisive walk was going nowhere, that the cockiness and all his other aggressive airs notwithstanding, the man in the black turtleneck was mainly groping for the familiar around the table.

"So say something, Jimmy. Less is less, right?"

Mahan couldn't deny it. Even since his last visit to the hospital three days ago, there *was* much less to see. Standing at the head of the table, McMillan wasn't a pastor, but only a gray-faced man inside an oversized sweater who was trying to make up in the rush and volume of his voice what he had lost in his physical presence.

"Don't ever work as a doctor's receptionist, Jimmy. You'll have them blowing their brains out in the reception room."

"Should you be here?"

"No, I shouldn't. In fact, I'm not here. None of you has seen me. I'm a ghost on the way upstairs to collect a few things to go away for a while."

"Away where?"

"Visit my sister in Providence," he said, picking up one of Ballinger's breadsticks. "She's been under the weather herself lately. I'll cheer her up by showing her what lousy looks like and stay until my next appointment with Rubenstein's torture machines. Wouldn't want to miss that." Lloyd bowed his head into his soup. "I would appreciate it, Jimmy, if you could finish what you got there and come to my room a few minutes. I'm sure Sara can keep your pheasant warm in the oven."

McMillan got his laugh from Ballinger as he went out. The clang from the hall a moment later, Mahan knew, was the breadstick being dropped into the tin trash can near the staircase.

"Looks fit enough," Lloyd said. "A little wan, but you have to expect that."

Mahan wasn't sure what to expect. When he went upstairs, he found McMillan moving his socks and underwear from a bureau drawer to a suitcase opened out on the bed. "Sorry to interrupt your supper, Jimmy, but there's only one decent train left tonight and I want to go over a few things . . . Sit, sit. Don't always be looking like you can't decide if your news is worse than mine."

He crossed the frazzled carpet to the recliner in front of the room's only window. A strong odor of Ben Gay hung in the room. "I gather Rubenstein doesn't know you checked yourself out?"

"Victor and I had a little chat. He told me what McMillan ought to do and I told him what McMillan would do." He took out the first shirt to come to hand, then thought again and grabbed every one in the drawer. "He called me unreasonable, and I agreed completely. In fact, I pointed out to him, as I have to you on several occasions, that one of the most astonishing statements a man can make is, 'But I refuse to be reasonable.' An assertion that recognizes itself while trying to get away from itself. Think about it. It's quite a radical statement—implying total change from its own existence."

Mahan didn't think about it. He had never dwelled much on McMillan's fanciful abstractions. They had always seemed so secondary to the man.

"But that's not why I got you up here. First off, anything I can help you with?"

"We went over that on the phone again this morning."

"Right. Just be careful if they send you Hartman to fill in. He'd like nothing so much as to get his foot in the door of this parish."

He had to laugh. "You've warned me about that twice, Gene. What in God's name has Martin Hartman ever done to earn this distrust?"

McMillan didn't reply; he was more concerned with glancing around to make sure he hadn't overlooked something. As small as the room was (too small for a pastor, according to Sara Dobbins), it had always struck Mahan as being even more impersonal. The personal objects—family photos on the bureau, a crucifix and school diploma on the walls, two muddy Rembrandt prints, a tattered Breviary on the prie-dieu, a bookcase stuffed with mysteries and spy novels waiting to be donated to the parish flea market—could have been anybody's possessions. Even the objects battered from use gave off no more sense of belonging to Gene McMillan than wares to be found in any second-hand store. The only thing truly Gene McMillan about the room was Gene McMillan himself.

"Told you about the bank, right?"

"Minimum five thou in checking."

"No. Maximum five thou."

"Maximum. I know, Gene."

McMillan thought a moment, then flopped down on the bed with a laugh. "Natural reaction when you leave Jesse James guarding the till."

Mahan smiled obediently, but even as a crack it was senseless. He had no connection to thieves or thievery. Had McMillan forgotten who he was?

"What am I going on about? I really asked you up to hear my confession."

He didn't know why he was surprised; he had been McMillan's confessor as often as anybody. "I'll get my stole . . ."

"Oh, to hell with the stole. Sit and be quiet a second."

Mahan knew the ploy: keep psychologically what was surrendered ritually. He had called the old man on it more than once.

"Bless me, Father, for I have sinned. It's been . . ."

"About a month."

"No."

"It is, Gene. I remember."

"By your calendar. By mine I'd say my last full confession to you was about nine years ago . . . Don't look so put out. That keeps you one up on Mike and Ed. To them I've never made a full confession."

Mahan shifted in the recliner; he felt himself already losing control of the sacrament. "Sure, I'm the one you want to hear this?" McMillan nodded, jovially "Because it'll amuse you in some way?"

McMillan shook his head. "I'm not sure about satisfaction, though."

"What satisfaction?"

The old man dropped his smile to the tight fists he had made on his thighs. But then, just as quickly, he jumped to his feet to issue one of his dramatic roars. "The satisfaction of the vain animal confessing his vanity, what else! And of course, letting other people hear it and deriving exquisite pleasure from their reaction!"

Mahan didn't grasp the words, but he was relieved to recognize the self-justification. "Ever ask those around you what they think?"

"What might that be, Jimmy?"

"I don't think you're vain. You just use that as a decoy to avoid real issues."

"Which, according to your lights, are . . ."

"Fear, for one. The fear you've come up short in your vocation in some way. The fear of good old-fashioned doubt."

"A greater sin than vanity in your lexicon, sounds."

"Goes with the territory."

McMillan found some coins in his pants pocket and began rubbing them together. "Think you know my situation, do you?"

"Tell me or I'll only be guessing."

He marked that as a reasonable reply. "Okay. Let's say it's the situation of the man who knows he's dying. The situation of this able enough priest who owes, he thinks, some of his suppressed thoughts and views to those close to him. Not because his confession will do him much good personally. In fact, the odds are it would jeopardize an important relationship. But because this imbecile of a dying priest still thinks his vocation is important and wants it protected even after he's long faded from the scene."

"Too vague. I need more than that."

McMillan nodded, but absently, as though he had already said more than he had intended. "You're right," he announced from his new distance. "Maybe you are the wrong one to bother about this. Excuse me a second."

Mahan felt like an idiot before McMillan's abrupt charge from the room and rush down the hall to the bathroom. He didn't know if he was more incensed with the man for being so cavalier or with himself for a spasm of jealousy at the thought McMillan was taking his cryptic misgivings downstairs to Lloyd or Ballinger. He jumped to his feet, gave the recliner a surly shove a few inches off the spot it had worn into the carpet, and went to the window. He tried to cool down behind the thought that he would wait for McMillan to return, that he would get him to understand escape wasn't so easy.

"The situation of the man who knows he's dying."

McMillan *had* said that, hadn't he? He had no right being angry with him. He had no idea how any human being could say "I'm dying" as calmly as he could "I want a beer" or "What's on TV tonight?" Weren't people like that already on another planet from him? How did he dare have any feelings about them? There was no way they could be the right feelings.

Across the street an elderly woman on a cane was being assisted into Sardi's by two stocky men. How many old women had McMillan watch come and go from Sardi's over the years? Their grief had to have dissolved into a huge featureless puddle for the old man by now; for sure, it had for James Mahan. He just couldn't feel for the mourners anymore, not the way he had promised himself at his mother's casket he would. Barely did he shake their hands at the cemetery or in a restaurant after a funeral lunch now than he began forgetting who they were. He wanted to remember them individually, but it was beyond him. God help him, the thought crossed his mind sometimes that he hadn't been meant to remember them, that it had been the nature of his vocation from the start that he lose himself within the dehumanizing quantity of those around him who had to mourn their mortality. He didn't want to accept that as true. But then why was the thought there in the first place?

"Excuse me, Father."

Sara Dobbins stood in the door with a cup of tea, looking dubious about finding him alone in the room. "Put it on the dresser, Sara."

She wasn't sure that was the right answer. "Don't forget your own supper, Father. I can't keep it warm forever."

McMillan's reappearance stopped him from saying something impatient. "Tea to the rescue," he said, his jauntiness back. "You're invaluable, Sara."

"I was just saying to Father Mahan . . ."

"I heard you and you're right. Take him down with you before he wastes away."

Mahan waited for the high sign he was sure would come as McMillan crossed to his tea. But even with Sara blocked out there was no signal; McMillan simply glanced at his clock and did some rapid dunking of his teabag.

"You go ahead, Mrs. Dobbins," he said on his own.

"No, no, Jimmy, go with her," McMillan said promptly.

"If you're sure . . ."

The merriment in McMillan's eyes didn't seem all that far from an admonition. "I'm positive. Anything else, we'll talk about it later. Plenty of time."

Sara walked out, leaving no opportunity behind her but the chance to watch McMillan squeezing his teabag. Trooping down the stairs after her, Mahan thought about telling her he didn't like housekeepers, even temporary ones, letting their stockings billow up around spindly legs. Then he told himself to keep his mouth shut.

✳ ✳ ✳

Mahan used the first-floor study for sorting through the mail. The room consisted of little more than a desk, three uncomfortable straight-backed chairs, and a glass-enclosed bookcase holding a collection of dusty, 20-year-old pamphlets. He had never understood what "study" it was supposed to have encouraged; he himself had never opened a book, not even his Office, within its walls. Like so much else in the parish house, the cold, dim room struck him as some calculated attempt to show how transitory his surroundings were.

He had just slit open the phone bill when the front door bell rang. With Ballinger and the sexton Tom around, he kept his attention fixed on the numbers in front of him, recognizing Lloyd's calls to his family in New Jersey and step-brother in Houston, the weekly consultations Ballinger held with a linguist friend in

Boston, and McMillan's talks with his sister in Providence and an old seminary crony down in Miami. As always, he was the most hidden within the numbers—no out-of-town friend or relative, barely a trace of him in the regular calls to the diocesan office, the school principal McIntire, Sardi the undertaker, and the scores of others he contacted on parish business. All his phoning had been included within the basic, the minimum, and the assumed, meriting no special category.

The second door ring sounded like a scolding, and with neither Ballinger nor the sexton around to hear it. He took off his reading glasses, got up, and went out to the vestibule. He could tell from the silhouette in the front door's serrated glass that the caller was a woman with a kerchief on her head. What he couldn't tell until he opened the door was that it was Barbara Hoag.

"Father Mahan? I'm Barbara Hoag. We met at my mother's wake."

He was dismayed she thought the introduction necessary. "Let me think. I see a tube of mints in your hand."

She smiled bashfully. "I was just over at Sardi's. Odds and ends."

"Bills."

"Those odds and ends."

Her awkwardness reminded him of his own. "I'm sorry, I've got you standing here like a salesman . . ."

She stepped into the foyer quickly, almost furtively. "I don't mean to interrupt anything," she said, pulling off the kerchief.

"Just some solemn reflections on message units. In here." She took one of the stern chairs drawn up before the desk. "What we call a study. Not like in one of those British mysteries, is it?"

She smiled at his inanity and looked around without seeing anything in particular. He couldn't see how her short hair had been affected by pulling off the kerchief, but she fussed with it anyway.

"I guess it'll be a relief when you finish with the odds and ends."

She drove her hands deeper into the pockets of her belted raincoat. "There's only the apartment to go. Charles made a pass at it yesterday, but I haven't gone back yet. It takes some leading up to."

He said he understood, and did. After his mother had died he had waited almost a week to go back to her apartment. It had always been there as some last resort for him, as the ultimate safety net under his vocation, and he had delayed accepting its disappearance as long as possible.

"One thing I've resolved, though, and thanks to you. John Luttinger? The man I couldn't figure out how he'd heard about the wake? Well, I kept thinking about what you said about my imagination getting the best of me. So I called him, and the explanation *is* simple. He knew about the wake because he was on his way to visit Mom when she had her attack. He was turning the corner when the EMS was carrying her to the ambulance." The smile was broader—and shallower. "What do you say to that?"

"They were friends."

She nodded as though she had expected that answer. "Ever get the feeling your head was one of those Slinky things? Those metal coils that go up and down the stairs by themselves? I've felt like that since talking to John. One second I'm a Slinky on the level that says good for Mom, she had this friend who stayed with her all the way to the end. Then Slinky goes toppling down a step and I'm thinking goddamn that woman, ridiculing my father all those years with a man he passed in the hallway and on the elevator every day. Then Slinky does another somersault and I'm telling myself I'm a sophisticated woman who shouldn't get excited one way or the other, an affair is just an affair, it's a loaf of bread or a can of peas, why even think about it twice. But just as I accept that attitude, feeling a way above everything that annoys common mortals, over goes Slinky again, and I'm back at one of the other levels."

"Slinky."

"No reflection on your advice, but there *is* something to be said for just imagining some things."

"That's why you're putting off going back to the house?"

She nodded. "It's not where we grew up, but it still has associations."

"What does your brother say?"

"That I can't put it off forever."

Mahan suddenly realized why she was there, why she found it difficult even to look at him. "Would I help that much?"

Barbara Hoag returned to the probing stare that had unsettled him at Sardi's. "I seem to think so. It came to me when I was leaving the funeral home. Suddenly I was crossing the street and ringing your bell. I'm usually not so impulsive."

He returned her gaze, feeling the loser for every second of it. "An exaggeration, maybe?"

"Why do you say that?"

"I'd guess you have a checkbook and a phone. Calling Sardi and telling him the check was in the mail would have been enough. But you came all the way here, and not just to go to your mother's."

She had the grace to look embarrassed. "Not so impulsive, then."

"I don't think so, Barbara. In fact, I think you're blaming me for something."

No concession. "Will you go with me?"

"If you think it'll help that much."

"Ever since Charles called me about Mom," she said steadily, "I haven't asked anybody for anything. Somehow it seems I should, that I have it coming to me. I feel like I'm being too stiff-upper-lip, squandering this once-in-a-lifetime opportunity I have to get something . . ."

"For free?"

She nodded. "Yes, Father."

✳ ✳ ✳

On the dank street Mahan listened to her the way he always seemed to listen to talk on gray afternoons: His company rambled on as he counted the steps still to be taken before he could escape the glum atmosphere and be safely back inside a building.

"So I guess you'd call me a municipal historian," she said. "Subways, statues, sewers—if there's a piece of metal plating or grillwork anywhere on it, I'm your girl."

He told her about the time his parents had taken him to the World's Fair, to a dark exhibition hall to show him an architectural model of every high-rise and house and store and parking lot in the city. Even his own apartment house had been recognizable in the illuminated glass case. Everything had seemed so incredibly containable that day.

"I get the same feeling with those flags. The miniature ones they make for all the countries? There's a man who works with me, he collects them and puts them all over his office. He can tell you in a second which is Kenya or Sri Lanka. Sometimes when he's out, I go to his door and stare in at them, thinking how . . ."

potential they look. They're all colors, different stripes and symbols. But they also seem to be part of a larger, invisible set, and I keep telling myself you should be able to do more with them than just stick them in an office."

"But that's really all they're good for."

"I know. They really don't have any potential at all, do they?"

He was surprised she understood that. "Just like that scale model of New York was good only for the exhibition hall. I couldn't take it home to play cops and robbers or World War III invasion. I couldn't even imagine myself running up the little streets. I was on a different scale. It just came up to my knees. It was just teasing me."

"But isn't the potential still fun to think about?"

"If you don't have anything better to think about."

✱ ✱ ✱

Barbara Hoag's destination was a twin of the building where Mahan had sneaked his first cigarettes with Al Moroni: a spottled-brick fortress of pillars and arches separated into two wings by a barren courtyard garden. He felt on very familiar terrain as he went through the glass door marked with a pretentious B WING. Even the cat odors in the hallway and the kerosene smell in the elevator seemed the same as they had that day with Moroni.

The late Elizabeth Hoag's apartment smelled merely sour. "I always said it was too big for her," Barbara said, closing the front door into a long hallway with several rooms leading off it. "Two bedrooms, living room, dining room. But when I'd say it, she'd stare at me like I was supposed to volunteer to move back with her. Funny how the older I got, the more I had foot-in-mouth disease with her."

He thought of Sara Dobbins as he parked gingerly on the edge of a sofa cushion. She unbelted and unbuttoned her raincoat and tossed it over a chair. She wore a dark blue shirt and black toreador pants, looked even thinner than she had at the wake.

"There's a drink around here somewhere. She had a thing for fruit brandies."

"Too early. Thanks."

She didn't insist, not even to propose the tea or coffee he would have accepted. Instead, as she unbuttoned her shirt cuffs and rolled the sleeves up to the elbow, her attention went to the knick-knacks cluttering the mantle of the fireplace. The main pieces were a set of ceramic gnomes—identical but for cap colors.

"My first set of flags—Happy, Doc, Bashful, and the gang. Shouldn't they do more than just sit up there?"

He didn't want to talk about her sets anymore. "Is there something I can get out of the way for you? Something heavy?"

She took the hint and went immediately to one of the hall closets. The clothes rack was a camphor-smelling jam of coats and jackets; a landslide of valises and overnight bags seemed about to erupt from the deep shelf above the clothes. "The two black ones. Careful of your head."

He was careful, and she was even more so. First through the closet for the coats, then to the two adjoining ones filled with hats, suits, and dresses, she worked quickly, dispassionately, hesitating over nothing, apparently having decided even before laying her hand on the hangers which jacket and blouse had to be cleaned before being given to somebody, which was right for only one relative in particular, and which was too frazzled at the collar to be suitable for anything but the garbage can.

Watching her from the sofa, stirring only to turn on a lamp against the thickening twilight, Mahan grew increasingly certain *the* moment wouldn't come. She could have hunkered down on the floor for hours, he thought, without coming across the one loaded object that would stagger her with the realization she was heaping together the artifacts of somebody who had carried her around in her womb, who had milked her and wiped her ass and dressed her, who had once been her entire existence, but whom she would never see again. Such an object, he was sure, didn't exist for Barbara Hoag. Just as when he had finally returned to his mother's a week after her funeral and found only Macy's and Key Food, Century 21 and Tedesco's grocery, he could sense Barbara Hoag discovering that no item that had once been mere merchandise available to anyone at all, could represent something personal. Rather than shed tears so incidentally, he knew, she would keep them locked up forever.

"Really sure there's nothing I can get you?"

"I'd settle for you telling me you're okay now."

Her hand froze over the skirt she was smoothing into a suitcase. "Time to come down?"

"You are down, Barbara."

"How do you know?"

He had no real answer, and she looked ashamed of something. "There was no way I could lose asking you to come along," she said, cropping at the rug under her. "If something got through to me, it would've been your fault for making everything so sobby. If nothing happened, it'd still be your fault—for forcing me to be on my best behavior. Either way, you came out indispensable."

Mahan smiled for her benefit, but he always felt lost when people talked about emotions they were determined to keep away or emotions they had already overcome.

"Thank you for absolving me of responsibility."

He hated her fatigued tone, and the fragility beneath it. He didn't know which felt suddenly more invincible—the weight on his thighs that wanted to sentence him to his rut on the sofa forever or the vacuum that seemed to suck him up toward the courtyard window to see the garden of gravel below.

"Could I ask you something, Jim?"

He nodded, and heard the customary question. No matter the words, it was always about why he had become Father Mahan.

"I was 15," he said, as soon as she fell silent. "We were playing stickball in the schoolyard. A friend of mine—kid named Al Moroni—uppercuts one that must've gone three stories above the school roof. I never saw a ball go so high. I thought it was going into orbit. But no such luck. Just hung up there for the longest time. Then it was like it got tired and wanted to come back down. Where? Where else but right down on me. Everyone saw it. Moroni was running and the guys on his team were yelling for him to get at least to second base. My team was yelling things like, 'Easy catch, Jimmy. Can o' corn, babe.' The whole game was coming down into my hands.

"Jesus, I hated that feeling. It was like I'd been picked out of a crowd, out of a whole skyful of possibilities. The Spaldine could've bounced on the roof, maybe skipped across the street, gone anywhere. But no, it came right down on me. I never felt so alone in my life. I was the only one who could catch it, who *had* to catch it. My whole body went stiff on me. It was like I had some great load over this second self. So I kicked out at it—literally. I just swung out my left leg while I kept my eye on the ball. I could see the black lettering as it came down, or at least imagined I could, and that's what I focused on. Grab the lettering, I told myself, and the rest will be all right. Grab the lettering in the center of the ball.

"And that's what happened. It was on top of me and I just reached for it. It came slamming down into my hands and stopped.

Perfect cup. Perfect sound of the cup catch. Not even all that hard. I caught the ball and held on. End of story."

✳ ✳ ✳

Mahan felt childishly proud. He hadn't touched a cigarette since second year at the seminary, and he hadn't been much of a smoker even then, but he managed to tap two Marlboros out of her pack on one try and had them both going with one match.

"Odd way to decide you had a vocation," Barbara said, reaching up from the floor for her cigarette.

"Saul doesn't take the road to Damascus every day."

"And the rest?"

He hadn't expected the nicotine to go to his head so rapidly. "Work is the rest. I'm a pretty good manager. I know a lot of ropes, even how to finesse the odd knot."

"And that's enough?"

"I've never met a saint, Barbara. I haven't even come across a visionary. I don't think this parish expects much along those lines."

"I didn't mean to imply they did. I guess it's just that I haven't heard any religious ideal in what you're saying. God knows I never expected to hear me saying this, but . . . some high purpose, the sense of being elected in a special way."

His third puff was one too many: He tasted the tobacco. "You get over that kind of romance at the novitiate," he said, extinguishing the cigarette in an ashtray configured as a thumbless hand. "One night you go to bed with it, the next morning you wake up and it's gone. That feeling of being elected, what you call it, becomes ordinary. That's the first really hard test. The discipline, self-denial, all the rules of the house—they're nothing compared to that loss."

"So what do you do?"

"If you feel sorry for yourself, like I did, you get afraid, confused. You wonder if it's you, if you've been found out as a fraud. Then your ego kicks in. 'What the hell did I give up everything for? If I'm not going to have a harem, scores of children, millions of dollars, and the Nobel Prize, shouldn't I at least be able to expect that perpetual religious glow to keep me warm?'"

He was grateful for her laugh. "So the humbling epiphany of a rubber ball."

"Not humility. Just the opposite—arrogance."

He turned away from her frown to Dopey and Sleepy on the mantle. He belonged up there with them, he thought; he belonged with Seven Dwarfs, on stickball teams, in religious orders, and in all the other sets where potential wasn't at all what it was cracked up to be. He belonged in a neighborhood where he knew everybody so well that, 15 or 20 years ahead of time, he could tell who would go down the aisle with whom, who would attend the bachelor parties, who would be the perennial maid of honor, who would have children right away, who would get fat, get sick, and get dead early. He had snatched the Spaldine, felt the fear of Hell itself leap from his chest, and then looked around at all the eyes fixed on him. None of them, not even Al Moroni or his pipsqueak brother Ralph, had been as they should have been. That day in the schoolyard they had all been years older. They had all been married men, fathers, or saloon skels. They had all been in adulterous affairs, all been promoted at their jobs as high as they would ever get. How free he had felt at the idea of escaping their destinies! Never again—he had known it as certainly as he had never known anything—would he be completely caught up with them in anything. How could he have been? They had applauded him for simply catching a ball. They had all looked so content with so little.

Barbara said nothing for a long moment. Then: "I didn't mean to pry. You ought to be going."

Mahan thought about asking if she wanted a blessing for the apartment, then remembered that Elizabeth Hoag was dead and that her daughter didn't give a damn about who would be moving in next. He forgot about the blessing.

✳ ✳ ✳

In his room that night Mahan found it hard to concentrate on his encyclopedia. Even with his window closed against the cold dark and the radiator clanking reminders that he was better off inside, he felt exposed in some dangerous way. The page under his nose—offering *Orange* (town), *Orange* (city), *orange*, *Orangeburg*, *Orange Free State*, *Orangemen*, and *Orange River*—didn't help with its suggestion of splashy, attention-getting colors.

He thought about Barbara Hoag, then about taking an extra run in the backyard, then about going down to the lounge to watch some television, then about praying. Each option seemed evasive. He tried again, imagining Barbara naked on a beach. That helped. His thoughts, he realized, weren't of her, but of her thinking of him. He pictured her face and hair, but barely. He put a thin ass on her that belonged to anybody, imagined breasts he remembered from one of the bridesmaids at the Santiago wedding. Her pubic hair was so generic it might have been from an anatomy chart. Barbara Hoag's body was important only in its transparency—a convenience for showing him to himself. How else to think of her but as an accessory as revealing—but also as flat—as a mirror?

He went back to the encyclopedia. He thought he could use a reference to one of the oranges in his Sunday homily. He might, for instance, illustrate some moral by noting that a town and a city had identical names but absolutely nothing else in common. Then again there were Carlos and Mireya, his two Bolivian foster children to whom he had passed on all his discoveries about Atlantic Ocean porpoises, Pacific Ocean algae, and Indian Ocean fish. The Orange River was hardly an ocean, but maybe his monthly letter to La Paz could somehow relate it to how Bolivia was landlocked.

He went on to the entry for *orangutan*. As he registered the Latin classification *pongo pygmaeus* in his notebook, he smiled to think it was precisely the kind of idiot information he had once showered on Al Moroni.

"Hey, Al, know how many presidents got assassinated?"

"Hey, Al, what side were the Russians on in World War II?"

"Hey, Al, you know that writer Hemingway blew his brains out?"

Pongo pygmaeus was the kind of thing Al Moroni would have never discovered for himself, but once told about, would have clasped as a vital part of their friendship—bringing it up again months later, maybe as a joke, maybe in total earnestness. What was it Ralph Moroni had said the night of Al's wake at Sardi's? "He thought you were better than a book, Jimmy," the runt Ralph had said. "He never remembered anythin' when he read it, but he did when you told him about it. Why don't you do that now, Jimmy? Why don't you go up there and tell him to get out of that fuckin' casket? He'll pay attention to you, Jimmy. If you tell him to stop it with all this bullshit, he'll listen."

Mahan laid aside his pen, took off his glasses, and sat back from his desk. He unblurred his eyes on the prie-dieu. He had knelt at it to cry for Al Moroni, to understand why he had been unable to weep for his mother, and to summon up an image of his father more detailed than the old photos in his mother's bureau drawer. He had failed every time. When had the kneeler become merely another piece of furniture for the room?

He scratched at an itch on his elbow and put his glasses back on. He didn't like such questions. The answers were always like dates without calendars.

The next entry was *Oratorians*, the secular priests who didn't take vows. Them he knew about. He had always looked down on them for not truly committing one way or the other.

* * *

Ed Lloyd was waiting in the vestibule; he was clad in sweats, mittens, and a Cincinnati Reds cap. "Mind if I jog with you?"

Mahan minded, but figured Lloyd was so out of shape he would last only a few blocks. "Not at all."

The chilly evening loosened him immediately, let him slide easily between the air and the asphalt. Moving alongside, the towering Lloyd rumbled, but not all that much; it was more heavy foot than congested lung. He wove out into the traffic braked for a light, then on to the slope that curved down past two blocks of private homes over to the park. Lights were on in the houses. Only a handful of children were still playing outside, and some of the nine-to-fivers were already coming up the slope from the subway. Lloyd said hello to Ann Fox and Alan Buddhoz, then knew enough to conserve his energy.

He kept Lloyd at his elbow across the avenue and on into the park. In the evening fog the bridge ahead resembled an old Navy carrier gutted of its conning tower and decks. As a kid, he had watched them build the bridge beam by beam, cable by cable. But when they had finished, and he had gone down to see what everyone was about to celebrate as an accomplishment, he had felt mainly the abruptness of it all. One day there had been hanging spars over the Atlantic, the next there had been traffic moving toward the center from both shores. What had happened to the *process* in the building?

"This looks easy when I'm watching you from my window."

"You're doing great," he said, as a marble-sized sweat glop ran off Lloyd's nose.

"You'll go to paradise for that lie."

"Why tonight?"

"Something I want to talk about and let it swim off with the sweat."

"We can stop."

Lloyd said no, and Mahan was glad; he didn't like breaking stride in the park. "It's about the bazaar. I was talking to Mike today and he said you've put him in charge over the Sodality."

"Mary Kennedy got a contract out on me already?"

"I wish we'd talked about it. Mike's got worlds of savvy in organizing a zillion things, but this is different. Kennedy's gang gets real pouty when you take away their pet things. I think they would've swallowed this a lot better from me than from Mike."

Mahan told himself to put on his gravest face. It seemed important the old man sitting on the bench with a Yiddish newspaper believe they were debating some major theological issue, not the ideal organizer for Derby Craps.

"When's the last time Mike ever stroked anybody? That's why the Sodality ladies come to me in confession."

He knew Lloyd was right, but was annoyed the Sodality's favorite nephew had ruined his run with such nonsense. The only way to end it seemed to be his promise to talk to Ballinger.

"Don't get the wrong idea, Jim. If the bazaar wasn't . . ."

Mahan sliced his hand through the air: The rule maker had heard enough. Lloyd understood, turning back to the track ahead. His rear end was dragging, his legs were getting lower in their lift. He looked like a ponderous moose about to collapse. "You may be overdoing it, Ed."

But Lloyd kept clomping on. No sooner did he fall behind a few yards than he found new thunder to come abreast again. His eyes became glassier, his snort continuous. Mahan grew more doubtful with every stride. He still had enough and then some to get down to the bridge, turn around, and meet Lloyd coming, but the faster he went, the faster the stubborn giant was certain to try to go, with who-knew-what consequences for his tormented body. Did he stay locked in stride? Quit altogether? Or maybe just air it out more so Lloyd would see his futility?

He aired it out more. "You don't have to keep up, Ed!"

The only reply was more snorting and more pounding. And even as he heard the ferocious noises so close, Mahan thought he shouldn't have been able to, that he ought to have already streaked yards away and been on his own. But it seemed to take so long to get moving, to get unstuck from the gluey sweat Lloyd was dropping all over the path. Was it already too late? Had he kept to Lloyd's pace for so long that he couldn't get back to his own? In a mere few minutes he would be passing under the belly of the bridge with only a yard or two separating him from somebody who should have collapsed even before they had reached the park. What a mockery! Every evening he had exercised while Lloyd had lazed around the lounge, napped up in his room, or, at best, shot stationary baskets in the schoolyard. And yet here they both were. He *had* to be better than he was showing . . .

"Jim!"

Mahan turned back to the cry. Lloyd was a good 50 yards behind on the path, nothing left to his trot, jiggling wildly. "Okay, Jim! Okay!"

Did he imagine the foolish grin as Lloyd used what remained of his strength to throw up his arms? There was so much he wanted to see that he didn't trust what he did see. The important thing, he told himself, was to keep going, to build his lead further. He wanted to be miles away from Ed Lloyd when he finally crossed under the bridge.

✳ ✳ ✳

Dear Jimmy,

By now you've noticed that Tuesday has come and gone without my threatened return. At least I hope you've noticed.

The truth is, Jimmy, I'm not sure when I'll be back. It could be next Tuesday or Fat Tuesday. As I mentioned, Annie hasn't been in peak health herself lately. She had a fall in June, did a marvelous job on her hip bones, and has been back and forth to the hospital ever since. Nothing to get morbid about, but it's shaken her up and reminded her of the frailty most of us try to overlook as our human lot. I don't know if she wants me around as a brother or a priest, but she seems to take comfort in railing at both of us for being able to sit down in a chair without wincing.

As for this one's frailty, no bother. I spoke with Rubenstein yesterday and, after his obligatory sermon, he arranged to shift my next round of treatments up here. A pleasing prospect, to be sure. It's like the buggers are waiting in ambush for me with their horse needles across every state border. Maybe the only difference between the original Inquisition and this one is that, whereas they used to torture you in the name of exorcising the devil, they do it now in the name of exorcising mortality.

I also called the diocese last night and had a chat with the Lord's Own, Jack Geis. Between one self-importance and another, he told me about your formal request for a substitute for me and how he intends sending you someone by Sunday. You've probably heard more about this, but why I bring it up is who he suggested might be available for filling in. You got it—the infamous Martin Hartman.

The truth is, Jimmy, there's no reason why the two of you shouldn't get along. I don't deny I've always found Hartman hard to take, but you're not me and you're the one who needs the extra hand. So try to forget those cracks about the man. He's my problem, not yours.

That's not exactly fair, either, is it? Come on, McMillan. Get it out. What is your problem with the man?

Actually, it's nothing exotic; just the usual pride and vanity. To put it baldly, Martin Hartman is the most intelligent man I've ever met in the Church. In fact, he's so bright he's alienated just about everyone in the diocese he's crossed paths with. He knows everything better than they do. If they suggest something, he'll point out he suggested something better last year. They think X, he'll tell them only an ass would do X when Y is so obviously the better choice. With what result? The inevitable one that Martin Hartman, age no longer to be added with small numbers, remains the humble cleric with little to show for his time but the Ingersoll hanging around his neck. From one parish to another, from one diocese to another, he's the one you'll find sitting on the bench—the 10th man who's got as much chance of getting his own parish as I do of playing centerfield for the Red Sox. In failure and in failure, Martin Hartman defines the word obnoxious.

*But I'll tell you a little secret, Jimmy, the secret of all this
vanity of mine. The man's obnoxiousness has never particularly bothered me. That isn't why I shudder at the idea of
ever having him assigned to me. Why in hell should it? No
matter how oppressive the personality, if it belongs to an
underling, it can be managed. He gets on my nerves, I'll pack
him off to do penance until I'm calm again. There's not much
to be said for the authority of a house master who feels
threatened by the personality of an assistant.*

*But where Martin Hartman does daunt me—and here's
where my pride comes in—is with his head. I don't know
how else to say it but that he is light years ahead of me in
those fairly basic categories of knowing something, conceiv-
ing something, and planning something. His brain and imagination are a single unit. It's not just a question of knowledge,
though I know nobody else capable of going on for so long
(as he has with me over the years) about Mike Tyson, the
Celtic invasion of Italy, Indian mythologies, inflation in Hungary, and Mae West's movies. Name the subject and Hartman will be off to the races. But—and mark this—not with
the pedantry of a fool who's memorized an encyclopedia,
but passionately, as if just the fact that he knows Spain and
Greece grow different strains of oranges is grounds enough
for ideological combat.*

*My own suspicion is that not a single one of the facts
Martin Hartman spews forth in his rushes is accepted even
by him as rock truth. The things he says, especially those
he's most ardent about, are like bait he's dropping into the
water. Come on, he's saying, bob up and steal this tiny fact
away from me without getting hooked, show me how care-
less I have been. And naturally, when nobody measures up
to the challenge, he has yet another reason for alienating
some diocesan bureaucrat.*

*What I'm trying to say, kid, is that Hartman has always
scared the bejesus out of me. Not just because I know he
has more brains than I do, but because I've become convinced after seeing him in action that he uses those brains
in a profoundly spiritual way. Underneath his arrogance
and acquired knowledge of this and that, he's a man who
takes a risk whenever he opens his mouth. Very conscious,*

deliberate risks. The risks of someone who says—"Here, here's all my humanity, all the reason and thought this particular creature has amassed with his time. Show me exactly where it's insufficient."

I have no way of demonstrating this to you. But if nothing else, you must accept this is what he's made me believe about him. And as long as I hold to that view, aberrant as it may be, I could never be at ease around him. I'd feel more like his acolyte than house master. I'd despise him for his arrogance, loathe him for making me attribute a spiritual courage to him. I'd end up going back and forth between being intimidated by his vice and by his virtue. I could never be in charge of a Martin Hartman. I don't know enough, I'm not strong enough, I'm not humble enough. At best, I'd encourage his presumptuousness still further, thereby forcing him to greater risks. Sure, I might even find a lurking thrill in some of it, the way a child enjoys watching a balloon being expanded until it bursts. But I have no right to such an entertainment. As far as this McMillan is concerned, Martin Hartman stays on the bench in the diocesan office.

I hope you've understood by now that what I'm rambling on about here is what I was trying to say to you the night before I left. I owe you an apology for that night, Jimmy. I abused both your office and friendship. If I have any excuse at all, it's the one I was stumbling through that evening—that when the vain animal confesses his vanity, he could be committing his vainest act of all. In admitting to his mental aggressions against others, he has to be a saint not to savor the very airing of those aggressions, not to enjoy seeing their impact. If his confessor also happens to be the target of his aggressions, the satisfaction can be more pernicious. It shouldn't surprise you that Ecclesiastes comes to mind. "Vanity of vanities, says Qoheleth, vanity of vanities! All things are vanity!" And again: "There is an appointed time for everything—and a time for every affair under the heavens."

Indeed. And now is the time for silence, until I can confess to you in the spirit the sacrament requires. I still want to believe that day will dawn. Maybe that's another reason Rhode Island suddenly seems so inviting: You aren't around to remind me of my failed responsibilities.

*But don't count me out. I've devoted half my life to resign-
ing myself to fates I reject as soon as I realize I'm heading
for them. My constitutional impatience surely has some fuel
left. And how can anyone with even a stem of a brain resign
himself to seeing nothing more than neon signs advertising
life insurance companies? Providence will not provide.*

*Think of me in your prayers, Jimmy. And pass on that
order to Mike and Ed.*

In Christ,
Gene

✳ ✳ ✳

Barbara Hoag proposed a downtown restaurant with a French
name and an Italian menu. Mahan put on a black corduroy jacket
that left him between sober and casual. She wore blue again: a
checked navy dress with an extra flap front that seemed to him
unnecessarily tight around the arms. He made no comment about
her clothes because he didn't want her making any about his.

"I was hoping you'd call," she said, aligning her silverware
fastidiously. "I don't usually treat people I hardly know like hired
help."

"Hardly. How've you been?"

The light from the table candle fell short of her chin, while
the subdued lights in the ceiling weren't strong enough to reach
all the way down to her. He wasn't sure he wasn't inventing her
smile. "Suffering from the bends. Ask me any idiot fact about the
subway system. Who tiled the stations. How many stations have
been closed and why. How many were built but never opened."

"Built but never opened?"

"The tiles, benches, garbage cans, even those chewing gum
machines with the little round mirrors—everything's there."

"Why weren't they opened?"

"No need for them," she said, lighting a cigarette. "There were
other stops on another line only a couple of blocks away. The
real question is why they were built in the first place. The old
pork barrel. Under the table contracts. Political debts. Election
promises. Sin, Father Mahan."

"I've heard of it. And what's your job?"

She told him: something to do with updating records. He listened to her thinking of his call three nights before to invite her to dinner. He had felt completely foolish—wandering around the empty rectory, listening to the rain pouring down outside, seizing on a whim that the only truly safe place in the house was out of sight of all the pelted windows, at its inner core at the staircase. Then he had been grateful to find her number so easily and to find her at home with his first call; tonight, he was grateful she didn't already suspect he needed her company for the same kind of reasons she'd asked him to go to her mother's.

"You helped me a lot the other day," she said.

"That's city history, too."

"Some parts are easier to forget than others."

"Like?"

"Like trying to convince myself returning to the apartment would be the worst of it. Rots of ruck. The worst has been since then. When I turn on the answering machine expecting to hear Mom bitching that I don't call. When something idiotic occurs to me and I think, 'Oh, I have to tell Mom that.' Boom! No, I won't tell her."

"I wish I could say something intelligent."

"You have, you have. And you should be flattered, too. I usually try hard to forget what men say to me. That was my big problem, according to Mom."

He drank more wine. She told him about her credentials for being the Hoag family's black sheep ("men who have been lovers and lovers who have never been husbands, rooms that have been apartments but apartments that have never been homes"). He told her about the purse snatchings at the church, about his foster children Carlos and Mireya, and about *pongo pgymaeus* and all the other animals he liked to slip into his letters to La Paz and into his sermons. And then he told her about McMillan and about how he was never going to allow Martin Hartman into the parish house.

"I thought McMillan said he wouldn't mind."

"I asked the diocese to send someone else, anyway."

"For you, then. Not for McMillan."

Mahan thought about the scorching anger that had led him to crumple up the letter from McMillan and toss it in the study basket. "It's not the nicest feeling in the world when somebody you've loved and respected tells you he has always regarded you as a mediocre priest. I felt really low."

"You mean mad."

"Mad. Furious. That's why he couldn't confess to me before going up to Providence. The one thing he couldn't confess, what he'd been carrying around all these years, was his opinion of me."

"Thinking himself superior?"

"On one level. That's his vanity. But apparently, he's also blamed himself for a second sin—lack of charity. The more he rationalized he was being charitable to me and the others by not saying what was on his mind, the more he was acting just the opposite. What he was really doing was denying me and Ballinger and Lloyd the chance to challenge his presumption. In the name of not hurting us, he was mainly protecting himself from our reactions. That's the wrong he really seems to be blaming himself for."

"But which he's now admitted to you."

"Between the lines."

"And you and this Hartman?"

He drained his second glass of wine; he wasn't going to ask for another on his own, but he wouldn't have minded if the waiter noticed his empty glass. "I'll have to get over it. But if I try to take it on now, the best I can see happening is trading in jealousy for envy. Not much of a gain."

She thought a long moment before saying: "On the phone the other night I heard a familiar voice. It sounded a lot like a woman who recently dropped by a rectory and made an awkward job out of doing the easiest thing in the world—asking."

"I'm not even sure what I'm asking, Barbara."

"More," she said, shrugging as though it were obvious. "More than what you get from your routines and rituals."

"Don't make that sound like nothing."

"Oh, no. They let you hope, pray, daydream, even believe. But your rituals don't let you ask. They're too big for that. They make you feel small even for wanting them to come down to your size."

Mahan pictured her as she must have looked outside the rectory ringing the bell. Twice she had pressed her finger on the button of the flaking metal strip of the door, then stood back for immediate satisfaction. She had come to get something—something free, as they had agreed—and she wasn't going to leave without it.

"That's what I was thanking you for before, Jim."

He nodded. Her gratitude didn't feel like a weight anymore. When the waiter arrived with the food, he didn't hesitate to ask for a third wine.

✶ ✶ ✶

From the restaurant they went to a piano bar. There they sat on a raised deck in front of the pianist and listened to standards he associated with the Capitol and Columbia LPs his mother had kept in her bedroom closet. When the pianist took her break, he told her yellowed stories that her attentiveness reanimated even for him. From the bar they strolled through narrow streets past garishly lighted store windows and dark parked cars. The air was still clammy with the memory of the rain earlier in the week, but he found it hard to believe that that same downpour had fallen over his near-frenzy over McMillan's letter. More than days seemed to have passed.

What Barbara found hard to believe was his casual attitude toward Sara Dobbins. "Eccentric?" she repeated incredulously. "It's just eccentric when you think aliens have landed and the only people who know about it are Jackie Gleason and Gerald Ford?"

"Don't forget Neil Armstrong."

"And Neil Armstrong. Pardon me."

"I know it sounds weird, but . . ."

She slid her hand through his arm with a laugh. "C'mon, Jim. When was this conversation—11 years ago? She was having a bad day. I bet she wouldn't even remember it if you brought it up."

"Yes, she would."

"How do you know that? You haven't talked about it since."

He didn't know why he was sure; he just was.

She guided him to the awning of a pocket-sized apartment house on a side street that still had patches of cobblestones in the gutter. "He hasn't opened the door for me twice since I moved in," she said, nodding toward a truculent-looking doorman sitting in the lobby with a newspaper.

"Titles can be misleading."

Her gray eyes seemed to draw on every shimmer from the lamppost behind him. "But not yours."

He shook his head. Hadn't they already dealt with that question? Hadn't he already tucked her away safely as a *friend*? "Doesn't mean I shouldn't get out of my ghetto more often."

"Well, you paid tonight, so I owe you one."

"Anything at all?"

"Within bounds, Father."

"I want to see one of your stations, the ones that were built but never opened."

Her dismay made the idea seem even better. "What for?"

"Because you're the only person I'll ever meet who can show me one."

"Wouldn't a home-cooked meal do?"

"Only after the station."

She fished her key from her bag doubtfully. "I'm not even sure I could get down there. I'd need an excuse."

"Research."

She considered another moment, then nodded. "Okay."

"You mean it?"

"I'll ask around. No promises, but I can ask."

"Great." It felt like an intimate enough promise to kiss her back on the cheek. She smelled of lilacs. "Thank you, Madam. Good Night."

She clenched his fingers in something like a handshake and smiled one final time. If not for the doorman coming alert, he would have lingered to follow her sashay through the vestibule to the elevators in the rear of the lobby. He couldn't imagine greater fluidity, more self-assurance—or recall another time when he had felt so much a part of it.

He waited only until the subway stop three blocks away to tell her. He was a child—a wafting, jellying, stomping child encircled by mountains of glittering baubles—and knew it was better to admit that at once rather than foster more adult fantasies about legs and genitals and breasts.

"So what you're telling me," she laughed from the secure distance of the phone, "is that it's not the priest who's aloof to all my vamping."

"Christ, no. The priest is turned on. But beware of the frigidity of the child Mahan. He's the one I'm always apologizing for. You have to understand the upbringing."

"Strict?"

He saw he had been standing in a dry black piss patch in front of the phone. He lifted a foot carefully and, miraculously, didn't leave his loafer behind. "Tacit."

"Then why are you talking about it?"

He was talking about it, he wanted to say, because it was one thing for a superior to accuse him of being a mediocre priest, as a superior had every right to do, but another thing altogether to accuse him, as McMillan all but had, of being a mediocre man. What he said instead was: "Because I have an APB out on him before I think of looking for somebody else."

Silence. Then: "You might find somebody who doesn't want to be a priest."

"Being honest?"

"I hope so."

"I don't think I want to find that somebody."

Through her new silence he sank into the radio in the token booth, into some screeching commercial for a rock concert. He pictured mobs of teenagers—the boys all wearing grungy clothes and smoking dope, the girls jiggling and vamping under lurid T-shirt slogans. Then she coughed and said: "In that case you better know what to ask for."

A train rumbled into the station downstairs. He thought of how long it would take for the doors to open, for passengers to get off, and for the doors to close again. He was still thinking about it when a heavyset Hispanic with a newspaper rolled under his arm popped up from the staircase and a chime downstairs announced the closing of the subway's doors.

"Jim?"

He laughed; falsely. "Don't be in such a hurry," he said, seeing that the man's paper was the *News*. "Happens to be my life in front of me."

"That's right. Yours, not what others want to be yours."

It seemed like a clear enough distinction: He was on one side, everybody else, including her, on the other. "Then I guess I better get on with it."

"I think so." Not all that much regret.

"Right."

"Right." Slightly more regret. "Good Night, Jim."

"Good Night, Barbara."

*** * * ***

It took Mahan a moment to recognize George Strickland. It had been four or five years since the kid had graduated from the parish school and since then he had grown by more than half a foot and lost 20 pounds. The bruises on his face from constant brawls in the schoolyard had given way to a mild acne.

As Mahan watched from in front of the rear confessional, Strickland executed perfectly all the moves and mutterings for Ballinger's prayers for the dead, the doxology, and the Lord's Prayer. He was offhand, a little restless, but then few his age wouldn't have been. Was he glancing around so often to be sure nobody was keeping an eye on him or merely to count the witnesses to the fact that he attended weekday Mass? Was what he was sizing up in the pew in front of him the shoulder bag on the kneeler between Rose Sardi and her daughter Donna or just Donna's ass?

Mahan kept watching. It was the third straight morning he had stood where he was, trying to believe he looked casual. He had yet to figure out what he would do if he caught George Strickland or anybody else stealing, but he didn't worry about it. He counted on his instincts to see him over hurdles. One of them was already pulsating: Since when had a teenager like George Strickland felt a need to join a handful of night workers, aged insomniacs, and parish nuns for a weekday Mass? Not even he had affected so much piety at Strickland's age.

The Kiss of Peace rewarded his watchfulness. While the Sardis exchanged kisses and hands flew up from the pews like a scattering of pigeons from a nest, Strickland rocked back on his heels, pretending an interest in the figures depicted on the stained-glass windows. His face was averted when Rose Sardi turned back to him, started to extend her hand, then pulled it in again when she saw she could not get his attention immediately. Only when the woman had turned back to the altar did Strickland lower his eyes from the windows and, just in case somebody was watching, go through an outsized gesture of regret he had missed the hand proffered to him. It was small enough theatrical effort for his confidence that the woman wouldn't remember him behind her.

As Ballinger turned from the altar and brought the chalice to the railing, there was the usual stumbling out of the pews into the center aisle. When the Sardis joined the drift, it was Strickland's cue to slouch down on his knees. Once he was sure the women were committed to the aisle, he started hunching and squaring his shoulders in a series of wrigglings that brought the top half of his body over the back of the pew. Mahan sucked in his breath as the kid made one last check of the people sitting nearby and then took an awkward swipe at the shoulder bag strap. Strickland missed, and couldn't get his arm back to his body fast enough—first running his hand through his sculpted hair as though that had been the purpose of his lunge in the first place, then again peering to the left and right to be sure he had gone unobserved.

The second try was artistry. Even tensing his concentration, Mahan felt a second behind as Strickland flashed out his hand directly from his cowering position and snatched the bag strap. He didn't worry about potential witnesses, didn't worry about Rose and Donna Sardi returning too soon. He simply yanked the bag off the kneeler, landed it with a heavy slap against the pew, then started rummaging through it. He had no idea that Barbara Fiorino, on her way back to her front pew, only had to raise her eyes a fraction to see everything. Strickland was blind to everything but the red wallet he pulled from the bag and then slipped into the pocket of his leather jacket.

The kid showed nothing when the Sardis came back from the altar. He sat motionlessly as the women bowed, swallowed, and meditated. Mahan began sweating before so much arrogance. The rip-off was audacious enough, but then to remain seated only inches away from his victims, risking their discovery of what he had done? By the time Ballinger neared the end of his prayers, he was ready to surrender to the heat of a profound loathing for George Strickland. He wanted to injure the thief in a way he had never injured anyone in his life; more than violent, he wanted to be *gratuitously* violent. He wanted to be one with Strickland's thievery: If it was pure chance who ended up being robbed, an element of whim should have been involved in when he let up on the teenage punk. He wanted George Strickland to feel the same injustice the Sardis were going to feel when they couldn't find the red wallet. He wanted Strickland to know the feeling of being without a choice, where even fear and courage were so irrelevant they could be taken for one another. He wanted George Strickland to realize—and realize *too late*—what he had done.

Sister Caroline jumped the gun, heading for the side door before Ballinger got to the blessing. Mahan couldn't feel his legs as he slid into the last pew, out of the way of the imminent rush to the door. Ballinger uttered the dismissal. Rose and Donna Sardi stood with their shoulder bags. Strickland stood as respectfully as the women. Ballinger conferred the blessing. Everybody—including George Strickland—made the Sign of the Cross.

The first parishioners up the aisle told Mahan how stunned he apparently looked. Maggie Pierce started to say hello, but then pulled in her jaw and continued out. Jeff Matukis, with more warning, just hobbled on without looking at him. And George Strickland, the cause of the carbonated rush to his stomach? George Strickland stood patiently in his pew, waiting for everyone else to go before he clogged the aisle with his body. He was the perfect gentleman—the perfect *blessed* gentleman.

Mahan let the Sardis go. He could always call them with the wallet later. As if winning another bet with himself, George Strickland slowly zippered his jacket to let Barbara Fiorino precede him up the aisle, making him absolutely the last to leave.

"George."

Strickland stopped. His leather jacket smelled of cherries. "Father?"

"Three things," Mahan heard himself announce. "First, the wallet you took."

He paused, wanting each of his commands to have separate life. The silence worked: Strickland removed the plastic red wallet from his pocket and handed it over.

"Second, if there's another robbery in this church or any other in the diocese I hear about, I will personally drag you down to the precinct. Is that clear?"

Strickland thought about not nodding, letting the redness of his face suffice, but then gave in—curtly but without bravado.

"And third, I don't ever want to see you in this church again. Never. Not if you live to be 100. Do you understand?"

This time there was no acknowledgment at all, and Mahan wanted to cry in the face of so much emptiness. George Strickland was 17 or 18, but he was also suddenly in a no-man's land between being a coarse, hardened adult and a yearning, disarmed child. How had it happened to him so fast? Hadn't they just been telling him the other day how cute he was?

"Goodbye, Strickland."

George Strickland blinked, his hope gone once and for all. Then he jammed his fists into his jacket pockets and, recovering swagger as he went, vanished through the main door.

Mahan stood frozen, hearing senseless things around him. The squeaking door as it swung down to stillness. The scraping of the sexton Tom as he came out on the altar to replace the cruets. Someone chigging a bicycle in the street. The sounds were soothing in their separateness, seeming to make everything infinitely postponable.

✳ ✳ ✳

In the days that followed Mahan had much less trouble praying. At Mass, in his room at night, at unexpected junctures in between, he felt swelling urges to focus his mind completely on some representation of vast cosmic splendor and to picture himself obscured within it; only the tinniness of his voice and callowness of his meditating betrayed his presence at all. He imagined stars millions of light years away, dark moons bursting with millions of mysteries, vapor trails that extended across cold universes. He thought of the representations as brilliant and solidifying even as he contemplated them, then envisioned them crumbling and vanishing because of his attention to them. He invoked a great, masterful Presence permeating everything he could conceive, then of the same Presence denying Its own existence because he had discerned it. He thought of himself as a small but intrusive entity; as sincere, but also as presumptuous. He wondered why his mind didn't stop nagging him or didn't stop functioning altogether once he had fallen to his knees and shut his eyes to surrounding distractions. He wondered how he could ask so many enervating questions of himself even as he was supposed to be aiming his ruminations outwardly, and he wondered whether the very energies of his efforts superseded anything he could feel through them, whether in fact his earnestness alone gained him a supernatural substance for his blood that readily identified him (YOU KNOW WHERE I AM) even to the most distant galaxies.

He hadn't practiced such agitated, contradictory, self-justifying meditation since his ordination. It was as different from his vocational praying—that sluggish routine on his bedroom prie-dieu he had lost the ability even to fake—as question was to answer. He didn't think of himself as a clergyman named James William Mahan; Father Mahan had never been so sloppy, so fanciful in his representations, so untrained in his expectations. This was somebody floundering and fleeing. Who this was was the 11-year-old who had once lain awake in bed begging the report card under his pillow to record better numbers before showing it to his mother and father in the morning. Who this was was the 14-year-old who had once sat in a movie house crying for Robert Redford and Faye Dunaway to bring back his father. Who this was was the 18-year-old who had once walked out of Sardi's telling himself that if he hadn't flubbed a couple of lines of the Apostle's Creed, Al Moroni might have climbed out of his casket. He was the 11-year-old, 14-year-old, and 18-year-old who had asked those things, and he was also the older man who had received none of them—whose report card had remained unchanged, whose father and best friend had remained dead. The track record counted for nothing.

Sara Dobbins told him he looked tired; he didn't believe her. Ballinger assured him George Strickland would be better off in the long run for the treatment that he had received; he didn't know what the long run was and hoped Ballinger was merely trying to be charitable in a way Police Officer Mahan hadn't been with George Strickland. He didn't believe in any answer to his prayers that had to do with James Mahan, and he didn't believe in any having to do with people influencing other people. Instead, and in particular when he entered the altar in the morning and knelt in his room at night, he felt himself hurtling backward at increasing speed from every belief he had ever had. It was a dizzy, exhilarating sensation. No longer a middle-aged man in inevitable orbit toward some greater incapacity, he was now a joker, a radical, the loosest of cannons. Others were being spun ahead against their wills, but he had managed to grab the handle to some powerful vehicle that was pulling him away from danger. He was free.

Except for the dizzy spells that hit him—first while coming off the altar one morning, then while going through the mail in the study two days later.

✱ ✱ ✱

Mahan heard what he had expected to hear from Rubenstein.

"You find stress funny, Father?" the doctor asked in his W.C. Fields twang.

"My housekeeper's been telling me the same thing."

Rubenstein kept on scrawling on his prescription pad. "Good. I feel useful in giving you a second opinion. Your housekeeper agrees with me you've been under more pressure without Father McMillan?"

"Nothing we haven't been able to handle."

"Really? Then why're you here?"

"I meant . . ."

"You don't know what you mean," he said, tearing off the prescription. "If these don't make you feel better in a couple of days, I want you back here."

"Fine."

"Not really," Rubenstein said evenly. "Get used to the pressure. I've just received the last X-rays from Providence. I'd say Father McMillan has a couple of weeks tops."

Mahan busied himself by folding the prescription an extra couple of times to put into his shirt pocket. "Is there something I should be doing?" he managed to ask.

"Depends if he wants to come back here."

"That'll be up to him. Does he know yet?"

Rubenstein glanced at his desk clock. "Within the hour. I've got a feeling he's going to want to come back. It's his parish. It's what a lot of them . . ." He stopped with a frown.

"What a lot of them do?"

The doctor was more amused than embarrassed. "Saying it to somebody else makes it an observation," he smiled. "Saying it to you makes it ignorance. Maybe you do have higher standards, Father."

Mahan smiled back; tactfully, helplessly. Rubenstein understood, and swung his chair around to the window that was surrounded by degrees and licenses. "Just be sure you don't make the same mistake I made when I heard my father was down to hours."

He thought about blowing his nose, but wiped his eyes instead. "What mistake is that, Doctor?"

"Don't miss Father McMillan yet. He's still with us."

✳ ✳ ✳

It took Mahan two days to work out the practicalities for McMillan's return to New York. He hired an ambulance service in Providence. In the guest room on the other side of the hall from McMillan's quarters he installed a male nurse recommended by Rubenstein. He had an oxygen cylinder set up by the old man's bed and (optimistically) a second one stored in the hall closet. He received Rubenstein's assurances that the doctor would never be further away than a beeper summons. For all that, it wasn't until a grimly emaciated McMillan came through the front door of the rectory, his loudest of indignant whoops aimed at the ambulance paramedics who insisted he be carried in on a stretcher, that Mahan was sure he had done the correct thing. As he led the way up the stairs, he was finally able to shake off the brittle reserve of his phone conversations with Annie McMillan and anxieties about McMillan's ability to handle the long drive down from Rhode Island.

"I hear this is all your doing, Jimmy!" McMillan bellowed, as the paramedics maneuvered up the staircase in a procession that also included Ballinger, Sara Dobbins, and the nurse Roy Webster. "Mind telling me where the money came from?"

"The diocese."

"The devil you say! They even get their furniture from flea markets!"

The paramedics laughed. Ballinger and Webster laughed. Even Sara made some kind of laughing sound. Mahan thought that was enough of an answer where his personal savings were concerned. Instead, he remembered what Rubenstein and the Providence doctor Henkle had told him about the Percodan and other drugs McMillan was on—that sometimes the old man would be lucid, other times not. Logical conversations weren't to be expected. Forthright responses might come to questions asked days before. All in all, it seemed like a solid reason for not having to pay attention to a damn thing Gene McMillan had to say.

He stayed in the hall while the paramedics settled McMillan in bed and imparted final instructions to Webster. The old man's grouchiness leapt another decibel at sight of the huddle, and didn't subside much with Ballinger's promise to return later with a deck of cards and Webster's list of 101 services in the offing. Only Sara escaped the rancor: "I have to warn you, Sara," he told her. "I've picked up a trick or two about shellfish in my sister's kitchen. We're going to spiff up the menu in this place." Sara Dobbins rushed from the bedroom dabbing at her eyes.

With the paramedics paid off Mahan had no more excuse for not going into the room. The man in the bed was some chalky version of the McMillan last seen at his bureau squeezing a teabag. An effort like that would have been beyond the skeleton in front of him.

"You're looking good, Jimmy."

"And you're fishing."

McMillan smiled, but his teeth had become too big for his shriveled mouth. "I think somebody told me you've put an end to this stealing business."

He could have spared himself the shame that washed over him at the thought of his ferocious dismissal of George Strickland. No sooner had McMillan got the words out than he closed his eyes and lapsed into what appeared to be sleep. He was dismayed, even after the warnings from Rubenstein and Henkle and his own experiences at hospices. He counted to 10 before being sure he wouldn't have to burden McMillan with the Strickland story, then tiptoed out and closed the door behind him.

In the kitchen downstairs Tom was serving tea to Ballinger and Webster. Mahan knew Sara would have never let the sexton enter her domain under normal circumstances, but he didn't know which she considered more abnormal—having McMillan back in the condition he was in or having the black nurse Webster around. He found her sitting on a garden bench. Legs crossed at the roll in her stockings, a tan cardigan thrown over her shoulders against the chilly afternoon, she had a handkerchief in one hand and a rosary in the other.

"Can I get you something, Father?"

"Nothing. Stay where you are, Sara."

Her doubtful eyes went back to contemplating the browned grass at her feet. "The Father is asleep, is he?"

"Dropped off like that."

"Long trip it was. He'll feel better after a rest."

He saw that Tom had made good on a promise to replace the cracked slat fencing off the Bonner yard, but hadn't bothered to replace a couple of others against the Fiorino yard. He was glad: Even a safe fortress like the rectory should have had an escape hole.

"In all the excitement, Father, I forgot to tell you. I got a letter from Della. She'll be coming back from Ireland the end of next week."

Mahan didn't know if that was good news, bad news, or no news. By now, he thought, Sara had trained him so well in awkwardness that he would probably be tongue-tied with Della Robinson, as well. "I was starting to think she'd stay over there."

Sara Dobbins answered something. What he suddenly heard instead was Barbara Hoag's reminder that 11 years had passed since the woman had gone on about her interplanetary creatures. "Can I ask you something, Sara?"

"Father?"

"The first day I reported to the house here. It was years ago, I realize, but do you by any chance remember how we met at Tedesco's and walked here together?"

She slipped her rosary into her sweater pocket; she was more alert, but not yet alarmed. "Yes, I think so."

"And do you remember what we talked about? How you'd seen a TV interview with Jackie Gleason and Gleason had seen these aliens?"

She shook her head without hesitation. "*He* didn't see them, Father. It was those presidents Nixon and Ford, they saw them and told Jackie Gleason."

"So you do remember telling me that."

"I think so. Why do you ask?"

"Well, this is going to sound odd after all this time . . ."

"Whether I believe it or not?"

Mahan had never seen her smile so heartfully; he might have stumbled into a cavernous chamber of her mind where priests were no more important as visitors than anybody else. "Yes, Sara. Whether you believe it or not."

"Why shouldn't I go along with it if people tell me it's true? What's there to gain by lying to me, Father?"

"But it's not reasonable, Sara. There's no proof."

"Yes?" It wasn't a question, it was a challenge.

"But that's important, Sara. It's not just some minor consideration. You have to be reasonable about what you're telling people. You have to be ready to demonstrate it."

She was baffled. "It's been so long, Father. I don't remember the exact words they used on the TV."

"I don't mean that. I don't doubt for a second you heard it how you remember."

"You don't?"

He was hunkered down at her knees before he realized it. She seemed to consider pulling away her legs, then made herself concentrate on what he was going on about. "Forget the obvious things for a second. Forget about the lunacy of somebody in show business, a comedian, saying all this. What I really want to know, Sara, is why, if you're so ready to accept what Jackie Gleason said, you're not . . . *different*."

She didn't like the question, and liked his urgency less.

"Think about it, Sara. Here you have a true revelation that would turn everything on this planet upside-down. You said it that morning—something that would upset all the apple carts."

"I was telling you what Jackie Gleason said," she corrected edgily.

"Okay, he said it, you didn't. But if you're willing to listen to what he said, accept it even as just possible, how can you . . . well, even just come to work every day? How in the world can you just go on lighting the oven and making coffee and cleaning off the table? Is it really the same for you today going to Mass in the morning or to Sardi's when somebody dies?"

This time she did move her legs away. "And what is it I'm supposed to be doing, Father? I can't forget my obligations. Is it a priest telling me to do that?"

"I'm not telling you anything, Sara. I'm asking."

As soon as he said it, he wanted to grind the pebble under his right knee into his skin so he could pay for his stupidity. She arched her back nervously and shifted still further away on the bench. "I should be thinking of supper, Father," she said. "Will that Mister Webster be eating with us now?"

Mahan stood up. Sara Dobbins hadn't counted on serving as a housekeeper for a black man. He thought about lecturing her on her bigotry, then thought about soaking his head in a shower—about the size of Niagara Falls. "Yes, Mister Webster will be with us as long as Father McMillan is. We hope that's a long time."

"That's all right then, Father."

"I'm glad you agree."

He made a point of dusting off his pants slowly so as not to have to see her expression as she sighed and stood up. When he finally did look up, he was surprised to see her standing her ground in her sensible black shoes. "You shouldn't be disappointed, Father," she said kindly.

"Disappointed?"

"The night I saw that TV show I was imagining some of the same things you're here asking. 'What a lot of frightening things this star is saying,' I'm thinking to myself. 'They'll be talking about nothing else tomorrow morning. The papers will be going on and people will get panicky.'"

"Yes?"

She plunged her hands into her pockets with a wry smile; a breeze tousled one of her small gray curls. "I wasn't even in my bed that night, though, before I'm back to worrying about all the everyday things. Getting my brother's breakfast in the morning. What I needed from the store. I prayed for my mother and father, like always. Or at least I thought about them." She blushed. "I had this silly notion, too."

"What was that?"

"About my mother and father. I remember thinking in bed *they* might be the alien creatures Jackie Gleason was talking about. Maybe it was my parents who'd come back to earth as these things. You don't have to tell me that's a silly one. I know that."

He moved his lips: Anything to keep her talking, anything to maintain the illusion of saddling up on her confusion and riding his own out toward clarity.

"Of course, there was never a word in the paper. Only ones who heard about the things Jackie Gleason said were the ones I told—my brother, Della Robinson, you."

"It's always stuck in my mind."

"Why would that be, Father? To read about him, that Gleason was what he was till the day he died. And I don't think Nixon changed very much."

He told himself to try once more. "But *shouldn't* they have changed, Sara? My God, they were going around saying mind-boggling things! *Shouldn't* it have made them rethink what they'd been doing with their lives?"

She tried to see his problem better by squinting. "Changed to what, Father?"

"I don't know. To whatever's necessary."

Sara Dobbins gave him another long benefit of the doubt before finally shaking her head; once again he seemed to have let her down. "If that's the kind of change they have to be making, Father, they don't have to be waiting for some Martians to come along, do they?"

He was five years old again, Mahan told himself. The only things missing were short pants and a striped polo shirt. Otherwise, little Jimmy Mahan was back to watching all the adults doing and saying things beyond his grasp. "Of course not."

"Common sense, Father."

"Absolutely. Common sense."

He kept nodding to her until she clapped the screen door behind her. He pictured her entering the kitchen, finding a great disorder, and scolding Ballinger, Webster, and Tom. He pictured her tasting Tom's tea, spitting it out into the sink, and turning on the tap for another kettleful of water. It was easy to imagine her doing things better.

✳ ✳ ✳

That evening Mahan initiated what he saw as Father James Mahan's last routine. He jogged to the park, took a quick shower, sat down to dinner with Ballinger, Lloyd, Webster, and McMillan's fill-in Kimball. Between dinner and Sardi's he took his turn in McMillan's room, going on about everything from Della Robinson to the Jets, while Webster patiently spooned out broth and McMillan grunted about having to sit up and swallow. He got McMillan to talk some about Providence, to laugh a couple of times, and to smile a few more times than that. Then he turned the room over to Lloyd.

He was the one who did the smiling at Sardi's. He smiled to hearten the Loschen and Robles families. He smiled because he was also glad to banter with Joe Sardi. And most of all he smiled because, for the first time since doing prayers at the funeral home, he was confident nobody would stand up to question his right to be there. He *knew* he was there as a minister in a real sense.

Back in the house after Sardi's, he stopped off to get a beer in the kitchen before retiring. The house seemed muted more than merely quiet, as though feverish things were happening all around him but behind closed doors. Passing the lounge, he heard the kind of mechanical laughter that went with a TV sitcom; he guessed the real laughter belonged to Kimball. The stairs creaked more than normal under his footsteps, as if to warn somebody in hiding he was coming. On the second-floor landing he stopped to work out the murmuring from Webster's room; a basketball game on the black-and-white portable?

He cracked open his beer can loudly, but the noise dispelled nothing.

He squeezed open the door to McMillan's room for a look. The heavy Ben Gay odor again assailed his nostrils, but two steps inside and it was gone again, and he knew he had imagined it from his visit weeks before. What the room smelled of was nothing. It was so aerated—if only through the sight of the oxygen cylinder—it was antiseptic. McMillan wasn't sweating, farting, or developing cotton balls in his mouth as he slept; he was just wheezing his chest up and down like a bellows, being purified.

Mahan deposited the flip top from the beer on the dresser and tiptoed over to the recliner near the window. McMillan's railing curled up his chest like fingernails on a blackboard, but he beat off his squeamishness by remembering he had handled it before, back in his father's bedroom. Then there had been medicinal odors—of iodine and of mercurochrome and of musty pill vials—everywhere, and on top of them the smells that were supposed to have eradicated the medicinal smells, worst of all the aerosol called Silken Rose. There was none of that in McMillan's room; even the dusty odor from the mysteries in the bookcase was gone. The only scent was from his beer.

He took a sip, wondering if tonight was going to be the night. He didn't really want McMillan to take off so fast. After all the years that McMillan had lived and that James Mahan had pretended to be a priest, what possible harm could there be in waiting another week?

He saluted McMillan and drank to his hope.

✳ ✳ ✳

McMillan was strong enough for visits from Geis from the diocesan office and from his seminary buddy up from Miami. But he wasn't so strong that he could pay attention to them for more than a few minutes. Mahan thought of him as hovering like the Spaldine he had once stiffened under: The sign he was looking for was that illusory moment when the ball appeared to travel laterally across the peak of its arc—the one and only warning it could no longer sustain itself.

"Geis tells me you took a long time requesting this Kimball character," McMillan said to him one afternoon.

"A little after you went up to your sister's."

McMillan was delighted by the lie. He sat in the recliner, practically smothered by the blankets up to his neck, a pair of woolen socks, and a black beret brought to him by his Miami friend. "Now, now, Jimmy."

"Who remembers?"

"According to himself, it was quite some time after I left."

"Could be. What difference?"

McMillan all but cackled. "I was just wondering if you took so long because you were being optimistic I'd be back soon or because you didn't want to be responsible for my little tumor pals. No, no, none of that look. I did it myself years ago when Jack Tam was on his way out. Just to ask the diocese for a new man, I told myself, was sentencing Jack to death."

Mahan had to laugh: He was glad he was so transparent to the man to the end.

"We're all arrogant bastards, Jimmy. We think of ourselves as so omnipotent we can change the very course of living and dying with the wrong kind of this thought or that. That's what superstition is—arrogance. And what ends up in the rubble of all our airs? Sometimes the most ordinary obligations."

He knew he was being scolded, but didn't know for what. "I think you're making a point."

McMillan lifted a bony finger to his nose and flicked at an itch. "Promise I won't blame you if I pass right on over to the Nethers if you carry out your office by giving me the oils." Mahan felt his face reddening. "You mind if we do it now? When we're both a little clear in the head?"

"I'm not sure anybody's around. Ed had to . . ."

"So we'll dispense with the community sing and go for the cut-rate anointing. How about that?"

He carried McMillan's sarcasm back to his room, where he removed his black leather kit from his desk drawer and checked it had everything. The half-filled vials of oil and water reminded him he would never have to fill them again. He accepted the idea calmly. It wasn't at all like the last night in his room before going off to the novitiate, when he had looked at his cassettes and posters and baseball card collection as though he were about to do them a great harm by leaving them behind forever.

McMillan was still awake, but looked more listless, when he returned. "Praise to you, God the Almighty Father. You sent your Son among us to bring salvation."

"Blessed be God who heals in Christ," the old man got out.

"Praise to you, God the only begotten Son . . ."

McMillan's forehead was cold and crusty to the touch, even after he had applied the extra dollop of oil Pete Harris had once advised him to lay on so the recipient could feel true contact. "Through this holy anointing may the Lord in His love and mercy assist you with the grace of the Holy Spirit."

"Amen."

He was surprised McMillan didn't help. The old man's hands were on top of the blanket, but not turned over, and his eyes were hooded tightly, like a blind man anticipating only what others could do for him. With the left hand he did what he could, slathering the oil down into the palm through the thumb and index finger, then laying more across the knuckles. He was about to do the same thing with the right hand when McMillan began trembling—just about everywhere except in his hands.

"May the Lord who frees you from sin save you and raise you up with Him."

McMillan replied again, still firmly. Caught off guard, Mahan was slow to remember the right hand. When he did, it seemed natural, even necessary, to do what he had done only once before—in the hospital with his mother. Emptying out what was left of the oil, he panned it into every groove of his palm as he gripped the old man's right hand and shook it. Immediately, there was the tightening of the return clasp and, although McMillan didn't open his eyes and the blanket never stopped shaking, the same voice that had been so assertive with its Amens said: "May the Lord who frees us from sin save you and raise you up with Him."

"Amen," Mahan said quickly.

✱ ✱ ✱

Once Mahan had dispensed the last sacrament, a new restlessness overtook him. He could no longer sit in McMillan's room and work at making conversation. So much seemed over but not really over. He was impatient. He was distracted. He rambled. It suddenly mattered to him equally that Roy Webster had taken to sitting with McMillan most of the day, that Barbara Hoag had called to say she had gotten permission to visit one of the never-opened subway stations, and that McMillan's replacement Kimball was annoying some of the older parishioners by polishing off his weekday Mass in less than 25 minutes. Everything seemed to be on borrowed time because, almost as much as McMillan was, he was. The big difference was McMillan's growing pain.

One afternoon, after an especially wrenching attack had abated, the old man gazed up through glazed eyes and asked him: "What's the worst of it, Jimmy?"

Mahan knew the answer, knew he had no right to share it, but knew too that he would never be able to say it to anybody else. "The worst of it," he said, taking McMillan's wet hand into his own, "is the third possibility—not an afterlife or just a coffin of maggots in the ground. But suppose you're going off into some other dimension where you'll exist in some way but where you won't recognize me anymore as somebody you know? I've always thought that possibility was the worst of it—with my mother and father, with Al Moroni, others. I'll never really lose them because I've always got my memories. But what about you, Gene? What about them? Do you end up in some place where you forget who I am, who I've ever been? That would be like never having existed for you. I think that's the worst."

"Good man," McMillan nodded, then fell asleep.

✻ ✻ ✻

Mahan hovered over every detail of the funeral. He arranged a room for Annie McMillan in the parish convent and was at La-Guardia to meet her flight from Providence. He wrote the obituaries for the neighborhood newspaper and the diocesan weekly, and he saw to the listings for the *Daily News* and *Newsday*. With Annie McMillan's help he called distant relatives in Delaware, Illinois, and California, giving them wake and burial dates but assuring them that their condolences would be just as sincere at some local service of their own. He nudged all the school, church, and neighborhood groups to dip into treasuries for flowers or parish donations in McMillan's name. He successfully lobbied Geis at the diocesan office to pledge the bishop's presence for the Requiem.

For the price of one room he persuaded Sardi to take down the door separating his two largest parlors to accommodate the crowds. He had no trouble talking the school principal McIntire into marching the older students into Sardi's class by class during the wake and shutting the school altogether the morning of the funeral. He had Tom call in extra labor to get the church in condition for the funeral Mass. He had Sardi explain to Annie McMillan all the financial and aesthetic intricacies involved in selecting a headstone, then accompanied her to inspect the burial plot. He rented the back room of the Zebra Crossing for the funeral lunch, winnowing down the entrée options to trout and roast beef with the owner Bob Forte. He had Sara Dobbins buy a bottle of the bishop's favorite bourbon, just in case. He filed all the necessary medical insurance claims. He paid off Webster. He turned over to Annie McMillan everything he had on her brother's bank accounts and put her in touch with Hal Barclay, the attorney entrusted with the will. He asked Ballinger, Lloyd, and Kimball to celebrate special Masses in McMillan's name.

And he asked Martin Hartman to say the funeral Mass.

His planning paid off. There was hardly a minute during the day that mourners weren't filing through Sardi's. On the two wake evenings they numbered in the hundreds; jungles didn't have more flowers. Old friends and acquaintances from New Jersey, Delaware, and Connecticut, more recent friends and acquaintances from Rhode Island, old teachers, one of Rubenstein's nurses, a security guard and an intern from the hospital, parishioners who had moved away, former students from the parish school, every single member of the local clubs, the regulars from Gregory's saloon and the neighborhood restaurants, representatives of the station house and fire house—they all came. So massive was the outpouring that on both evenings Mahan felt obligated to go into Sardi's other two parlors to lead the prayers for the dead being waked there, to reassure the families that their sorrow was no less because it wasn't drawing the attention that McMillan's passing had.

Mahan assigned himself the Requiem eulogy. This entitled him to sit at the side of the altar with Geis as bookends to the bishop. It also enabled him to have a closeup look at the thin, sandy-haired Martin Hartman, whose selection as the celebrant had brought dismay from Ballinger, clucking from Lloyd and Sara Dobbins, and casual questions from Geis that weren't so casual. He didn't care. What his choice came down to was that Gene McMillan deserved Martin Hartman as his celebrant and that Martin Hartman would probably never again have the opportunity to commemorate somebody who had made so much of an effort to understand him.

As he sat waiting for his cue to go over to the pulpit, Mahan couldn't help admiring Hartman's deft performance. The man's elocution and projection were precise, his movements economically authoritative. Mahan knew he wasn't as good, remembered the bishop wasn't, and suspected Geis was their third. Martin Hartman was the smooth, no-frills professional in everything, and that included not inquiring why he had been chosen to say the Mass. He had simply walked into the rectory 45 minutes ahead of time, asked Sara for a cup of instant Maxwell House, and then proceeded to the sacristy to get dressed for another guest assignment. The man knew he was significant in some way; he just wasn't impressed by it.

Finally, Hartman tripped down the altar steps, genuflected briskly, and, flanked by his altar boys, moved to the bench on the opposite side. Mahan stood up, feeling abruptly dislodged from his seat and hurled toward the pulpit by some sudden barking coughing in the back. The first thing he saw was that Tom had forgotten to throw away the sheet with the Sunday announcements; having the old copy on the lectern was a stabbing reminder that McMillan had still been alive when he had read from it.

He lifted his eyes above the pulpit to the packed pews. He picked out Annie McMillan sitting next to the coffin, but knew he couldn't talk to her. He'd known her only with McMillan's death, and it wasn't the dead McMillan he wanted to commemorate. He decided to focus on the school kids grouped together in the side pews and on Gregory, Fiorino, and the other members of the neighborhood association sitting midway back in the center pew.

"In the name of the Father and of the Son . . ."

✹ ✹ ✹

Mahan was comforted by the sudden motion from so many areas of the church. It was one thing to have an iceberg of faces in front of him, much more to have hundreds of people raising their arms for the Sign of the Cross independently of one another. He was addressing individual beings, each one capable of personal movement. Was even George Strickland lurking somewhere among them, casing another handbag?

"Whatever Gene McMillan knew," he heard his voice quiver, "he knew from you, he knew from us."

He pictured the expressions behind him. The bishop would be curious, Geis suspicious. Martin Hartman? Hartman, he was sure, would be impassive to the end.

"Gene McMillan was a home team. Seldom did he go out on the road, and when he did, he couldn't get back here fast enough. To the neighborhood where he was born, schooled, moved to take up his vocation, worked his entire life, and where, he always knew, he would die. What we represented was adequate for Gene McMillan. He wasn't a man consumed by the envies of ambition, sloths of fantasy, or greeds of knowledge. There was no anger for what others had, no resentments for what he himself might have had. His flaws and imperfections were our flaws and our imperfections—the ones we gave him and he embraced as sufficient . . ."

Sardi's pallbearers stood like impatient sentries at the back door. Klippstein and Perez and the others couldn't wait to march down the center aisle to get their shoulders under the casket and speed McMillan along his way to the cemetery. Was it only the eulogy delaying them?

". . . Call it our sense of community. That was the unifying bond that accounted for Gene McMillan's life, as it now accounts for his death . . ."

There were so many things he had to say before the pallbearers received the signal to move in. He knew the signal: It came when Joe Sardi himself slipped into the church, took in where the Mass was, then murmured the word to Klippstein or Perez. He had seen it with his father and mother and Al Moroni, with everybody: When Sardi slinked in from his other morning duties to gauge what part of the Mass he was interrupting, he became the last call. At no other point during wakes and funerals was it so obvious that Joe Sardi was somebody who *disposed of* people, who took bodies from the church to *get rid of* them. Once Sardi did his whispering, those in the coffins could never again be looked upon, not even in death, and the bereaved realized—too late—that they'd still had something of their parents, spouses, and friends even in the caskets in church.

Mahan talked, and remembered. Sitting with the Fiorinos, Teddy Lewis burped a laugh and crossed his arms across his thick chest as if to say, "Ah, indeed, no end to the stories to be told, all right!" What he couldn't imagine ever sharing with Teddy Lewis was his certainty that Sardi would end up disposing of every single person in the church, even the kids in the side pews. He himself would go on standing at the pulpit, prattling on as he was now, registering how, one after another, those listening to him vanished. Teddy Lewis would stop looking entertained. Annie McMillan would stop gazing at some spot above his head. Miles Harkleroad, Sara Dobbins, Mary Kennedy, Gregory and Billie Duffy—they would all make the blond varnish of their pews look even blonder by dissolving. Only he would be in demand, for his priestly function. He would be working in concert with Sardi, his talking serving as some Magic People Remover. He would talk, Sardi would enter. He would talk, Sardi would size up the situation on the altar. He would blink away some parishioner with his gab, Sardi would send his men down the aisle to haul the unfortunate's remains away. One by one, the parishioners would create holes in front of him until there were more holes than parishioners and then so many holes that the holes themselves wouldn't be visible.

He kept talking. He knew the cloth rustling behind him was the bishop's cape. If the bishop was growing restless, was Geis already a nervous wreck? He didn't care. He already had his hands full trying to protect those who were still there from Sardi. There was no more time for fretting about what was an appropriate eulogy and what wasn't. He wanted to head off deaths, not accept them in the name of commemoration. Too many people were already gone because he had worried only about his place at the pulpit. They had been deprived of the protection he owed them. It was as though they had been good only for dying so he could get up and lather their corpses with creamy sermons. He had to reassure everyone that wasn't the case, that as long as he was there physically for them, they would be all right. He had to tell them they didn't need an intellectual or spiritual priest, only a physical one who was there for them to see, that everything else was extra.

Some of them began coughing at the idea. Bart Teresi from the bank hawked so deeply from his chest he turned red. One of the nuns—Beatrice, was it?—had the look of a martyr as she dropped her eyes to her lap. Mary Kennedy was getting twitchy, and would have been more so if her glances at Della Robinson weren't being ignored so pointedly. Sara Dobbins kept raising her chin at him as though it were only for her to look higher to comprehend what he was saying.

But volume, not sense, he thought, was what mattered. The old stories and jokes—he recalled them in detail, knowing he had to rid himself of their every particular if his silence after today was going to be truly effective. He stumbled over the thought that he had too much to unload, that his own memory was too disordered to gather up everything, that he couldn't possibly finish before Sardi's arrival. But then he recovered again with a reminder of his encyclopedia studies. *A* was for Al Moroni, *B* for Barbara Hoag . . . He was fine.

What was the hardest memory to throw away? He went back to his bedroom the night before leaving for the novitiate, saying goodbye to his clothes, team caps, and cassettes, hoping they wouldn't hate him for leaving them and making them so vulnerable to the garbage can. He went back to his father's room, astounded that a mere half-hour nap in the old beach chair had cost him some last cry, some visible move from life to death. He went back over to Sardi's, wondering why he couldn't have taken a turn at hitting a high pop fly to Moroni, helping Al to shake off the neighborhood in the way Al had helped him. But none of these was the hardest memory to shake off, he was surprised to realize: The hardest was the sight of a confused George Strickland walking out of the church, his hands in his jacket pockets, having to brave the great unknown. That memory came back to him in waves of warm shudders, making him tremble in embarrassment and burn in admiration. He couldn't deny it: The memory *thrilled* him. George Strickland gone off—clearly caught and firmly judged, but off and gone without any obligation for restitution.

Mahan laughed. He would never get beyond *A* if he kept recalling things. There was Teddy Lewis with his arms still crossed over his chest, but now examining something on his knees. There were all the apes answering to *pongo pgymaeus*. There were Sara Dobbins's aliens. Had his life been far too full, after all? The silence he was heading for seemed to recede further and further away . . .

"Jim."

Martin Hartman had somehow crossed the altar to the pulpit. Mahan's immediate thought was that Hartman was annoyed with him for going on and on. But then he saw that Hartman wasn't irritated at all, that his clear blue eyes were searching for, not resenting, something. "Am I getting a little scrambled, Marty?"

As soon as he asked it, he regretted the question was the first thing he had ever really said to the man. Shouldn't their first exchange have been something a little more personal or theological, maybe a combination of the two? Maybe like: "Tell me honestly, Marty, don't you feel sometimes that we're in the business of asking people to believe in belief?" And Martin Hartman, he would have looked amused and replied wisely: "Why should we want to devote our lives to doing something stupid like that, Jim?"

What Martin Hartman in fact said was: "I think so, Jim."

Mahan smiled at the firm grasp on his wrist; he knew it was intended to bolster him, not restrain him. "Sorry. I was just trying to let everybody know I was here."

Martin Hartman nodded, then withdrew his hand. Without a word he pivoted around sharply and hastened over to the foot of the altar steps. The altar boys, bewildered, jumped up from the bench and scurried after him, barely arriving for a genuflection in unison. Then, just as rushed as he had been, Martin Hartman stopped abruptly and waited. His back was to everyone, but his ear was pointed to the pulpit. Ritual was still ritual.

Mahan knew he had to end everything formally—in the usual name of Father, Son, and Holy Ghost. But he couldn't do it, even with some other names he would have preferred substituting. He really couldn't manage anything, it occurred to him, but what he couldn't control. Certainly, he didn't *have* to admit the moan that felt as though it were gathering together every tissue of his stomach and chest as it rose. He didn't *have* to let the moan flee out from him until it seemed to rattle blue Jesus in the green temple, yellow Joseph on his brown carpenter's bench, golden Mary next to a white angel, and all the bald men with double chins and enormous black eyes who had draped their togas over the stained-glass windows to diffuse the sun. He *didn't* have to give in to any of it, but he did anyway—surrendering control in some gratuitous agreement with his will and then feeling the church—from Martin Hartman at the altar to Joe Sardi sneaking in through the back door—fuller than he had ever known it to be.

✱ ✱ ✱

Physically, the station was as Mahan had pictured it: the platforms right and left instead of a single center strip, the lights ancient wall globes dimmed by decades of crud. He had sat with Barbara Hoag on the wooden benches a dozen times, just as often had joined her in studying the florid tile lettering with the station's name. Now that he was really there he didn't want to drop a coin into a glass peanuts ball to chew on 60-year-old nuts, but the penny was still in his fob pocket.

But for all his mental meanderings he hadn't anticipated the feeling of standing inside some great vacuum cleaner bag, hadn't provided for the tickling of his arm hairs or the folds he seemed to have to widen out of his eyes to focus completely. Neither had he figured on a lurch in his stomach every time a rat scampered loudly down the track alongside the third rail. He just hadn't prepared enough for being where he was.

Barbara led him down to what had been projected as the platform entrance. The turnstiles had been pulled out, leaving the darkened change booth protected only by a floor-to-ceiling gate that stopped abruptly where the turnstiles should have been. Two staircases, fenced over by rotted boards, had been recessed into the walls to the left and right of the booth.

"They built everything, then just stopped?"

"No need for it," she nodded. "And they knew it from the first day."

"Knew what?"

She marked her steps carefully over to the booth. Something she saw in the low ceiling confirmed her suspicions. "The staircases are too close to each other," she pointed. "Follow them up and they'd be piggybacked on the same sidewalk."

"Not very practical."

"They weren't meant to be. They knew from the start the stairs would never be opened out into the street. That's why they built up, not down. Maybe they had a twinge of conscience about hacking up the street needlessly, but it was all a charade."

The strength of her conviction excited him. Suddenly he had a clear image of the contractor who had swindled the city. From the first day the contractor had been invited to City Hall he had been set on stealing. Through months, maybe years, of negotiating with licensing agencies, planning boards, transport unions, and electrical workers, from Point A to Point Z, everything the man had said, answered, promised, regretted, and apologized for had been an evasion from the central objective of building something that would profit him and him alone.

"So what do you do about it now?"

"Leave it. What else is there?"

A train was approaching in a clatter. She smiled as though that were an extra surprise she had arranged for him, then moved on up the platform with the same sashay she had shown him the evening he had walked her to her apartment house. His feet felt nailed down. He couldn't see the train coming, but heard that it was plowing down on him, following a pre-established course that would bring it oh-so-close but not exactly where he was. He remained still until it finished rattling past him—behind a cement wall, invisibly.

She used a Kleenex to wipe off the small circular mirror of the gum machine. "What do you think I'll see if I look?" he asked.

She looked relieved he had finally broken the ice. "Come see for yourself."

"That's all I've been doing lately. With professional nudging from Dr. Richard Mooney, of course, but for myself. I was fishing for an outside opinion."

"You mean a judgment."

"If I don't like it, can't I appeal?"

She thought about it while she scrounged around for cigarettes and matches in her bag. He winced for her pale blue blouse when she leaned against the post for lighting up. "I think you look like somebody who's just staggered out of bed after a deep sleep," she said, tossing her dead match down on the track. "You're woozy. You're not quite sure where you are. I don't imagine you even feel rested."

"That, no."

"But underneath . . ."

That much he knew for himself. "Underneath I know I've put a stop to a couple of little somethings that needed stopping. I know a nerve or two are better off than they were. And I know, at least I hope I do, that I will eventually feel the difference and be amazed I waited so long to feel it."

"It's automatic?"

"No. But with friends and the psychiatric gifts of Richard Mooney . . ."

She smiled cannily, as she had at the restaurant when he had told her about the letter from McMillan. "But no monumental decisions for now."

"They've waited this long, they can wait a little longer."

"Maybe you're looking for too many guarantees."

"As many as I can get. But that won't be an excuse. Promise."

She took another puff and glanced around her skeptically. "I don't know a lot about that kind of choice."

"I think you know more about it than I do."

"Ha!"

"You knew what to ask for that day in the rectory."

"Self-pity's easy."

"Now it's self-pity. That day it wasn't."

She didn't want to debate. "Long time ago, Jim."

"So tell me something more recent."

She nodded, as much to her feet as him. "I think I once told you about the man with the flags."

"Right. In your office."

"Between you, me, and all this dust, the flags were my real objective. But he's not so bad, either."

"I'm happy for you, Barbara."

She let a thought pass, then abruptly straightened up and discarded her cigarette on the track. "Pepsin," she said, pointing to the gum machine. "They still make that?"

"I don't know."

She took his word for it, then ambled off to see what else there was to see. He *was* happy for her and the flag man, he realized. It made her completely independent of him, made her somebody he would be able to know as a distinct human being. And he had been running out of those.

"So what're you going to ask for, Jim Mahan?" she asked, her voice picking up an echo with the increasing distance between them. "What exactly is it you're going to decide you want if you ever decide?"

Another train was coming. There seemed to be no reason to fear this one in the least. Festooned with flags from every nation on earth, it would take him home, then be there again the next morning to take him anywhere he wanted to go. This one wouldn't pass the station behind a wall, he thought, it would inaugurate the station. Finally.

"To call this world home!" he yelled to her above the roar.

✳ ✳ ✳

Dear Carlos and Mireya,

I hope you're both well and enjoying your summer. It's winter up here now, and sometimes it gets very cold. I don't know about you, but I have always liked the worst heat more than the slightest cold. Maybe my blood isn't thick enough. What do you think?

A friend of mine was showing me a flag of Bolivia the other night. It made me think of how little I really know about where you live. All I've got here are big books, and none of them talk about you. Could you tell me some things I won't find in big books? I would really like that, and if there is something I don't understand, I'll write back and ask about it.

God bless both of you.

Love,

Jim

✳ ✳ ✳

The unwarm sun hung over the bridge. As he chugged toward it, Mahan imagined some infinitely asbestos creature looking down on him from it. The creature had no human qualities. It didn't care whom he helped, whom he harmed, what he stood for. All it grasped was the run he made toward it every evening. As long as he jogged into the park at the same time every evening, the asbestos creature would remain curious about him, and more than that he couldn't expect.

Jerry Simpson was coming toward him, keeping his eye on the collie that was sniffing out a spot under one of the benches for peeing. He wondered how long Jerry Simpson would stay in the neighborhood after college. Not long, he decided.

He nodded to the boy and pushed on. The rush came to his head earlier lately. More and more, he needed the fire brigade of help from the storekeepers to go the final blocks. He didn't mind. He was there for them, and they were on the scene for him. He liked blessing them for that fact—and liked telling Richard Mooney he did. The shrink clearly thought him arrogant in some fervid way.

The belly of the bridge loomed larger. He still missed the fact that it hadn't been opened to traffic more gradually. When would he ever get a chance again to see a bridge being built over an ocean?

Mahan ran on.